Vampire Mine

Aline Hunter

An Ellora's Cave Publication

www.elloraescave.com

Vampire Mine

ISBN 9781419971570
ALL RIGHTS RESERVED.
Vampire Mine Copyright © 2013 Aline Hunter
Edited by Ann Leveille.

Electronic book publication August 2013
Trade paperback publication 2015

With the exception of quotes used in reviews, this book may not be reproduced or used in whole or in part by any means existing without written permission from the publisher, Ellora's Cave Publishing, Inc.® 1056 Home Avenue, Akron OH 44310-3502.

Warning: The unauthorized reproduction or distribution of this copyrighted work is illegal. Criminal copyright infringement, including infringement without monetary gain, is investigated by the FBI and is punishable by up to 5 years in federal prison and a fine of $250,000. (http://www.fbi.gov/ipr/)

This book is a work of fiction and any resemblance to persons, living or dead, or places, events or locales is purely coincidental. The characters are productions of the author's imagination and used fictitiously.

The publisher and author(s) acknowledge the trademark status and trademark ownership of all trademarks, service marks and word marks mentioned in this book.

The publisher does not have any control over and does not assume any responsibility for author or third-party Web sites or their content.

Dedication

To my amazing editor Ann, as well as the art department at Ellora's Cave for inspiring me to write this story sooner rather than later. I'd also like to thank the readers who support the Alpha and Omega series and my crit partners and beta readers. This one's for you.

Prologue

Pain—raw and intense—slammed into Sadie Dumus.

Like a living creature it snaked its way through her system and clawed at her insides. The result of starvation, her body demanded the sustenance it needed to survive. Horror swept through her as she shoved a hand to her abdomen, willing the agony to disappear. Her muscles rebelled, flexing beneath her contorted fingers, creating more misery. The dryness in her throat made it difficult to breathe. Hunger and bloodlust roared to life, no longer willing to be contained.

Not now. Goddess. Not now.

She was so close to her goal, standing right at the finish line. Finally, after months of work, she'd managed to track Aldon Frost to his nest. It was the one place he'd be vulnerable, the only place she could learn his secrets. It had taken so much time, so much patience. He excelled at hiding his tracks, leading her down one path only to lose her on the next.

Tonight she'd finally managed to stay on his ass.

She'd followed him successfully, using every resource at her disposal. She phased, she hid and she watched. The bastard had finally taken her down an alley, toward what she was certain was his domain. Sadie's coven viewed Aldon as a threat to the city. He was a rogue vampire drawn to the dark side of magic. As their protector and enforcer, it was her job and duty to take him out for her sisters-in-magic. What she hadn't known was how defenseless she'd be when the opportunity finally struck.

As weak as a newborn kitten.

The magic inside her dimmed and the final reserves her ravaged body had managed to store ebbed away. She fought, willing her depleted muscles to keep going for just a little longer. She'd put herself at risk by using power she didn't have, afraid that if she didn't find his nest soon she never would.

Her heartbeat slowed to a horrific thudding in her chest. Without essential nutrients her organs were shutting down. It was only a matter of time. She'd known that. She'd thought she was ready for the moment to arrive. Her existence had become a cage of mirrors, reflecting her past back to her piece by morbid piece. They served as a reminder of what she'd done to herself.

She was going to die. It was inevitable.

There was no one to blame but herself.

Her feet shuffled, creating a dangerous sliver of sound she couldn't afford.

Shit.

Leigh had told her to come clean with the coven about her circumstances but she hadn't. If they ever found out she'd fed from a werewolf they'd shun her or kill her. Despite the fact it would leave the coven temporarily defenseless, they wouldn't take any unnecessary risks. A vampire who was blood bound to a werewolf was the ultimate weakness in an enclave. She'd never feed from another, meaning she couldn't heal herself by drinking from a passing stranger if the need arose. She also wouldn't be able to move from place to place if her sisters-in-magic decided it was time for a change of scenery. Her importance depended on her ability to adapt. They required her to be ready and willing for whatever they needed.

She was their enforcer, the one entrusted with their protection.

Her stomach churned as a ball of fire erupted in her gut, begging for something—anything—to ease the persistent torture. Pushing her balled fist into her belly, she prayed for relief. She'd known it would come to this. The last few weeks had been hell. Each day was like sand slipping through an hourglass, each grain lost becoming another nail in her coffin. Her torment went beyond hunger at this point. The last blood she'd successfully ingested was long gone, dried up and all but forgotten. She'd been lucky to have lasted this long—a little over two months—without the nourishment necessary to survive.

The man she'd been tracking froze. His nostrils flared, his thick blond hair skimming over his shoulder as he turned. She tried not to panic, to rely on her training. Vampires could smell fear and she didn't have the strength to mask the scent. Not with her shields falling so quickly, each breath she took like a ticking time bomb.

"Don't bother trying to hide. I can feel you. Reveal yourself."

To her utter mortification her magic chose that very moment to vanish.

Son of a bitch.

Here she was, face-to-face with a threat she couldn't take down. In her current state Aldon could snap her like a twig. She couldn't phase away, nor could she defend herself. Her vision blurred, the slow thudding of her heart ricocheting in her head. Damn it. She was fading faster than she thought possible.

Thankfully, he didn't know that.

Not yet.

He took a step closer, sizing her up. He was so tall, like a fucking building hovering over her. His shoulders were much broader than hers, muscles visible beneath his trench coat. Although pale—as all vampires were prone to be—his skin had a swarthy hue. He'd blend in with mortals and immortals alike, beautiful to behold even if impossible to touch. As though he needed another weapon against helpless victims who would be powerless against him.

Bastard vampire.

"Why are you following me?"

"Who says I'm following you?" Thank the Goddess her voice sounded strong, her statement coming across as confident. "It's a beautiful night to hunt. I decided to take advantage." She arched a brow, giving him a thin smile. "Nocturnal creatures are known to cross paths from time to time."

"True." His expression revealed nothing as he studied her, his sky-blue irises vibrant in the dark. "Yet somehow I don't think that's the case."

She wanted to think of a witty retort but a wave of exhaustion prevented it.

Fatigue swept through her, white dots speckling her vision. Pride kept her from falling on her face. She extended her arms, attempting to remain upright. How had she gone on for so long like this? How had she managed to convince herself she was still in control?

A memory flashed through her mind, making her withering heart skip a beat. Even now—with all the time that had passed—she ached when she thought of *him*. Her eyes burned with unshed tears, yearning and heartache forming a knot in her throat. She remembered Trey resting on his side, his beautiful amber-tinted irises hidden behind closed lids, a sprinkling of dark shadow lining his jaw. He'd seemed so different then, unable to defend himself, trapped in a cage like a damn animal.

The sight had angered and terrified her. The man was more than capable of taking care of himself but he'd gotten himself into trouble. Captured by Shepherds—religious zealots determined to destroy shifters one by one—there would have been no happy ending. They'd have broken him down, using every weapon in their arsenal, before they snuffed him from existence.

No way. She hadn't been able to let that happen.

One bite had sealed their fates.

In saving his life, she'd sacrificed her own.

Even now she could taste his blood, feel her pussy clasp in response, her weakened body tingling in multiple wicked places. The first swallow had been the best, cascading down her throat like ambrosia, so good she knew she'd never find its equal. His being a shifter had meant she'd started healing immediately, despite the severity of her wounds. But that hadn't been her focus. Instead she'd fought off an orgasm unlike any other, mortified at the thought of using him, of taking more than he was willing to give.

It was bad enough to take his life's blood without consent.

A whimper seeped past her lips and she dropped to her knees. She focused on the memory, not the pain. This was all that was left—the past. Memories of what she wanted but would never have. Death didn't frighten her. In fact, the thought of passing into the next realm brought a strange sense of calm.

No more pain.

No more heartache.

Only peace.

Arms wrapped around her and the world shifted. She shuddered as she felt a chest against her shoulder, followed by Aldon's hushed order, "Easy."

Confusion swamped her, breaking the spell of Trey's memory.

Had she died? Was her brain reacting to her demise like a dream that made no sense?

Aldon Frost was evil. The head of her coven—Geneva—told her so. During private meetings when she'd been given instructions on how best to guard the coven the mistress of the group had told Sadie that Aldon had to be monitored more closely than any other. Once his nest had been found, Sadie had to destroy the vampire. He threatened their race—was a danger to their very way of life.

Why hasn't he killed me yet?

She felt the firm press of his hand as he lifted her head. She didn't open her eyes, remaining lax as he scented her neck. The position to vampires was the same as bearing her belly to a predator, a sign of submission. As much as she detested herself for it, there was no other alternative. Not now. His teeth sank deep, easily penetrating her skin. She wasn't the hunter but the hunted. His contented sigh reverberated through the cold night air. She shivered, trying to think of Trey, wanting to remember him in her final moments.

This is it. I'm about to die.

Then he was done, pulling his fangs from her abused flesh. "Stubborn creature," he stated matter-of-factly. "So certain of yourself. So arrogant. So predictable. You wear your pride like a shield. I suppose I should thank you for simplifying things."

When she attempted to struggle—determined to at the very least slap the hell out of the bastard—she felt it.

Magic.

Warmth seeped into her chest, the first relief she'd felt in months. But it wasn't coming from her. It was coming from him. She fought the compulsion of succumbing to his will and tried to stay awake. It was a trick, the inviting allure of dark magic. If she gave in, her soul would be lost. She had to fight to maintain the hold on her sanity.

"Sleep," Aldon commanded, the order a siren's song too powerful to deny. "Sleep."

She tried to open her eyes and see the face above her. Instead darkness rose, wrapping its arms around her, trapping her in its embrace. There was no fear, only comfort and reassurance. The feelings disoriented her, breaking her tenuous hold on reality. The abyss overcame everything, shrouding her mind and body like a blanket, directing her thoughts to another time and place.

She sank into eyes the color of cherished whiskey, felt the rasp of Trey's breath against her face as their lips had met for the first time. The grass had cushioned them as he'd settled his weight against her, his form molding to hers as though they'd been made for each other. He'd smelled so good—too good. He had been a part of herself that she'd never truly known.

Like this, they would have forever.

Maybe this was the end. She'd finally arrived.

And what could possibly be better? What more could she ask for in the afterlife?

Trey was his own version of heaven.

Chapter One

Trey Veznor gasped in ecstasy as he felt the prick of teeth against his skin. A gash had been made in his throat, creating a small trickle of blood. Sexual need rushed through his body, engorging his cock, drawing his balls taut. He growled at the sharp scrape of teeth against his neck, the sweet flick of a tongue sweeping across his flesh. Despite the ache in his muscles he tried to reach out when his lover moaned—the sound a symphony in his ears—and discovered he was unable to do so, trapped in a body that refused to function.

Fury made him want to scream in frustration.

The need to touch the female—his female—increased.

She'd been hurt. He scented the metallic rustiness of her blood, sensed her wounds through their flourishing connection. Misery consumed her, the pain unbearable. She'd been injured in a way that terrified him. He'd never seen the woman destined to be his mate in a weakened state. She was strong, fearless and fierce. He knew her, could feel her. He'd thought about her so often she was in his thoughts even when he didn't realize it.

Sadie.

His skin parted in welcome as her tiny fangs pierced his throat. Her lips moved, surrounding the punctures, sealing them off. The suction of her mouth as she drank was so sweet and hot. He wanted to grasp her tiny waist and place her on top of him. A few thrusts and he'd come like a randy schoolboy, unable to hold back long enough to even think about sinking his cock inside the haven of his mate's body.

Desire amplified, his dick straining against his jeans.

So close...so fucking close.

He'd hurt her before, reckless in his outrage against her kind, but he was determined to make things right. Once he found her he wasn't letting her go. He'd warned her not to make promises she couldn't keep.

No more barriers. No more bullshit.

Teeth slid from his skin and her tongue skimmed over his wounds.

"Sadie," he whispered, trying to lift his arms and open his eyes.

He felt her move away, her succulent scent beginning to fade.

Damn it. He wouldn't let her go. He'd tether her ass to his bed and force her to face what they were to each other, even if it meant being locked in a room with his mate for days.

"Sadie," he roared, fighting to lift his lids, to see her angelic face. "Listen to me." It felt as though his soul was ripped apart, torn in two as she vanished. "Damn you! Listen to me!"

This time when he tried to move, his arm worked.

Then something shook him hard. "Wake up."

He swung at the thing pulling him away from the warmth of Sadie's touch. His wolf's anger merged with his, his growl a threat to the idiot stupid enough to try to come between him and the one female destined for him.

They'd waited too long. Time had transformed into an enemy he'd become tired of facing. Each second was pure agony. Too much more of this shit and he'd break like a rubber band stretched past its limit.

More shaking against his shoulder, harder this time. "Trey, wake the fuck up."

His eyes flew open, his hand flew out and he wrapped his fingers around a throat. Even with vision blurred from sleep he made out the form of a dumbass fucking male who'd intruded where he wasn't wanted. When his opponent didn't fight him he slowly came down to earth. His fingers loosened as he recognized a vital member of his pack, the one person who was aware of his situation and of the loss he experienced with each passing day.

"Easy, man," Nathan—his Beta—grumbled. "I'd have left you alone but you were getting loud." Trey lowered his hand and Nathan moved away. The Beta ran his fingers through his hair, shaking his head. "You're going to have to get hold of that shit. If we have guests and they hear you they'll know something's up. Hell, they already suspect something's off."

"I could say the same about you," Trey replied, shaking off the memory of Sadie's silken lips against his neck. He sat up and ran his hand over his face. "You've not exactly been June Cleaver."

Nathan's lips formed into a sardonic smirk. "Unlike you, I've only got a few weeks left. I've waited this long. A few more days aren't shit."

Fucking bastard.

"If she shows," he taunted, unable to prevent the sliver of jealousy that arose. "She could blow you off."

Humor faded from Nathan's face, replaced by anger. His Beta's eyes turned, irises shifting from brown to amber. "She gave me her word."

Nathan's mate—a vampire who'd somehow been involved when Sadie had saved Trey's life—had promised to return after a period of three months. Nathan hadn't wanted to give her that space but current events had prevented him from stopping her departure. Fortunately, due to their circumstances, the men had been able to share their concerns about taking vampire mates. In the shifter world such unions were forbidden. Vampires were magical creatures, with some of them being able to turn the animals inside shifters into familiars.

Such a thing could render a shifter—male or female—powerless.

"Listen," Nathan said, this time in control of his emotions. "When Leigh shows up I'll find out about Sadie. As soon as I know where she is I'll tell you. You can talk to her and sort things out."

Sounds like a great plan. Too bad she doesn't want to talk to me.

The intimate time he'd shared with his mate had gone badly—very, very badly. He'd been drunk, relying on his friend Mr. Daniels to assist him in grief. Sadie'd paid the price for his spiral of gloom. All it had taken was a few words—words he hadn't meant to speak aloud, for fuck's sake—for her to promise he'd never see her again.

The way she'd looked at him...the hurt he'd glimpsed in her eyes... Christ it made him feel like a total piece of shit.

Nathan walked across the bedroom toward the door. "Diskant called right after you crashed. He's arranged for a meeting with the pack at noon."

"Let me guess." He swung his legs over the side of the bed, flexing the muscles in his back. "We're hosting."

"You're Alpha," Nathan responded over his shoulder. "What do you think?"

Nathan vanished around the corner, leaving Trey staring at the empty entranceway. After Diskant had moved he'd handed over the keys to his former home—an old fire station, of all places—to Trey. The place had always been used for meetings. Since Trey had been reinstated as Alpha—a responsibility he'd abandoned to search for those who'd killed a large portion of his pack months ago—he'd been in charge of all werewolf business in the city.

He'd thought pack business would be a welcome distraction. Something to ease the memories of a woman he wasn't sure he'd ever see again. Instead each gathering with his kind served as a reminder of how moronic he'd been. Yes, he was Alpha. As such he'd always care for those who turned to him for protection. However, as a shifter it was impossible not to do the same for his destined female.

She was equally—if not more—important.

As he walked to the adjoining bathroom he thought about the time that had passed. Sadie had rescued him from a Shepherd cell eight weeks ago. For two months he'd wondered where she was and if she was safe. Nathan had hesitantly told him about what he'd seen when Leigh had brought him home. Sadie had been in the car, bleeding all over the place. Nathan hadn't had the opportunity to inspect her wounds since she'd vanished into thin air.

Phasing.

That's what vampires called it. Some vampires were born with the talent, able to move from one place to another instantaneously. It allowed them to protect themselves from harm and to move around undetected.

He turned on the shower and considered contacting Aldon Frost. The vampire was the only person he knew who could give him answers. Unfortunately contact with the leech wasn't welcomed by the pack, which meant it was done on the down-low. They knew Trey did the vamp's security and accepted Aldon returned favors but that was as far as their knowledge went. Aldon had been curious about Trey's interest in vampires but hadn't asked questions. That was one perk of running a private and exclusive security business.

He chose his clients and worked when he felt like it, was his own boss on his own terms.

As his client, Aldon would answer questions without hesitation, sharing information in exchange for state-of-the-art technology. Not to mention Trey's services came with complete confidentiality. No one would know where Aldon lived, what kind of system he'd purchased or what kind of traps he had in place for unwelcome visitors.

Sliding his head under the hot spray of water, he thought of Nathan's promise.

A few weeks.

Sure as fuck, it sucked, but he'd wait.

Like a premonition of bad things to come, Sadie's warning returned to haunt him.

After tonight, you'll never see me again. You have my word.

"I warned you not to make promises you can't keep," he growled in frustration, closing his eyes and enjoying the hot streams of water beating down his back. "Once I find you, you're mine. There's no running from me."

Not now.

Not tomorrow.

Not ever.

He didn't take his time, glad that he'd gotten his hair cut and didn't have to primp or preen. Toweling off, he studied his reflection. Since he'd stopped drinking his coloring had returned to normal, although he still had shadows under his eyes. That came from restless sleep—most nights consisting of dreams of Sadie. On good nights they'd engage in pleasures of the flesh, exploring each other's bodies in all sorts of wicked, delectable places. On bad nights, such as the one he'd just woken from, he'd be trapped in his body, unable to move, knowing after Sadie had taken his blood she'd leave.

The doorbell rang, which was odd since the pack usually just barged inside the house whenever they felt like it. He got on track and pulled on his clothes. Black T-shirt, worn blue jeans and a beat-up pair of boots. It wasn't anywhere near noon—maybe six or seven if his inner clock was ticking right. Perhaps it wasn't the pack and Ava had decided to swing by. Usually if she had an appointment with the doc, who'd started monitoring her pregnancy more closely, she liked to drop off leftovers from dinner.

His mouth watered just thinking about it. The woman certainly knew how to cook.

Diskant and Emory were lucky bastards. Their mates— Ava and Mary—had become close in recent weeks. The women made meals, talked and spent their free time together. The men in their lives reaped the rewards of the friendship. Not only did they get to eat homemade food every night, they also got to take their mates to bed after they finished. It was the good life—one Trey wanted for himself.

Stop that shit. Get your head on straight. Pack business today. Remember?

He tried to listen to sound reasoning, going through the motions.

Then logic flipped upside down and turned on its motherfucking head.

A scent drifted through his door, hitting him like a well-aimed sucker punch.

The hair on his nape rose on end, his sense of smell kicking into high gear. The fragrance was familiar but he couldn't quite place it. Flashes of memory bled together. Wasn't the scent from the nightmare he shared with Sadie? Every single time she took his blood then left him high and dry there'd been someone else with her. He'd always known there had been—had been able to feel the weight of the outsider's stare—but didn't really give two dog dicks about it. All he wanted to focus on during the encounters was his female, not some idiot who'd decided to enjoy the show.

He dragged in a deep breath, senses going into overdrive.

Damn. The smell was so fucking recognizable. Deep down he knew it from somewhere. Worse? He also identified traces of Sadie's scent along with it. His mate's sweetness was there—faint but there.

What the fuck?

Two and two. Simple fucking math. Bringing everything together.

He ran from the bedroom and rushed down the stairs, heart pulsing, muscles in motion. He'd recognize Sadie's luscious scent anywhere, delicious and vibrant, an aphrodisiac that went straight to his head. She wasn't close but someone who'd been in her presence was. God help the person who'd come to his home. He wasn't in the mood to ask questions. He was going to demand answers.

He didn't hesitate when he spotted the stranger in his kitchen—a tiny and helpless female. Sadie's scent was stronger now. Despite the fear that he felt coming off the woman across from him, he could smell traces of his mate. Moving forward and ignoring the alarm in the young girl's face, he growled low in his throat. Before he could reach her Nathan blocked his path. Trey snarled, the wolf within gaining ground, wanting to take control. His Beta grasped his arms, harsh fingers digging into his skin. Trey snarled when he felt the male's power—the ability Nathan had to control the beast of others—attempting to calm him with touch.

"Get your fucking hands off me."

"No," Nathan snapped, pushing Trey back, getting in his face. "Go for her and there'll be blood. I'm a Beta by choice. I don't fight battles. Not because I can't but because I choose not to. Don't forget that."

Trey's wolf howled—in pain, anguish and fury—and tried to push past his defenses. Too long denied what it needed, the beast sought an outlet. Trey was aware this would happen eventually. The animal could only take so much for so long. He'd been afraid he'd frighten Sadie when they met again, consumed by the desire of man and beast.

"Listen, Trey. That's my female you're threatening." Nathan snarled in warning, nails forming claws that broke the surface of Trey's skin. "Calm. The fuck. Down."

Calm down? Is he serious?

Wolf and man came together, wanting to slam the female who was staring—eyes wide in terror no less—at him from across the room. The words computed but the meaning wasn't entirely clear. Why should he care who the fuck she was? The female was a means to an end, a way to get what he needed most. He'd been denied for so fucking long—too fucking long.

Sadie.

"Let go of me, pup," he ordered, words garbled.

"You will calm down." Nathan's eyes changed color, becoming an unrecognizable shade of neon green. "Right fucking now!"

Power slammed into Trey's body with the force of a train. Anger, frustration and need bled together, collected into a fireball of anguish. In an instant the feelings slid from his skin, taken from him before he could prevent it, there one second and gone the next. The wolf went silent, no longer snarling in his head, forced to retreat.

Nathan let go, wincing as though pained. Trey watched the Beta sway from side to side, spreading his arms for balance. Nathan almost toppled over but landed against the counter, using his arms to remain in an upright position. He bowed his head, taking deep breaths, his face no longer tan and healthy but sickly pale.

"Oh Goddess," the small female pressed into a corner whispered, her fear so potent the smell burned his nostrils. "I shouldn't have come here."

"Don't be afraid," Nathan said, sounding as weak as he looked. He tried to move to her. "I won't let anyone hurt you."

Trey knew the Beta wasn't in any shape to get to the woman. Until Nathan regained some of the power he'd used to subdue Trey's wolf he'd be weak as a newborn. He took a step back, knowing better than to approach the girl. Even in his current state Nathan wouldn't allow anyone anywhere near his female.

"He needs your help." Trey commanded quietly, "Go to him."

"I don't think that's such a good idea." She glanced between the men and then stared frantically around the room, as though she was pondering the best way to escape. "Neither of you seem stable."

Nathan eased his head upward, pivoting just enough to see his mate. "Leigh."

"Help him," Trey said, keeping his tone light. "He won't hurt you."

"You don't know that," she countered, her sapphire eyes almost too large for her face.

"Yes, I do. He can't hurt you. Not ever. It goes against our very nature to harm our mates." Nodding at Nathan, he informed her, "From now on you have that man by the balls. There's nothing he wouldn't do for you."

"Y-Your mates? What the hell is that supposed to mean?" she squeaked and squirmed out of the corner, moving toward the door, keeping as much distance between herself and the men in the room as possible.

The human reaction coming from a vampire confused him.

Sadie had phased with ease. He'd seen it with his own eyes.

Why isn't she using her ability if she's so afraid?

Nathan moved—his body graceful, muscles flexing with the motion—faster than Trey anticipated. The Beta trapped Leigh against the wall and wrapped his arms around her waist. Then he bent so his head nestled at the crook of her throat. She tried to fight her way free, slapping weakly at his arms.

"What's wrong?" Nathan's words were strained but steady. "You're sick. I want to know why."

"I'm not sick," she snapped, as though his observation pissed her off. Despite that, it was obvious the vampire was weak. Her struggles didn't gain her an inch of freedom. "I just...I'm fine. Let go!"

The Beta slid one hand up her side and twined his fingers in the hair at her nape. He forced her to look at him, tilting her head back, examining her face. After several seconds he found what he was looking for. It was impossible to keep secrets from Nathan. The male excelled—and was a master—at reading people.

"No, you're not." Nathan growled. "You're fucking starving. I scent your hunger. I sense your pain."

Shit.

Shifters experienced shame and outrage when they didn't see to the needs of their mates. It was instilled from the moment of conception. Then, to make sure the message hit home, the males of a pack always led by example. A female was to be cared for. The male provided shelter, comfort and nourishment.

Unexpectedly, Leigh's fear faded and she narrowed her eyes. "I didn't come here to discuss my eating habits, thank you very much." She whipped her head around and looked at Trey. "I came because Sadie's in trouble. I'm not sure what she's gotten herself into but it's got to be bad. She hasn't returned to the coven and she's not been to our healing caverns."

Terror lanced Trey's chest and he stopped giving a shit about Nathan's reactions or how terrified the woman in his Beta's arms might be. "How long has she been missing?"

"Almost a week."

Normally Nathan's influence kept the wolf in a tranquil state for a few hours. Trey hadn't thought it was possible for the beast to go from zero to sixty following the sapping of emotion. The transfer of hate and animosity to understanding and tranquility was stunning. Some wolves put their tails between their legs for months after Nathan gave them an ample shot of his mojo.

So much for that.

The wolf roared in his head, returning with a vengeance, causing his vision to change. Crimson tinted the objects in the room, making Leigh's eyes appear pink instead of blue. He wanted to rage at the female, to ask her why in the fuck Sadie had put herself in harm's way. Afraid he might do just that, he grasped a nearby chair and sent it soaring across the room. Wood splintered, breaking into pieces. The tips of his fingers prickled, his nails lengthening to claws.

"That's why I came." To her credit, Leigh didn't sound scared. Even if he could smell her horror at his behavior, she was attempting to hide it. "I can find her."

"How?" The question came out a snarl, the man and wolf asking at the same time.

"The same way we found you after you went and got yourself in trouble," she muttered, her gaze turning to a glare. He scented her hostility then, as though she viewed him as an absolute piece of shit and detested being in his presence. He wasn't sure why. What reason did she have to dislike him? "I have something that belongs to her," she went on. "I can trace her with it."

"Why not go to your coven?" Nathan interrupted. "Why come to us?"

"They don't know she's missing." Leigh lowered her head and fidgeted. "I've...uh..." Forming her hands into tiny fists, she continued, "I've been covering for her."

"Why?" Trey asked, grateful he'd started gaining ground over his bestial half. The wolf was still there, pissed as ever, but at least it was listening.

The sound of a door opening was the most unwelcome noise Trey had ever heard. He spun on his heel, braced for his unexpected guest. He immediately identified the visitor's scent—a combination of leather and Dial soap. Just great. Anyone else he could boss around and order to get the fuck out. This one, however, would smile in his face and take a seat at his table.

Fucking A.

The only human in the pack—Caden Stone—waltzed in. The enormous motherfucker had ditched his facial piercings—keeping only the earrings that stretched his lobes—but that didn't make him less intimidating. The bastard's size alone screamed fuck with me and die. Since Cade had covered himself with a leather jacket so his numerous tattoos didn't show—and he wasn't scowling, which brought attention to the wicked scar along his chin—Trey hoped Leigh wouldn't freak out and rush from the room screaming.

"Honey, I'm home," Caden said as he strode over the broken chair at his feet. "Looks like I made it just in time."

Fine. The cocky asshole wanted to take part in the mix? Then by all means.

"You sure did," Trey drawled, taking a step to the side to block Leigh and Nathan from full view. "Since you're here, I'm guessing you know about the pack meeting at noon. I have some shit to do so I've got to jet for a while. How about you entertain the guests and take notes. Be my secretary for the day."

"Like hell," Caden retorted, standing like a fucking brick wall in the kitchen. He folded his arms over his chest and spread his feet shoulder width apart. "I'm not your bitch."

"Diskant has new information on Shepherd compounds. They think they have a line on the group who does their dirty work," Nathan offered. Trey heard shuffling—more than likely Nathan and Leigh rising to their feet. "You've been waiting for this. There's a good chance you'll get the names of the men you've been searching for."

Several emotions flickered across Cade's usually non-expressive face.

Disbelief. Hope.

Happiness?

Then his gaze became troubled, almost desperate.

Everyone knew to leave the human alone. He'd suffered more than any man should, losing his wife and unborn child in the most violent way. Afterward, when he'd lost all hope, Shepherds had swooped in. They'd tricked Caden, telling him shifters had been responsible for the death of his family. It

Vampire Mine

wasn't until he'd met Trey's pack that Cade had learned the truth.

The horrible information and knowledge he'd gained had nearly destroyed him.

Those first few weeks with the pack had been tough. Cade was a smartass at heart and loved to push people's buttons. Then he'd taken a break and returned. Something had changed, although Trey couldn't put his finger on precisely what it was.

"You're sure?" Cade asked, sounding grave.

Nathan appeared in Trey's peripheral vision, his arm snaked around Leigh's waist. He'd turned so she wasn't entirely visible, her face hidden by the long fall of her dark hair. "I got the call last night. Diskant wants to reach out to other packs and share information but he promised you first dibs."

Trey knew Nathan was nervous. He and the Beta had agreed it was best to inform the pack about their mates after things settled down. Right now the members didn't trust anyone who wasn't a shifter. If both of them came clean at the same time—confessing they'd mated to vampires—chaos would certainly ensue.

Which meant Cade couldn't know who or what Leigh was.

Thankfully the gargantuan man was distracted and caught up in his thoughts. His gray eyes were glazed over. He seemed to be looking through everyone, toward something no one else could see. With a wave Trey sent Nathan and Leigh from the room. The wolf didn't like waiting—wanting to go to Sadie right then and there—but he managed to maintain control. He had to take care of Cade first. Then he could put an end to his own misery.

After the couple disappeared he put a hand on Cade's shoulder. "You can go it alone or you can let us help you. As a member of the pack you have a voice in this. We're bound to your decision." Cade didn't respond, staring ahead, jaw clenched. "This is your choice," Trey reminded the man. "You call the shots this time around."

"Go take care of your shit," Cade said, remaining still. "I'll cover until you get back. I need to think."

Not wanting to push, Trey lowered his arm. He didn't want to leave Cade alone but he didn't have any other alternative. Once Sadie was safe he'd return for the meeting. The pack would decide what they wanted to do and they'd have their vengeance. Then he could come clean, introduce Sadie to the pack and see what waited for them in the future.

It's not going to be that easy and you know it.

Pushing negative thoughts aside, he left the kitchen and went in search of the tiny vampire who was about to start a domino effect. Actions always had consequences. Like any other individual, he'd just have to face them as they came. Even if it wasn't going to be happy or nice, he'd find and claim his female. Like it or not she was stuck with his stubborn ass. He'd waited what seemed like forever to find her. He wasn't going to let her slip from his grasp a second time.

After tonight, you'll never see me again. You have my word.

Fuck, it wasn't going to be easy.

Not by a long shot.

Chapter Two

You're such an idiot. Leigh tried not to panic as she yanked her arm from Nathan's grasp and rushed across the room he'd brought her to. *What did you think would happen? That they'd sit down and listen to what you had to say over a nice cup of tea? They're werewolves! Not people.*

The way he'd touched her said it all. The delusional man thought she was his mate.

Like hell.

It didn't matter that she was attracted to Nathan. It also didn't matter that she'd had numerous fantasies about him since their first meeting. The man looked like a freaking Adonis—all muscles, tanned skin, perfect features and big brown eyes. She'd have to be *really* dead not to notice how good he looked. Her fascination was physical, nothing more. Emotional stuff was something else entirely. She'd sworn she'd never give her heart to another man.

How could she when it belonged to someone else?

Brett might not know she was alive but that hardly mattered. As long as she lived she couldn't betray him. They'd vowed to love each other no matter what. Even if she couldn't go to her childhood sweetheart and tell him what she'd become, she was determined to uphold her end of the promise. It was her fault she'd gone out on an errand too late one night and had ended up in the path of a crazy vampire who'd destroyed everything innocent about her and ruined her life.

"No you don't," Nathan chided.

A step to the side to avoid him didn't work, her freedom short-lived. Whatever had happened to him earlier no longer affected his strength and coordination. He slid his big arms around her waist and tugged her toward his chest. His smell swamped her — so clean, so tempting.

"You're so weak you can hardly stand," he murmured. "That won't do."

She fought her hunger as he palmed the back of her head and bent so his neck was directly in front of her mouth. His pulsing vein beckoned, so close she could almost feel the splash of his blood against her tongue. He'd taste spicy and sweet. She knew he would. Shaking the notion off, she shoved at his chest. Perhaps he didn't care what would happen if she sank her teeth into his throat, but she did. Sadie's current predicament painted a vivid picture. Even if he smelled like heaven — even if she wanted him like hell on fire — she couldn't chance a taste.

"Stop crowding me." Hearing the despair in her voice, she gritted her teeth and demanded, "Back off."

"No." The huge man met her determination with his own. "I won't have you hurting. Especially when there's no reason for it." Nathan yanked her upward, lifting her feet off the ground. Her nose bumped his throat in the process, the aroma of his blood so strong she couldn't see straight. "Take what you need from me, imp."

For the first time in months her body responded to the closeness of a male. Her nipples hardened to points as a ripple of arousal rushed from her tummy to her sex. Her canines threatened to extend, her gums tingling and burning. The fantasies she'd had of him took over — of her lying beneath him, welcoming him into her body, begging him for more. Sweat coated his chest, allowing her fingers to glide over his pectoral muscles with ease.

Another man's face flashed through her mind. He was nowhere near as big or handsome as the man holding her tight but he was beautiful in his own right.

Brett.

You're forgetting him.

Her heart lodged in her throat and the burgeoning sense of hope in her chest shattered. She realized how quickly she'd let lust and hunger cloud her judgment. All it had taken was a lost moment with Nathan and she'd all but forgotten her promise.

No. No. No.

Her magic—although weak from her lack of nourishment—flared to life. Desperate, she sent a burst of pure energy shooting from her palm, hitting him directly in the center of his chest. If she hadn't been mortified at the result, she'd have laughed. While the mild electrical current would have shocked the hell out of a human, it didn't do squat to a werewolf. Her legs folded beneath her, no longer able to bear her weight. Thankfully her would-be meal rescued her, swooping down to catch her, lifting her as though she weighed no more than a bag of sand.

"This ends now." While the statement was firm, there was so much concern in his voice it made her heart skip a beat. He strode toward an empty chair with purpose. "You will take from me, mate." She shivered at how possessively he said the word, as though he'd finally been given leave to announce it to the world and he had no intention of taking his proclamation back. "It's my right and privilege to care for you." He gentled his tone, rubbing a hand down her back. She wondered if he sensed her feelings somehow. "Best you accept that. I'm not letting you go. The last couple of months have been hell."

Days of worry, frayed nerves and lost sleep caught up with her, changing the flaring bit of tenderness toward Nathan to full-fledged resentment. The last couple of months had been hell? What did he know? He hadn't watched his only friend slowly starve to death. Sadie had suffered horribly as she'd felt the effects of malnutrition, the muscles from her training becoming nothing more than skin and bone.

She kicked out with useless legs, scrounging up the last energy she had left. "You've suffered? What a crock! You have no idea what suffering is. Not a fricking clue."

"Settle down," he grumbled, taking an elbow to the gut with a soft grunt.

Like hell. "I don't think so."

The tighter he held her, the more she squirmed. She didn't have the strength to get away but she wasn't going to make things easy for him. When he gained the advantage and brought her mouth to his neck, holding her in place with a hand at the back of her head, she ground her teeth together. It was agony smelling his blood and knowing he'd put an end to her thirst, but she'd weathered worse. Hunger was something she'd learned to ignore and overcome. She didn't have to drink blood all the time. In fact she could go weeks without it.

Hold strong. It'll go away. It always does.

This time the reminder didn't feel so reassuring. Nathan brought feelings she felt incredibly uncomfortable with to the surface. Not only did she want to sink her teeth into his throat to curb her appetite, she also wanted to hold him close and breathe him in. Her vampire nature—the thing she hated most—wanted her to lose control of her inhibitions and give herself to the man. To surrender to the desires she'd denied since her transformation.

Get hold of yourself. Sadie's in trouble, remember?

"We're wasting time," she huffed, wriggling as much as she could.

"Then take what you need." Nathan's rebuke was firm, his grip unbreakable. "I'm not letting go until you do."

"It'll kill me." She let her fangs drop but made sure her teeth remained clear of his skin, hoping that a half-truth might get his attention. With a tilt of her head, she met his amber gaze. "Is that what you want?"

He froze, staring her in the eye, the muscles in his arms like granite. "What are you talking about?"

Good. He was finally listening.

"Once a vampire drinks from a shifter they become bound to their blood. No other source will do. If something ever happens to you, I'll starve to death. Rumor has it your pack is in the middle of a war. Force me to drink from you and I'll be gambling with my life. If you go, I go. I'm not willing to take that risk. Now," she tried to force her fangs to retract, hating the way her gums burned and itched, "back the hell off and give me some room."

"I don't believe you."

One firm tug on her hair and she had to meet the werewolf's intense gaze. *Oh hell.*

Three months ago she'd been able to walk away. No fuss, no muss. But now? His woodsy scent called to her, his face sexy and captivating. Her breath caught and her pussy flooded. Time had definitely worked in Nathan's favor. No longer neat and tidy, his dark and unkempt head of hair went perfectly with the goatee he'd decided to grow, taking him from a man you introduced to Momma to the bad boy you welcomed each night through the bedroom window.

"Sadie," she blurted, grappling to stay focused. Why was it so hard to think clearly? Why couldn't she get her raging hormones under control? This wasn't the time or place for her libido to kick into high gear.

"What about her?" Trey snarled.

Nathan's fingers slipped from Leigh's hair, allowing her to whip her head around and address the man who'd been listening to their conversation. A hot wave of embarrassment crept up her cheeks. Not only had Nathan gotten under her skin, the bastard had also lowered her guard. Anyone could have heard what she said, which could have been devastating not only to her but the coven.

"If she's hurt, you're the one to blame." She tested Nathan's grip, grateful to discover he'd decided to let her go. Sliding free from his embrace, she rushed to drive her point home. "As soon as she drank from you, she was doomed. She can't feed from anyone else. That's your fault." Humiliation hit, an awareness that she'd caused her friend's slow demise.

Sadie had tried to warn her of the consequences but Leigh hadn't listened. Instead she'd forced Sadie to drink from Trey, naïvely believing the asshole werewolf would do right by the woman who'd saved his life. "If I'd known how things were between you two, I wouldn't have pushed the issue."

"What are you talking about?" Trey snarled.

Nathan surged to his feet, taking a stance between Leigh and his Alpha. Another prickle of awareness made her lightheaded, a dizzying hum droning inside her skull. Trey had been unconscious when Sadie had taken his blood but Leigh had assumed he'd remember some small part of the encounter. Even though he'd been fully clothed, she'd seen the enormous tent in his pants. And the scent of his and Sadie's combined lusts had stunk up the basement where he'd been held captive. Leigh had assumed he wanted Sadie as his lover and partner but after that night he hadn't attempted to seek her out.

But what if he didn't have memories of that night?

Was it possible he had no idea what he'd done?

Nathan hadn't believed her when she'd told him how things worked when a vampire fed from a shifter. It was very possible Trey didn't know he'd sentenced Sadie to a slow death after he'd given her his blood.

That changed things.

She studied Trey, watching his movements, relying on her instincts to gauge if he were being honest or avoiding the truth. "You don't remember me, do you?" Considering he'd charged at her earlier, she'd thought he might. Now she wasn't so sure.

"Should I?" A warning flashed through his eyes, the muscles in his jaw clenching.

Holy crap. Oh no. "Yes, you should." She took a deep breath and slowly rose from her seat. Time to get answers. "Do you remember anything about the night we found you? Do you have any memories of what happened?"

"I know Sadie managed to get me out of the hands of Shepherds." He balled his hands into fists and shifted his feet, his eyes glowing yellow. "I know she brought me home before she hit the road without so much as a goodbye or see you later. She left me high and dry. I couldn't even thank her."

For the first time in weeks, Leigh felt a pang of pity for the man.

He'd been unaware of the suffering he'd caused.

"It wasn't easy to get you out," she informed him softly, treading carefully into treacherous waters. "There were a lot of men to go through and we had to fight our way to the basement. Sadie got hurt." Guilt assailed her when Trey's tan face paled and his fingers unfurled. Struggling past her emotions, she continued, "Once we found you, we realized we'd have to carry you out, but we were so weak and tired... "

He'd seemed so large to Leigh back then, almost impossible to lift. Of course she was always weak since she refused to give her body what it needed to thrive. More shame and embarrassment struck. If only she'd taken more blood before she'd gone with Sadie—if only she'd given in to her thirst for once—things could have gone so differently.

"Tell me," he ordered, the words a harsh rasp. "I have a right to know."

"It came down to a decision," she whispered, hating to be the bearer of bad news. "Drink from you or leave you to die." Fear made her pause. Trey was barely holding it together. What would he do when he learned how much Sadie had endured once she'd left the only person she could feed from behind? "Once she'd taken what she needed, we managed to get you to the car and bring you home. Afterward she went to one of our healing caverns but by then the damage had been done."

"Damage?"

Up until then, Leigh didn't realize one word could convey someone's absolute devastation. Trey's reactions were totally honest, holding nothing back. He was prepared to listen to whatever she had to tell him, even if it destroyed him in the process. Her plan to storm into his home and put him in his place had drastically backfired. Although there was a chance he'd heard what she'd told Nathan, she decided to put everything out in the open.

No more secrets, to hell with misunderstandings.

"She started starving to death." When his eyes bulged she hurried to finish. "She couldn't drink from anyone else."

"She what?"

"Vampires can't drink from shifters. Something happens when we do. We become tied to the person we drink from." She couldn't mask her nervousness, not when she could feel Trey's rage from across the room. "It makes it impossible to gain sustenance from any other source—from any other person."

He took a step forward and Nathan countered the movement, standing directly in Trey's path. She didn't think she'd be thankful for Nathan's interference but she released a shaky breath just the same, finding that she preferred having the imposing werewolf on her side.

"Where is she?" Trey sounded panicked but resolute. "Take me to her."

Peering around her protector, she looked at the man who'd caused so much harm yet hadn't known it. It was time to reveal her hand. She removed the pair of earrings she'd stolen from Sadie's bedroom from her pocket. "I can do that but if she's in trouble—and I think she is—I'll need help."

Approaching footsteps drew the attention of everyone in the room. Nathan thrust her behind him, hiding her with his much larger frame. She caught a glimpse of Trey rushing from the room, instructing over his shoulder, "Get her outside. I'll come around and meet you. It's not safe to talk here."

Nathan didn't argue, taking her by the elbow to guide her around a couch. She hadn't noticed the door in the corner, too transfixed by Nathan and then Trey as they'd come at her like Mack trucks. As she stepped outside and breathed in the morning air, she said a small prayer of thanks.

Despite it all.

Even at her worst.

She managed not to cave to her thirst.

Thank heaven for small favors.

Her gaze swept over Nathan's sublime body. There wasn't a single inch of him covered in fat. Beneath the layers of clothing was a body gods would envy. Another tidal wave of lust surged through her, heating her in ways she'd thought she'd never experience after losing her mortality.

And she'd thought denying bloodlust was hard? So much for that.

Every minute in the man's presence was going to be sheer torture.

* * * * *

Trey intercepted Cade before he could make it into the living room. His stomach had formed into a hard knot, anxiety making all of his senses sharp. His heart pounded in his chest, his skin itching as he restrained the animal inside him. The wolf had risen to the surface a long time ago, trying to fight its way free. The beast knew its mate was in trouble and wanted to bring its female home. It felt it alone could protect her, shelter her.

Nourish her.

The disgrace that swamped him made it difficult to breathe. He hadn't seen Sadie for months. And in all that time she hadn't been able to do the one thing that would give her life—the poor thing couldn't fucking *eat*. As a male it was his duty to see to the needs of his mate and he'd failed at the most basic level.

Images from his dreams were like a sucker punch to the face.

Now he knew they weren't dreams but memories. Everything that had happened—her fangs at his throat, the tiny pulls at his skin as she fed—had been real. He'd given her what she needed most only to rip it from her hands. Why hadn't she come to him? Had her pride gotten in her way? Had facing starvation been preferable to coming face-to-face with him again?

He winced. It must have been.

He was aware he hadn't been easy on her. He'd practically taken the gift she'd given him and thrown in back in her face. Vampires were dangerous to shifters, able to turn them into familiars with no free will. Despite that, he still wanted her.

Hell, how could he not?

The night he'd finally gotten hold of her, trapping her lithe body between his and the ground, he'd known they'd be perfect together. She'd been so hot, her pussy weeping for his touch. One kiss had set them on fire, turning the world upside down. He wanted to hammer into the softness of her cunt and hear her cries of pleasure. She'd been right there with him too, as caught up in the moment as he was.

Then he'd opened his mouth and fucked it all up.

After tonight, you'll never see me again. You have my word.

He was so deep in thought he barreled right into Cade. The human grunted and shoved Trey to the side. "What the fuck? I thought you were leaving."

Trey hurried to make an excuse—any excuse. Even if Caden wasn't a shifter he had spot-on instincts. The man had been an investigator once upon a time. Years had honed his intuition, allowing him to detect skeletons in anyone's closet.

"I forgot my wallet."

"Uh-huh," Cade responded and leaned against the closest wall. "Since when do you explain yourself to me?"

Fuck. "Since you're playing secretary, it's the least I can do."

Cade brought a hand to his chin and stroked the scar marring his skin. His steely eyes saw far more than Trey liked. "Why do I smell bullshit?"

"Maybe you've been kissing too much ass?" The Alpha in him wouldn't allow Trey to sever eye contact but he did move away from Cade, putting as much distance between them as possible. "Members of the pack could start arriving at any time. I suggest you get things ready."

"What the fuck are you up to?"

That was typical Cade — brash, ballsy and arrogant as hell. Trey found the man's bluntness refreshing, even if he'd never admit it to anyone in the pack. As an Alpha, it was rare that anyone would go tit for tat with him. However, Cade tended to overestimate his worth in the pack. While he was worth having around and had managed to get in the good graces of Diskant Black — the Omega and head of all the shifters of New York — he wasn't above the rules.

This time Trey didn't ask, he ordered, "Get ready to greet the pack."

Even if Cade liked to push buttons, he'd been around long enough to know he'd have to answer to Diskant if he stepped out of line. And it wasn't good to bother Diskant right now. His mate, Ava, was in the early stages of pregnancy but had finally started to show. Anything that tore the Omega's focus from his female wasn't welcomed.

"Whatever you say," Cade drawled, each word laced with sarcasm. Despite his apparent annoyance he was smart enough to lower his gaze as he moved away from the wall and started walking toward the garage. "I live to serve."

Trey waited for Cade to exit the residence, listening as the back door opened and slammed closed before he rushed from the hallway. Nathan couldn't leave the property with Leigh on his arm. The guards would ask him too many questions. He wondered where he might find his Beta and unexpected guest as he ran to the small door that led to the back of the property. To his relief he spotted them as soon as he stepped outside. Nathan had taken Leigh to the side of the building, keeping her hidden among the bushes. The man had boxed her in the cage of his arms, standing protectively over her.

"Would you stop?" Leigh's soft reprimand drifted to Trey's ears. "I told you I'm fine."

"Don't lie," Nathan growled. "Not to me."

"Children," Trey interrupted the two before their argument escalated and drew unwanted attention, keeping his voice low, "stop fighting."

The instant Nathan lowered his guard, Leigh took advantage. She ducked under his arm, gaining her freedom. "It's about time you joined us," she hissed, tossing strands of her long, dark hair over her shoulder. "I was starting to think you'd changed your mind."

He had to force the wolf back, struggling to whisper instead of howl. "No way in hell." Looking past her, he started working out an exit strategy. His motorcycle only allowed room for two. They needed a vehicle. Unfortunately he wasn't in a position to retrieve his keys and get to his car. "How did you get here?"

"I drove," Leigh snapped, her blue eyes shooting daggers in his direction. "The car's parked one street over."

His gaze drifted to Nathan. "I'm going to distract the guards while you two slip out."

Nathan nodded and wrapped his hand around Leigh's wrist. "Hurry."

Trey didn't have to be told twice.

They were lucky to have gone undetected for as long as they had.

He strode purposefully toward the line of trees along the back of the property. Members of the pack rotated keeping guard, taking shifts that lasted anywhere from eight to twelve hours. Trey approved the schedule but didn't go so far as to make it. As long as he had eyes on the place he didn't care how the pecking order was decided. Movement caught his eye, a subtle shift of color that would go unrecognized by the human eye.

Bingo.

"It's me," he called out. "Reveal yourselves."

One by one, they did.

He held his head high, approaching the wolves with total confidence.

Any display of weakness could create total chaos.

He stopped several feet away and called on his wolf. The beast responded, revealing as much of its power as Trey would allow it to. As he anticipated, the members of his pack immediately backed down. They lowered their gazes, taking on subservient stances.

This was it.

Showtime.

Chapter Three

Sadie fought the welcoming arms of sleep and struggled through the heavy fog keeping her from complete awareness. Her head slowly cleared, thoughts no longer splintered. Opening her heavy lids, she blinked rapidly and willed her eyes to focus. Shapes and colors bled together, making her head spin. She ignored the dry tickle at the back of her throat, drawing a steadying breath as she fixed her gaze on tiny crack in the ceiling.

How long had she been under?

Days? Weeks?

Months?

She resented the fear that slammed into her. After all, she was responsible for her current predicament. She hadn't been captured. No sir. She'd walked willingly into the devil's arms, moronically believing she'd finally meet her end and find some semblance of peace in the afterlife.

Stop. Pull yourself together, damn it.

Despite her weakened state, she managed to shift her arms and legs. A white-hot stab shot up her back. Her cold and tired muscles protested the movement, stinging as they stretched and flexed. She relied on years of training to push through, willing her body to ignore the pain. She didn't know what Aldon wanted with her but it couldn't be good. If she'd learned anything over the last few months it was that the man had a plan—even if she didn't know what that plan might be—for everything. Her captivity wasn't random. She served some sort of purpose.

And you handed yourself over to the bastard like a dessert on a dainty platter.

Moron.

Aldon was far more powerful than she'd thought, staving her hunger and using her weakened state to keep her incapacitated by sleep. Each time she'd woken he'd appeared and handed her back to the Sandman. There hadn't been time to question his motives. One minute she'd been aware of her surroundings—groggy but aware—the next her eyes had slammed closed and she'd gone nighty-night.

Which is why you should stop wasting time. Get your shit in check.

Pay attention. Right now.

She held her breath and gritted her teeth, trying to block out the fire that slithered up her torso as she rolled onto her belly. Decimated muscles groaned in protest, burning with the effort. Each panted breath tore through her chest, her lungs feeling as though they might burst as she attempted to remain quiet. At first she thought the pounding in her ears was due to adrenaline and the slow thudding of her heart. Then she realized it was actual sound resonating from beneath her. She closed her eyes, relying on her astute sense of hearing to listen.

A lock unlatched—the snick loud and crisp in her ears—and a door protested as it creaked open. Judging by the distinct sound and the clarity of her hearing, she realized she was only a floor or so away from the entrance to Aldon's lair.

Good news if she could get to her feet and find an alternative exit.

"Isn't this a pleasant surprise?" Aldon's deep voice drifted to her ears as he welcomed his visitor.

"Pleasant surprise, my ass."

Her heart skipped a beat and then lodged in her throat when she heard the corresponding acknowledgement. She screwed her eyes shut, fighting back tears. She knew that voice, had thought about it so often she wondered if perhaps she hadn't woken at all but remained snared in the land of dreams.

It couldn't be. How could it?

Trey.

A stupid, inflated belief in romance tried to influence her thoughts, tempting her to believe he'd come to rescue her. He'd barge in, order Aldon to hand her over and she'd find safety in his arms. He'd lift her to his chest, kiss her, promise to protect her, take her to his family and home and never let her go.

As-fucking-if.

Painful memories from the past suffocated hope.

Trey wasn't her lover. Hell, he wasn't even her friend. He might be willing to fuck her silly but that was it. No strings attached. No permanency. Her body attracted him but her nature disgusted him. At best he might text her for booty calls on the down-low. If she played her cards right he might even be willing to offer her the one thing she desperately needed to survive — his blood — in exchange for a bit of pussy.

Her self-loathing didn't last long, not when she heard Trey snarl, "You just fucked with the wrong bull." She jerked as the sound of a fist connecting with bone resonated from below, followed by an enormous thump as someone landed on the floor.

A cold chill shot down her spine when Aldon laughed. "Is that the best you've got?"

"Not even close," Trey growled, his voice shaky, indicating he was already in motion and prepared to dish out some serious damage. "That's my version of a bitch-slap."

What the hell was going on? Why was Trey here? And why was he fighting Aldon?

Last time she checked the two were on speaking terms.

They shared common interests…or so she thought.

She knew the moment they engaged in combat. Even though she couldn't see what was taking place, she knew how the fight would go. Vampires were fast but werewolves were strong. Aldon would try to wear Trey down while Trey tried to rip out his opponent's throat as quickly as possible. Assuming Trey wanted to kill Aldon. If not he'd be lucky if he could put a dent in the vampire. Aldon was too powerful. She'd only glimpsed a portion of his strength but she knew he wasn't a normal black mage vamp.

He had a secret, one that made him lethal.

A sharp creak ripped her attention from the ruckus downstairs. She turned her head, ashamed that something so simple took effort. She watched, shocked, as Leigh opened the door to the room. The poor girl looked like death warmed over. Her skin, while always pale, was now ghastly white. Dark shadows decorated the area beneath her eyes. She'd pulled her hair from her face, securing it at her nape with an elastic band. Sadie opened her mouth to speak but remained silent when Leigh's eyes bulged and she shook her head.

"*Quiet,*" Leigh instructed telepathically. "*You can ask questions later.*" Advancing forward, she questioned, "*What did he do to you? How bad are you hurt?*"

"*He didn't do anything.*" Sadie's pride rankled at the confession. "*He knew I had been tracking him. When he confronted me I lost consciousness from hunger. He brought me here.*" Speaking of which. "*Where is here, by the way? How did you find me?*"

Why is Trey with you?

The last thought wasn't meant for Leigh but the young vampire heard it anyway. Sympathy smoothed her tired features as she reached Sadie's side and placed a comforting hand on her arm. Leigh felt so cold, her body in desperate need of blood. Sadie cringed. Leigh shouldn't have come here. The girl was newly changed and unable to defend herself. She needed to learn to harness her magic in order to face the world.

"*Don't worry about that right now. We're going to get you out,*" Leigh thought. Lifting her head she whispered, "I'm going to need some help. She can't move."

A large form stepped through the door. Even though Leigh blocked most of him from view Sadie recognized his voice when he murmured, "I'm here."

Nathan. Trey's Beta.

Sadie didn't know much about the male, although their paths had crossed in the not-so-distant past—after she'd killed off a few Shepherds and saved Diskant's mate, Ava Brisbane. Nathan had been there too, injured himself but trying to defend the mortal woman. They'd formed an unlikely truce, agreeing to work together to save Ava's life.

The prism of confusion shined brighter, becoming dizzying.

First Trey appeared. Now Nathan was with him.

What were they doing? Didn't they know better?

Nathan slid his arms beneath Sadie's stomach and rolled her over as he lifted her to his chest. Her head fell back, one arm tucked against the man holding her, the other hanging like a broken branch at her side. She must have looked like a tattered china doll, hanging together by fraying pieces of thread. The last time she'd seen Nathan he'd been bleeding at her feet.

Humiliation tore through her, the most unwanted and damning of sentiments.

Somehow things always came full circle. It was almost poetic in a sickening and perverse kind of way. She was supposed to be the strong one, defending the weak. Never had she imagined herself like this. Cradled in a werewolf's arms, unable to stand or walk. The roles had been reversed. Now Nathan was the one watching over her, keeping her from harm.

Leigh led the way to the door. Once she'd peeked outside, she exited the room.

Nathan followed, staying close, allowing Sadie to get a glimpse of her surroundings.

She was definitely in a home, not a condemned building or bunker as vampires were known to use when they wanted to capture and cage prey. Framed pictures adorned neatly painted and papered walls with expensive crown-molded ceilings. They were on the top floor of the residence, a place that was old but well restored. Pristine wooden slats sped by as Nathan quickened his pace.

The delicious aroma of blood assailed her nose, thick and hot, coming fresh from the source. She knew that smell, could identify it anywhere. She should have been worried about Trey's wounds—he was quick to heal but had been injured severely enough to bleed freely—but she felt her fangs drop. The need to feed became her sudden and primary focus. Even in her current state she felt her muscles tense in preparation for attack. Her nature was ready to give it all one last hurrah in order to survive.

"Fuck!" Trey bellowed, so close she could not only smell his blood but also hear the steady beating of his heart. "Nathan, heads-up! He's on the move!"

"Leigh," Nathan snarled. "Behind me. Now."

Leigh did as she was told, darting past Nathan and vanishing from Sadie's line of sight. Aldon appeared, standing only a few feet away from them with an arrogant smirk on his blood-splattered face. His nose had been busted but he'd already started healing. The world spun and Sadie's stomach plummeted when Nathan dropped her and charged the vampire. She hit the ground, her head cracking against the hard floor. Through pained eyes, she watched Nathan sprint toward his enemy.

Aldon disappeared and Nathan rushed through empty air. The male staggered, trying to stop. Trey appeared at the top of the stairs and Nathan barreled directly into him. Watching the enormous men crash to the ground would have been comical if the situation wasn't so dire. She felt nauseous, wanting to vomit.

The men couldn't see what was right in front of them.

Aldon wasn't trying to kill Trey or Nathan.

He'd been luring them.

Clarity didn't always come easy. Sometimes a person discovered things they should have seen long before—things that could change or alter someone's life—often when it was too late. She didn't like having her moment then and there, lying on the floor, useless and forgotten.

"*Stubborn creature.*" Aldon's observant words were no longer cynical but disturbing as they echoed through her head. "*So certain of yourself. So arrogant. So predictable. You wear your pride like a shield. I suppose I should thank you for simplifying things.*"

Damn her to hell. She deserved to burn.

She hadn't been smart when she'd tracked Aldon. She'd been stupid.

If the coven had been spying on him, likely he'd been spying on them as well. It wouldn't have taken much. Their defenses were solid but he wasn't like any vampire she'd ever seen. He could have spied on the house from a safe distance, collecting all the information he needed. He'd known she'd been following him. That much was clear. The conceited prick had probably encouraged it. She'd walked right into his trap, caught in his web, giving him an advantage.

She remembered the way he'd bitten her—the way he'd sighed in contentment—drinking what little blood she had to offer. Yet he hadn't taken more. It hadn't been enough to sustain or nourish him because he hadn't meant it to be. He'd taken her blood to access her memories, confirming whatever suspicions he must have had.

He wanted something…or someone.

But who? There wasn't anyone of notice in the coven. Not really. The strongest of them was a newborn who didn't know how to cast a spell. And Leigh hated using magic…

A veil lifted, giving her free sight.

Leigh.

It all made sense.

One mouthful of Sadie's blood and Aldon had seen what Leigh could do. With the fledgling's help he'd be able to locate people with simple objects and influence the minds of others. And that was just the tip of the iceberg. Leigh detested blood but once she accepted what she was and embraced her full potential she'd be as formidable as a demigod.

Goddess, save us.

With Leigh's powers, Aldon would be unstoppable.

Terrified and unable to do anything more than witness what was to come, she shouted out to Leigh with her mind, putting as much warning into the thought as possible.

"Run."

Trey didn't stop to see if Nathan had been harmed during their collision. As soon as his feet were steady he rushed for Sadie. Fuck, she was pale. So damn lifeless it terrified him. Right then he didn't care about anything but getting to her. Something warned him if he didn't he might not get a second chance.

The yards that separated them felt like miles.

Leigh plunged to her knees, sinking to Sadie's side. She gripped Sadie's torso, babbling words that made no sense. The moment she had a decent grip on his mate she fell on her ass and tugged Sadie closer. Aldon appeared behind them and snagged Leigh by the back of her neck. The frail female struggled, screaming in fear, holding on to Sadie for dear life. Nathan's outraged bray carried through the hallway, informing Trey his Beta was right on his ass.

Sadie's voice seemed to roar through his head, pounding in his ears, her desperation palpable. *"Don't let him take her."*

For the first time Aldon's self-assured smirk vanished. He bent at the waist and pulled on Leigh's neck, ripping one of her arms free from Sadie's limp form. Leigh thrust her legs out, wrapping them around Sadie's waist and locking her ankles together. Each yank from Aldon lifted Leigh and Sadie from the ground. Leigh's dark hair cascaded around her face and shoulders, the knot she'd placed it in falling apart. It was the craziest fucking thing Trey had ever seen, a tangle of arms, legs and hair.

For a moment Aldon, Leigh and Sadie seemed to flicker as though their bodies were dissipating before his eyes. Panic and terror sent Trey's senses into hyper-alert. He moved faster than he ever had in his life, building speed. Aldon was trying to phase them out. If he succeeded Trey might not ever find his mate again. He'd rip the entire goddamn building apart before that happened.

"Do it and I'll fucking kill you!" he thundered.

Aldon lifted his head, staring Trey in the eye. The vampire's irises changed color, going from dark to icy blue. His white-blond hair lifted into the air as he called on the magic inside him. Although being a natural born Alpha protected Trey from the compulsion to shift forms or fall prey to Aldon's dark magic, he couldn't stem the way the energy felt and the way it seemed to charge his skin.

Motherfucker.

He snarled when the tingle of magic flittered over his flesh, infuriated and petrified for his mate when his feet left the ground. An invisible force thrust him aside, knocking the wind from his lungs. He threw up his arms, trying to shield himself as his body flew toward the upstairs railing. There was no way he could prevent the collision so he braced for impact.

Wood splintered and parted as he broke through the beams, several spindles snapping and hurtling to the lower floor. He almost went over the edge with them but managed to extend his nails, slamming down his hands, burying his sharp claws into the wooden floor. His lower body hung over the lip of the walkway, legs kicking into empty space.

Don't let go. Get back up.

Nathan's livid growl had him flexing his fingers, digging his claws into the floor. He held on tight, commanding his muscles to bear his weight. The wolf inside him backed the order, rising to the surface, giving him strength. He lifted his head and watched Nathan slam into Aldon. The vampire released Leigh but the impact broke her away from Sadie. His mate came at him, sliding across the floor, stopping just shy of the jagged railing. She was so close if his hands were free he could reach out and snatch her.

I'll fucking kill him. Nice and slow.

Glancing at Aldon and Nathan, he collected his energy to make it to the upper level.

Then he felt the soft brush of Sadie's lips over the back of his wrist.

In his dreams her bite was the most erotic thing he'd ever experienced.

This time, however, it wasn't quite the same.

Her fangs scored the delicate bones in his wrist, her aim not true or clean. He hissed when her lips surrounded the torn tissue and she sucked. She drew so fucking hard on his skin he wondered if she'd rip the shit away from his bones. Although he wanted to provide for her, he tried to force her away. He'd feed her as soon as this was over. He had to hurry.

Aldon and Nathan had taken their fight to the floor.

Nathan wasn't strong enough to take down the vampire. Fuck, Trey wasn't sure who or what *would* be capable of such a thing. In the past Aldon had been one hell of an ally. Now? He was a bitch of an opponent. Trey knew the man was resilient. But this? He'd never imagined such a thing.

"Sadie, baby," he murmured, trying to get her attention. "Let go."

Her hands lashed out, wrapping around his forearm. The suction around his wrist increased, blood seeping past her lips. He watched, amazed, as color returned to her cheeks. Her fingers changed, filling out. To his amazement the rest of her did as well. Her face plumped, softness padding her bones. Each swallow resurrected her from death, bringing her back to life.

Lightheadedness assailed him and white speckles danced over his eyes.

Fucking shit.

He was going to pass out. If that happened, he couldn't protect her.

No way in hell. I'll die first.

"Enough!" Aldon yelled, breaking Trey's attention from his mate.

Nathan flew from one side of the hallway to the other, collapsing in a heap on the ground. The Beta didn't try to rise, still and unmoving on the floor, meaning he was out for the count. Trey hoped like hell the damage wasn't permanent. He didn't think it was. He felt each and every death in his pack. Nathan wasn't done, not yet. He must've lost consciousness. It was the only thing that would prevent him from getting up and charging at Aldon.

There was no way Nathan would leave Leigh unprotected.

Leigh tripped over her feet when Aldon turned toward her. She backed away, kicking out with her legs, shuffling along with her hands. Her huge blue eyes were full of panic, her pale pink lips parted in horror.

Son of a bitch.

Aldon was going to take her and there was nothing Trey could do about it. Sadie had taken so much blood he wasn't sure he could maintain a grip on the floor much less take on a vampire with immeasurable strength. Aldon advanced—one more step and he'd have Leigh in his grasp—and lifted his right arm.

Sadie disappeared—there one moment and gone the next.

The miserable burning at his wrist vanished.

Before he could react to her loss, Sadie reappeared in front of Leigh.

Her artic-blue eyes blazed in warning, her hands splayed open at her sides. She hadn't bothered removing his blood from the corners of her mouth, the liquid making her lips appear cherry-red. In the blink of an eye she formed a fist and planted it directly in the middle of Aldon's face. The blow carried more power than Trey would have thought Sadie capable of.

Aldon staggered back several feet, lifting a hand to his bloodied lip, narrowing his eyes.

Sadie stretched her arm behind her, reaching toward her fallen comrade. A silent communication took place between the women, a mental message from one vampire to the other. One moment Leigh was terrified and on her ass and the next she was on her knees, reaching for Sadie's wrist. Leigh bared her fangs and lowered her mouth toward Sadie's pale skin.

"Not so fast," Aldon barked, moving so quickly Trey didn't have a chance to let go of the railing or get out of the asshole's range. The vampire's hand wound around Trey's throat, Aldon's grip so tight it felt as though it crushed his windpipe.

Fuck me.

"Don't." Sadie didn't sound as confident, her voice cracking. "Leave him out of this."

"All it'll take is a flex of my fingers." Aldon's hold on Trey's neck intensified, depriving him of oxygen. "I'll snap his neck like a twig."

He totally could too. His fingers were locked tight.

Trey gagged, needing to draw a breath.

"His pack will avenge him." Sadie's words were laced with venom. "I'll make sure Diskant Black knows what went down here. They'll come for you. They'll hunt you down."

"Consider it a risk I'm willing to take."

Trey choked, cursing his failure as an Alpha and male. He'd never felt so weak or useless in his life. Here was, just shy of losing consciousness, when his mate needed him most. Sheer willpower had him directing his gaze toward Sadie, needing to convey his failure, sorrow and shame to her.

Leave it him to fuck things up in the most monumental way possible.

It wasn't bad enough he'd made her suffer for months. Oh no.

Now, when there was nothing left and he was going to die, he was leading her into her grave as well. He'd seen how bad she was—realized that Leigh had told him the truth about Sadie's condition the moment he laid eyes on his female's thin and fragile form—and knowing he was about to force her to endure the same torment...

Fuck, it tore him up inside.

Never.

His wolf rose, taking over, and he let it. His body started shifting. He didn't fight it, deciding it was all he had left. The beast readily answered his call, eager for blood, hungry for the kill. This is what he should have done from the start.

Enter. Destroy.

Claim.

Fur sprouted from his skin as his bones contorted. The animal wanted to tear out Aldon's throat and howl in victory as the life faded from the vampire's eyes. It would destroy the male who dared threaten its mate, sending a warning far and wide of what would happen if anyone fucked with what belonged to the wolf and the wolf alone.

"Make your choice," Aldon warned, maintaining his grip despite Trey's shift from man to beast. "Three...two..."

A hand snaked around the back of Aldon's neck, Nathan's fingers taut as he snarled, "Remember me, motherfucker?"

Trey dropped when Aldon released him, falling rapidly toward the ground. He finished his shift midair, trying to land on his feet. Power coursed through him, brought on by the change. The effects of his recent blood loss evaporated. He hit cushiony carpet with a dull thud, covered in shredded pieces of clothing. Shaking the garments from his body, he stood on shaky legs. His sides heaved as he fought to breathe, rotating toward the stairs as he gained his balance.

He heard the fighting upstairs.

His Beta would give it all he had but Nathan could only hold Aldon off for so long.

While his second-in-command was strong, the vampire was built like a fucking Viking, not to mention Aldon had some serious mystical juju at his disposal. Trey rushed up each wooden slat, racing against the clock, determined not to fail his female this time. His wolf snarled, its jaws clenching in anticipation. Arriving at his destination, he discovered Leigh was gone and Nathan was on the ground beneath Aldon. Sadie was bent over the two, her arm wrapped snugly around the vampire's waist.

"Let him go," she ordered and fisted her fingers in Aldon's hair, snapping his head back.

Aldon jerked away from Nathan and reached behind him as he rose. "You stupid little bitch."

His nails lengthened, becoming sharp as he raked them along Sadie's back, tearing through her shirt and skin from mid-back to shoulder. She didn't scream but Trey heard her whimper. Fury consumed him, coating the world in a haze of red. He'd kill the stupid piece of shit. Break every bone in his goddamned body.

"Fine, we'll do it your way," Aldon whispered. "For now."

A solid burst of magic sent Sadie away from Aldon and Nathan, her slim form rushing across the distance toward him.

He felt hopeless in that moment, knowing he couldn't shift fast enough to catch her, wishing that somehow he could.

For once—thank God—he wasn't left with an enormous amount of shame as a mate.

Sadie righted herself like a cat, using momentum and speed to rotate her torso around. He moved aside, watching in awe as she landed on her feet. She rose with her fists balled, ready to face Aldon. She radiated beauty and strength, a true sight to behold.

Magic blasted from her.

It felt different. Not as dark. Almost pleasant in a way. The sensation bristled over his fur and settled comfortably against his skin. It calmed him, soothing the wolf, giving him a sense of strength he'd lost when she'd drank from him.

Before she could use her power or wield her magic Aldon raised his hand, saluted her and said, "This isn't over."

Then he disappeared, leaving Nathan on the ground, Trey growling at empty air and Sadie standing over the two of them—braced for war with no adversary in sight.

Chapter Four

Protection.
Find what you need.
Sword, sword, sword.

Sadie's training kicked in, directing her as though she were on autopilot. Aldon could reappear at any moment. In order to defend herself and everyone else she needed her weapon. She closed her eyes and focused, calling on her magic. The blade she carried had been attuned to her by blood.

If it was nearby she'd sense it...

There.

She didn't hesitate, launching herself over the railing. The instant she landed she moved, hurrying toward the hum of magic. It didn't matter why Aldon hadn't kept the sword instead of tossing it in the trash. His stupidity equaled her gain. She saw the sheath, identifying the leather she painstakingly oiled once a week.

Yes. This is what she needed.

The instant the hilt hit her hand she pulled the weapon free of the casing.

Movement caught her eye. She reared back, ready to dish out some heavy damage, sending a surge of magic down her arm and into her weapon. She'd expected an attack. Aldon would come at her blindly, ready to take her down immediately. What she hadn't anticipated was Trey — naked as the day he was born — wrapping his arms around her waist as he sank to his knees. The thrill of impending battle had her blood pumping but Trey's touch sent her thoughts in another direction. A split second, the weight of his body leaning steadily against hers, and she was doomed. She lowered her arm and peered down, gazing at his dark hair and tanned, muscular shoulders.

She'd been so wrong.

Memories didn't do him justice at all.

In person he was bigger, stronger—sexier.

Licking her lips, she savored the small sampling of blood she hadn't bothered wiping away. She should have asked for permission but she hadn't. When she'd bitten him earlier she'd been too focused on her hunger to think about consideration or lust. Now, however, she was more than aware of the man. She could smell him, feel the heat of his body and hear the hurried rhythm of his pulse.

"Easy, darlin'," he murmured, his voice like gravel cascading over silk. "I've got you."

Her eyes burned as she struggled to hold back tears.

If only that was true.

She wanted so desperately for it to be, for Trey to hold her, keep her...

Love her.

Months of longing had brought her to this moment, confronting her own worst enemy. Even if she'd tried to convince herself that she'd deny the male, she wanted him too much to do so. She could have died without experiencing any of the things she yearned for most with the man at her feet. The blood she'd consumed rushed through her body, suffusing her muscles with life, bringing on a desire so strong it could devour them both.

Her nipples hardened to points, the fire in her belly pulsing downward to her clit. His hair brushed her forearm when he feathered his lips over her free hand, the teeniest of touches yet goose bumps spread all over her skin. How would those prickly strands feel against her thighs if he went down on her? Would he take his time? Or would he go at her like the wild man she imagined he'd be?

He'd know what he was doing. Men like him had years of experience.

"Leigh." Nathan's appearance at the foot of the stairs—as well as the name he uttered—iced the heat in Sadie's veins. "Where did she go?" he demanded, snarling. "Take me to her."

How selfish could she possibly be?

One touch and she'd forgotten about her responsibilities. Leigh's safety wasn't important. Nothing was. All she could think about was Trey—his scent, his warmth, how good he felt.

Damn her for being so weak and vulnerable.

She deserved whatever she had coming to her.

"Where is she?" Nathan shouted.

Sadie wanted to respond but wasn't certain what she should say.

Leigh had taken enough of Sadie's blood to flee but was her friend safe? Had she taken shelter at the coven? Or had she ventured to a safe house? Sadie hadn't had enough time to think ahead or ask her sister-in-magic what her plans might be. Since Aldon had made it clear he'd do whatever it took ensure Leigh's capture—and the fucking prick was strong enough to phase her out of any location—she had to make sure Leigh would be safe. The coven had power but was only capable of so much. They weren't physical creatures and never had been.

That was her job.

You've got to go. Find her. Formulate a plan.

Shifters—to her knowledge—didn't read minds, but Trey might as well have. "No," he growled, holding her tighter. "You're not going anywhere." She wondered how it was possible, thinking maybe she'd misdirected a thought in his direction when he said, "You belong to me, baby. Leigh told me everything. The moment you drank from me you sealed the deal. You're stuck with me. Don't even think about trying to escape."

What the hell did that mean? She belonged to him?

Fuck no, she didn't.

He'd turned her away not so long ago—even as he confessed she was the female intended for him—and she'd been humiliated. She remembered the agony of his dismissal, his rejection corroding her heart from the inside out. Even if he wanted her physically he didn't have the balls to claim her as his mate to his pack. There was too much at stake. Shepherds had attacked Trey's city, the werewolves he protected needed him more than she did and they both knew it.

Nothing had changed since then.

He wanted to fuck her. Maybe even to keep her on his terms.

But at what cost?

Suddenly the sword felt too heavy, the air in the room too thick.

To her shame she admitted that she'd be whatever he wanted her to be.

"Why are you even here?" She found it odd she felt so detached from the words, as though someone else had posed the question rather than herself. "Why did you come?"

"Leigh brought us," Nathan answered, talking in a rush of words, his brows furrowed as he wrung his hands. "She told us you needed help—she told us everything." He lowered his arms, his hazel green gaze so intense it was difficult for Sadie to meet his eyes. "She's my mate and belongs at my side. I have a right to know where she is."

What in the ever-loving hell? You've got to be shitting me.

Perhaps it was fatigue or shock that made her laugh at the possibility of such a thing. She tried to wrench herself from Trey's embrace. When that didn't work she lifted the sword clutched in her hand. He intercepted her mid-swing, capturing her wrist. He maintained his grip on her waist with his other arm, keeping her snug against him. Like this, she couldn't move. She was trapped once more, unable to do anything.

"Your mate?" she snarled, blood pounding in her head, emotional demons from the past whispering in her ear. "You expect me to believe that both of you mated with vampires? Contrary to what you might assume, I'm not a total idiot. She's a member of my coven. I'm responsible for her protection."

No way would she stand by as Nathan cast Leigh aside. She knew how deeply that wound went. He'd break the young woman's heart, ripping her chest open and watching her slowly bleed to death. Leigh had been through enough. Sadie would be damned if she let the woman be hurt on her watch.

Bolstered by fury, she snapped, "She doesn't need or want you, asshole. If she belongs by anyone's side it's mine."

Nathan took a menacing step toward them.

"Don't let her bait you," Trey ordered and rose, keeping his arms locked around her waist. Part of her recognized what was happening but another part of her had risen above the scene, causing her to witness what was taking place rather than actually participating. "She's crashing, man."

"What are you talking about?" Nathan should have sounded closer, not farther away.

What the fuck was going on?

Why couldn't she hear?

Why did her vision seem so out of focus?

Her body felt weightless, as though she was no longer of substance. Then her mind fogged over, thoughts tumbling out of sequence. Concentrating, she attempted to piece them together.

Leigh and Nathan. Mates?

Absolutely not.

Trey coming for her? Rushing in to secure her safety?

Only if the world had come to an end.

It didn't make sense. Something in her mind clicked—like an openhanded slap to the face—and she got wise to what had been taking place. Of course. That was it. None of it was real. She'd managed to delude herself yet again.

It's another dream.

It made total sense given the circumstances.

What better way to live in captivity than to create your own dreamworld with characters manipulated by mental puppet strings? The turn of events was created in her mind to cope with her situation. She tried to focus, to take the dream in a different direction. She'd take herself way back—to the only night she'd had with Trey. Only this time she'd make him say and do the things she wanted him to. She'd obtain some level of satisfaction even if she had to fake it.

To her frustration nothing changed, no matter how hard she tried to coerce her mind to another path. Trey remained, so tantalizingly close she could smell him. His pulse beckoned, his muscular body taunting her with pleasure that always remained out of her reach. Was that what was about to happen? Would he turn her away a second time, laughing in her face, tossing her aside like a secondhand toy?

Hadn't it been enough that he'd starved her body?

Did he also have to pick apart her soul?

Left with nothing else, she did as she'd longed to for days.

Why not? It wasn't as if anyone would hear. If this was her future it was time to lance the wound, remove the infection and start over. Her heart had to come to terms with things once and for all. Otherwise she'd remain trapped in demented nightmares she couldn't escape.

Just like this one.

Dropping the sword, she threw back her head and released the scream of anguish that had been contained for far too long. She focused on the sound—finding it fitting that her shriek started out fierce but quickly turned into a miserable wail—and found peace in doing the only thing she could.

Finally—after all she'd been through—she let go and accepted her fate.

Trey wasn't a version of heaven.

He was her tormentor in hell.

Damn it!

Even now, holding Sadie tightly against him and promising her safety, Trey had failed his mate. He'd sensed her turmoil and confusion but had attributed it as a natural response to Leigh's departure. Prior to her shift in mood he'd scented her desire, his cock becoming hard as a rock. She's been ready for him, primed for whatever he wanted to give her. If he'd wanted he could have lifted her off the ground and taken her to the wall. She'd have let him. She'd been so hot, the sweet and heady fragrance of her cunt right below his nose.

Then Nathan had appeared and flipped a switch inside his mate.

Once again, much-needed knowledge came too late. Her behavior wasn't a case of nerves or transgressions gone awry. His proud and unshakable mate had slammed into a wall she couldn't demolish. He'd never seen her like this—unable to control herself, crumbling right before his eyes.

"She's been through hell and back. It's time to pay her dues," he snarled at his Beta, keeping Sadie pressed to his chest, loathing the anguish he heard in her cry. "Her emotions are all over the place. Use your nose. Scent the goddamn air. She's about to have a mental fucking breakdown."

"We don't have time for this." Nathan's desperation beat against Trey, the Beta seeking the security and guidance of his Alpha. Instinctively his wolf reached out to Nathan's, trying to settle the raging beast. "We have to find Leigh. It's too dangerous to wait. Aldon—"

"Can't you see I have my own shit to deal with?"

He got Nathan's concern—he really did—but he couldn't focus on the Beta's anxiety over Leigh, nor could he devote time to ease his pack mate's worries. For once he had to put his needs—his female's fucking needs—over the wants of others. He'd known she needed him but had grievously underestimated just how much.

Why didn't she come to me before this?

"Get the car and bring it 'round. Grab my clothes outta the trunk. We have to split," he instructed, thankful when Sadie's cries died down. Then he saw her posture, the way that she tuned out everything around her.

Damn it.

He expected tears, or perhaps her to cling to him for support. She did neither, remaining where she stood like he wasn't even there. Lifting his head, he found Nathan gawking at the two of them. The wolf snarled its disapproval in his head, rising once again to display its dominance over its pack mate.

"That wasn't a request," he roared, allowing his fangs to drop, giving the Beta proper warning. "Get the goddamn car!"

"Where in the hell do you think we can go? The pack is waiting for you at the station. You can't take her there."

Fuck. Nathan had a point. Thinking fast, he blurted, "Diskant."

"Are you insane?" Nathan shifted his feet and folded his arms over his chest. "He'll tell the pack. It'll cause an uprising we can't control."

"She saved Ava's life," Trey reminded him. "Diskant owes her."

Nathan frowned, his eyes glowing bright yellowish-green. "That's true but she's a vampire. He doesn't trust her."

"I don't give a flying fuck." So help him, if Nathan didn't do as he was told soon, Trey was going to blow a fuse and take the man's head off. "Get the car."

Thank God Nathan finally listened and stopped arguing. They'd parked a few blocks over and walked the remaining distance to the brownstone Leigh had directed them to. Ironically, Trey knew the location well, having been the one to install Aldon's security systems. That was how he'd created a tentative partnership with the man.

One the pack knew little about.

Fuck. Fuck. Fuck.

When they got wind of what had happened, the shit was definitely going to hit the fan. He wasn't sure how things were going to go down from here. He and Nathan had planned on preparing the pack for their big reveal after they exposed the truth to his friend and the Omega of the city, Diskant Black. Circumstances, as they often did, altered his strategy.

He'd have to come up with a different arrangement.

Something he—and the unraveling woman in his arms—could live with.

"Sadie." He glided his fingers into her hair and cupped the back of her neck. Then he let her go and brought his other hand to her jaw, using the backs of his knuckles to lift her face toward his. "Look at me."

His heart sank when their eyes met.

Her irises—normally as vibrant as the sky on a cloudless summer day—had dulled over.

She's staring right through me.

Acting in the only way he knew, he gently cradled her face and brought his lips to hers. She smelled so fucking enticing, wildflowers with a dash of incense. Their mouths met in the barest of touches, a mere whispering of contact. Still she didn't react, motionless as a statue. He upped the ante, bringing the hand nestled in her hair down and around. Grasping her ass, he yanked her hips to his. His desire for her hadn't diminished, his cock was thick and fully engorged. He let her feel the entire length, rolling his hips for added measure, sliding his dick up and down her leather pants.

Her lips parted and he accepted the invitation, guiding his tongue into her mouth, keeping things slow and sensual.

As much as he wanted to pin her to the floor and fuck her hard and fast—leaving her marked with his scent and branded by his teeth—it wasn't the time or place. She needed to be lured from the darkness that held her. He groaned when she placed her hands on his biceps and squeezed, her sharp little nails digging into his skin.

That's it, baby. Just like that.

Kneading her ass, he rotated slightly, trapping his cock between them. It didn't take much—a slight lean to the left, a footstep to the right—to position the bulging length firmly against her pussy. Her soft little moan nearly undid him. His wolf howled in victory and tried to take control. Trey prevented it, keeping the animal in its place.

This was how he remembered her—responsive and soft, sweet and sexy.

Hell yes.

"Please." She gazed into his eyes, words raspy. "Tell me this isn't a dream. Tell me this is real."

"It's real, darlin'." If he could have taken away all of her pain, he would have. He wanted to do whatever it took to make things right between them. "I'm right here."

He pushed her to the closest wall. Once there he released her ass, lifted her right leg and hooked it over his hip. He brought his hand to the apex of her thighs, cupping her cunt. What he found sent a sharp spasm from his balls to the head of his cock. Heat radiated from the area he palmed, warming his hand. If it weren't for the clothing between them she'd have drenched his fingers.

"I've waited so long," she whispered, eyes closed. "I've wanted this so bad."

"Rock against me." He rubbed his hand over the area, applying pressure. It wasn't possible to find her clit. Her leathers were too tight, covering her too fucking well. He let her guide him where she needed him to be. Paying attention to her ragged inhalations, he let her thrust against him. She keened when he hit the right spot, snapping her hips. "Damn. That's good. There you go. That's my girl."

As she leaned forward, combing her fingers through the hair at his nape, he knew what she wanted. He turned his head, bearing his neck, inviting her bite. Last time her fangs had ripped a hole in his ass. He hoped this time she'd take more care. Her slick and clever little tongue bathed his flesh, lightly skimming over the area. Then he felt her teeth score his skin. There wasn't pain. No burning pangs as she sucked. Not this time around.

Holy shit.

It was lust to the millionth power, slamming into them both. Not only did the wolf howl through his head, the damn thing felt as though it were right there with them enjoying the moment. It shouldn't have been possible, yet somehow it was. His own canines lengthened, his wolf-half wanting to mark her as his for the entire world to see.

No, not yet.

He felt her desire, could smell how wet and ready she was.

He'd give her this. Hell, he fucking *owed* her this.

His mate came with a lengthy groan, her entire body going taut. Shock tore through him when his sac tightened. He yanked away from her, the tip of his jutting erection aimed at the wall. His cock jerked and he followed her right over the edge. Stroking his length, he bent his head, allowing the release to flow through him. His spine tingled, dick pulsing with each jet of his seed against the cream-colored wallpaper. It wasn't what he wanted for their first time but he'd take it. So what if he'd lost control like a horny kid? This was what he needed. What he'd ached for.

Next time, he'd do things right.

They were both breathing hard when she pulled her fangs from his throat. She nursed the area she'd bitten, taking her time, lapping at the punctures. A part of him resented his ability to heal. In his dreams her ministrations went on forever. If he'd been human she'd have needed more time to close the wounds. As it was, she stopped after only seconds.

He heard a car door slam and within seconds Nathan burst through the door. Trey turned his head, meeting the Beta's damning look. "I know you're pissed but you're going to have to get over yourself. The sooner we get to safety, the sooner we can find Leigh."

Nathan heaved the clothing and boots in his hands to the floor. "Then I suggest you put your clothes on."

Trey almost moved away from Sadie—almost. Then he recalled how he'd trapped her before, using his touch to prevent her from phasing away. The moment she'd broken free, standing several feet away, she'd vanished without a trace. He couldn't trust her not to run and he wasn't sure what was going through her head. Even if she had to come to him for blood to survive, he needed her help if he was going to assist Nathan. The Beta wouldn't let this go. He'd do whatever it took to find Leigh, claim her and keep her by his side. The man's patience only went so far.

"Take her," he instructed Nathan, moving Sadie from the wall, hating the confusion that swept over her face. "Don't let her go."

"What?" Sadie finally spoke, sounding clearheaded.

Trey forced her into Nathan's arms. "I mean it." He guided one of Nathan's hands to Sadie's waist and then his other to her throat. "Don't let go. No matter what she does."

"What do you think you're doing?" She struggled, fighting for her freedom. The smell of her anger suffused the air. "How could you? After what just happened between us? You selfish son of a bitch!"

Guilt did come but Trey pushed it aside. "We're going to Diskant for assistance," he said as he retrieved the clothing and footwear and started to dress. "He's got security posted around his compound. Aldon's not stupid enough to fuck with an Omega. He might be able to get the jump on a shifter but he can't surprise the only one of us who can change at will."

"So you're going to tell the pack?"

Trey stopped buttoning his jeans, peering at Sadie across the distance.

He heard the desperation—the fucking hope—in her voice. Emotions he'd caused by his callous treatment of her. Was he going to tell the pack? Eventually. But he had to be certain he was fully prepared for the aftermath. Some serious shit could very likely go down. Since the Shepherd attacks everyone remained on edge. He didn't have the balls to look her in the eye and say that, so he bent at the waist and tugged on his boots.

"I have to talk to Diskant first. We'll have to discuss how we want to handle the issue."

"The issue. Of course." There it was again, that god-awful deflation in her tone. He resented the hell out of it, even if he understood. She didn't trust him, not one bit. And he didn't blame her. "Well then," she continued, "I'm sure you understand I have issues with my coven to address. You need to let me go. I have to tell them what's happened."

"Don't take this the wrong way, baby, but if the coven really gave a shit Leigh wouldn't have had to come to us for help." Nathan quickly tied his boots and stood. "I got the impression she was afraid to." Able to meet her gaze, steeling himself for the hatred he expected to see from her, he was surprised to see a flicker of remorse in her eyes. "Do you really think they'll help you or her?" he queried gently. "Do you think they're more capable of protecting your friend than we are?"

"Diskant Black will never agree to help me or Leigh." She'd stopped fighting Nathan, passive in the man's hold. "I'm the enemy, remember?"

"You saved his mate's life," Nathan reminded her. It was an important detail. "Ava means more to him than anything.

Without you he'd have lost her. He owes you and he knows it. His pride won't allow him to turn you away."

"If you say so." She lifted her arms in mock surrender. "You don't have to hold me. I'm not going anywhere. We have the same agenda."

"If you say so," he chimed, throwing her words back at her.

Her glare of sheer disdain wounded him more than a solid punch in the gut ever could have. *Fuck it to shit.* He'd meant to be playful, not push her buttons. He approached her, strides steady. Once he reached her he wrapped his fingers around her wrist. He knew it pissed her off when Nathan let her go and Trey pulled her into his arms but fuck if he cared. She was here, in his world, where she belonged.

He wasn't letting her go.

"Until I know that for sure," he lifted her from the ground and marched toward the door, "I'm not letting you out of my sight." Glancing over his shoulder, he told Nathan, "Get her amazing Ginsu knife and bring it along, would you?"

"What are you? A caveman?" She snorted and shook her head, waves of her thick blonde hair cascading down her back. "Why don't you just drag me out of here by the hair?"

Maybe he was a bastard for laughing but who could blame him? His mate was feisty, smart and ballsy as hell. The pack had no idea how lucky they'd just become. This woman wouldn't back down from anyone or anything, including him.

Striding for the car, he bent his head. "I'm going to be whatever you want me to be, Sadie. No more running away. No more bullshit. You're mine, darlin'. All mine."

"Barbarian," she huffed, sounding indignant.

"If that's what you want."

Nathan opened the door and Trey sank into the passenger seat, situating Sadie on his lap. He gave her hair a soft yank, chuckling when she wriggled her ass against him. His body responded, the wolf reminding him they'd yet to fully stake their possession over her. The quick and sensual act against the wall had only been a prelude of what was to come. He wanted to see his female beneath him, her blond hair fanning over the pillows, and look into her eyes when she came next time.

Soon.

Even with danger knocking at their door—despite the threat of Shepherds, Aldon Frost and everything else he had to deal with—the future looked brighter than it had in weeks.

Chapter Five

ɞ

A multitude of thoughts ran through Sadie's mind as she tried to formulate a plan. Nathan had been correct. The coven wouldn't have come for her. Even if Leigh had pleaded Sadie's case and attempted to sway them to take up arms for the cause, they weren't strong enough physically to face a threat. As a whole, her sisters-in-magic weren't the most powerful nest of vampires in the world. That was the reason they'd approached her so long ago. Up until then Sadie had remained with her family in Alaska. Many supernatural creatures lived there, in a place far from mortal society.

She recalled accepting their offer, bidding her mother and father farewell, knowing there was a decent chance she'd never see them again.

Some vampires attached themselves to covens. Others — who found their brides or grooms and wanted to live their lives in harmony — generally floated from place to place. She'd assumed that one day she'd see her parents again but there was no guarantee. The opportunity to live her own life had been too tempting, so off she'd gone in search of adventure and her own place in the world.

Leigh.

That poor girl's situation had been so different. No one knew who'd bitten her, changed her and left her to face the transformation alone. Anyone else probably would have died. Leigh's heritage — one she didn't know about — and having mage blood advanced the transition.

Much like Ava Brisbane...

Diskant's mate was telepathic but Ava'd had no idea of her mage heritage when Sadie had mentioned the possibility to her. The Omega's partner had seemed confused, wanting to know more before Sadie had been forced to leave. Often mortals with abilities didn't know they came from a magic wielder somewhere in their bloodline. It wasn't unheard of for traits to skip generations and manifest decades later in family trees.

A nagging feeling ate at her gut.

Had Geneva—the leader of the coven and vampire in charge—known what Leigh was capable of? Had the secretive and oftentimes bitchy head of their nest suspected something? Usually the coven voted on who entered their home. With Leigh, Geneva had simply held a meeting, told them of the young girl and her circumstances and pretty much welcomed the fragile vampire into their domain. It wasn't unheard of but it was suspicious. Not to mention Geneva had seemed too protective of the girl—encouraging Leigh to stay indoors, indicating it was good that she take her time to accept what she'd become.

Recollections of her meetings with Geneva flashed before her eyes.

Her leader had seemed so intent on destroying Aldon the last few months. Sadie agreed a rogue vampire was a danger but what if there was a reason behind Geneva's fear? What if Leigh somehow played a key role in Geneva's plans? All of the members of the coven had secrets. Despite their bond, they didn't share everything. Their leader was more aloof than most, appearing mostly when the coven gathered to address issues.

They lived under the same roof. How often did she really see Geneva?

Her heart raced and her palms went clammy.

Not much.

Driving for several miles, they came to an enormous set of gates in the middle of nowhere. Nathan rolled down the window, said something to the man who approached the side of the car and suddenly the mechanism keeping the barrier in place parted wide. Nathan drove past the guards, hands clutching the steering wheel, his knuckles almost white.

Like it or not, her heart went out to the man.

He'd said Leigh was his mate. She hadn't wanted to believe it but his behavior told her he hadn't been lying. He hadn't spoken as they'd driven, jaw clenched, eyes pained. She knew how possessive and protective werewolves were of their females. Before Trey, she'd thought nothing could keep a shifter from its mate.

Maybe Trey hadn't meant to be a total douchebag.

He'd been drunk as hell when he'd attacked her harshly with his words. Maybe she'd gotten it all wrong. Maybe there was a reason they'd found each other again.

Or maybe your brain is fried and you can't think worth a damn. Listen to yourself. Yuck, yuck, yuck!

"Promise me you won't run." Trey's unexpected rasp against her ear sent a prickle down her spine. All of her mental observations flew out the window. "If you do, I don't know what'll happen. Think about the people this could impact. Not just Leigh. Not just me and you. This will hurt everyone in the pack, including men, women and their children."

Damn him.

The magic words—women and children.

White mage vampires never harmed the innocent. It went against everything they stood for. Knowing she could be the cause of suffering sent a pang through her chest. Once again she didn't have much choice in her decision. Hurt others and save her own ass? Or stand and face the firing squad? Neither option seemed all that promising.

Her word meant everything to her so it wasn't easy to whisper, "I promise."

Putting her thoughts on hold, she surveyed her surroundings.

Well, well, well. Trey hadn't been kidding.

Diskant Black had pulled out all the stops. She wasn't able to see the shifters guarding the area but she sensed them. An enormous house appeared in the distance, large enough to be a freaking mansion. A building had been erected nearby, possibly for livestock, although she didn't see Diskant Black as much of a cowboy. The man liked to ride motorcycles, not horses. Glistening water reflected rays of the sun, drawing her eyes to a swimming pool.

Damn. The sun.

Unlike stories depicted, she could venture out in the day. All vampires could. But the sun drained their strength quickly and their skin had a definite aversion. She'd been shielded inside the vehicle but that would all end once they climbed out of her Camaro. If necessary she could bear the rays for up to an hour, but no more than that.

Relief rushed through her.

Thank Goddess Leigh had driven Sadie's vehicle when she'd gone to see Nathan and Trey. The windows were properly tinted, keeping her safe as she drove around New York and the surrounding areas. If it had been any other mode of transport she probably would have been forced to duck and hide in the back.

Where was the fun in that? She had the best seat in the house.

She flexed her ass. Trey rewarded the movement by squeezing her thigh. He'd been hard as a baseball bat when they'd first settled in the car. Slowly his erection had stopped poking her buttocks. Now, however, she felt the hard ridge resurface.

Her eyes drifted closed.

She'd waited so long to feel him lodged inside her. After seeing him fully nude and witnessing his impressive build, she knew he'd have to force his way into her body. Once there she'd feel every single inch, his thickness more than enough to tease her pussy. She'd come harder than she ever had in her life, she was certain.

Trey chuckled and she winced. Rookie mistake. He could smell her arousal.

Stop acting like a horny teenager!

Nathan pulled to a stop several yards from the domicile and cut off the engine. "We're here. Get your shit together. It's game on."

Before they made it from the car, Diskant Black appeared. Huge, foreboding, angry. He stormed toward the vehicle with a tiny pixie behind him. He stopped moving and spun around to face his mate, his shoulder-length dark hair whipping around his face. Ava didn't back down, her blue eyes blazing, short blonde hair with pink tufts scattered all over her head. She placed one hand on her hip and rested the other over her slightly bulging belly as she gave him hell.

Dread swamped Sadie, giving her an ample dose of fear.

She hadn't known. She'd had no idea.

No wonder the Omega seemed so pissed.

The last time she'd seen Diskant's mate she'd been slim and teeny. Not so much now. With her petite size, it was easy to see her condition. Ava—the tiny female who'd brought the most powerful shifter in New York to his knees—was pregnant.

"I told you!" Ava snapped, easy to hear as her voice rose. "She's not a threat. I listened to her the moment they arrived at the gate." Taking the hand from her hip, she tapped her temple. "I'm able to do that, remember?"

Considering her age and experience, Sadie didn't usually get embarrassed about sex. But knowing Ava had heard her thoughts about Trey made her cheeks burn hot. She knew the tiny female was powerful telepathically but she'd never imagined she could listen in to others' minds from such a long distance.

Then she remembered the locket she'd learned was in Ava's possession.

How could she have possibly forgotten something so important?

With a zephyr Ava's powers would magnify tenfold. No wonder she'd been able to hear Sadie's thoughts so easily. Craig Newlander—the master of the Villati who researched and stored information about the paranormal world—had told her that Ava possessed the thing. Apparently Aldon had been too late to get his hands on the relic. Sadie decided it was for the best. Ava wasn't power hungry enough to unlock the darkness of the magic and Diskant could keep his mate—and therefore the locket—safe. She'd thought it was the proper place for the mystical thing.

Before she could dwell on her monumental slip-up Trey opened the door and climbed out of the car. Guards appeared, all of them armed with weapons. They surrounded the three of them, eyes darting from the Omega and his mate to their unexpected guests. Sadie's senses went on alert. The sun did drain her but with Trey's blood she'd be able to protect herself. She gauged the threat, thinking of who she'd take down first. She wouldn't kill them but she could cause enough damage to keep them down.

"She knows about me," Ava continued, pointing a finger at Diskant's chest. "She can answer so many questions I have. You will not send her away. She needs our help. Stop being a Neanderthal and pull your head out of your ass."

"I guess Ava told you we were coming?" Trey asked, seeming totally at ease.

He cautiously lowered Sadie to the ground. She wondered if he'd put space between them. He'd indicated he wouldn't unless they were pried apart by a tire iron. Their bodies brushed and she felt her feet settle against the hard earth. Ready to step back, she gasped when he took her hand and twined their fingers together.

Holy shit.

That was a public display of affection and he'd done it in front of everyone.

"What are you doing here?" Diskant snarled, whirling away from Ava to face the car. "Isn't there a pack meeting you're supposed to be in charge of?"

"Cade's got it covered," Nathan replied, maintaining his sense of calm. "We had to come here. You need a heads-up about some serious shit."

"You know better, Trey." Diskant's fury didn't ebb, his irises prismatic as they shifted into various colors. "You know not to bring danger to this place. I've killed men for less."

"Diskant." Nathan inserted himself into the conversation. "You should listen to him. Don't let your temper override reason."

"If I want your opinion," Diskant rounded on the werewolf, "I'll fucking ask for it!"

"Take a chill pill, D," Trey said. "We're not the enemy."

"Like hell you're not!" Diskant snarled.

Shit.

Tempers would only escalate. Sadie knew that. She'd been in the middle of enough conflicts with her coven to see where things were headed. Diskant would defend his interests. Trey and Nathan would do the same. There was one way to communicate everything that had happened and show Diskant everything he needed to know. But that would require taking an enormous chance with her coven, Nathan, Leigh's life and Trey's future. Even if she showed Diskant the past in images, would it be enough to persuade him to help?

She glanced at the enraged male.

He wasn't functioning on a sensible level. He was in full protective mate mode.

How could she take such a plunge if the reward wasn't worth the cost? What if her plan backfired and she didn't avoid a fight but instigated one?

What other choice do you have?

A yank of her hand was all it took to get free. Her fingers slipped from Trey's and she stepped away. She phased the moment she was no longer physically tied to him, reappearing behind Diskant. She grasped the ginormous man's arm, collected her thoughts and sent them into his mind.

For the first time he'd see Ava's attack through Sadie's eyes. It wouldn't be pretty. Ava had almost died thanks to Shepherds. When Sadie had given her blood to survive, her intentions had been pure. There had been no agenda. No hope for a debt owed. She'd done it simply to give Ava another lease on life.

Once those memories had passed, she allowed other memories to rush into Diskant's head. She showed him why she'd had an interest in Ava in the first place, clarifying the reasons their paths had crossed.

Ava's amulet.

The zephyr.

When she'd tracked Aldon, she'd discovered he'd been after something valuable. It had taken time but eventually she'd uncovered what the vampire had wanted—the zephyr Ava possessed, cleverly hidden inside an amulet passed down from Ava's mother. With it he could kill millions of people. Control the world. Dominate everyone and everything he pleased.

Holy fuck! She heard Diskant's thought, felt his alarm.

Relieved he was finally getting the picture, she redirected her thoughts to her capture and rescue and the threat Aldon posed. Making sure she included every single moment so Diskant could see who he was dealing with—a vampire undaunted by shifters. She made sure she added Nathan's link to Leigh in her thoughts, hoping that the Omega—even if he didn't have any sympathy for Sadie's position—might soften when it came to the other couple.

For added effect, she also gave him brief portions of Leigh's past and how much the young vampire had suffered following her change, including the pain and heartbreak Leigh had yet to overcome.

Someone snatched her away from Diskant. Her yelp of alarm carried through the open area. She hit the ground as she spun, driven away from the Omega. Lifting her head, she saw Trey crouch in front of her. His growl was feral, his fingernails forming into claws. Diskant looked like he'd been waylaid with a dummy stick. Swaying on his feet, he shook his head.

"No way," Diskant murmured, "not possible."

"She showed you the truth." Ava sounded shaken. Chancing a glance at her, Sadie saw Ava had paled. "Think about it. The night we met you saved me from vampires. We never knew why. Then the locket and Thomas…it makes sense."

"Thomas?" Sadie had to ask, determined to put the puzzle pieces in place.

"My brother," Ava sighed and raked a trembling hand through her hair. "I don't have the necklace. He took it when he left town."

"He took it?" Horror, disbelief and terror poured over her. "Where did he go?"

"We don't know." Ava reached for Diskant and in an instant he was there, wrapping an arm around her. She leaned against him, revealing just how small she was in comparison. "He disappeared. We were going to hire an investigator but I decided it wouldn't matter. Thomas is Thomas. He does what he wants, when he wants. If he doesn't want to be found, he won't be."

He doesn't want to be found.

There was one way to find him, whether Thomas liked it or not.

Just like that—click-click-boom—Sadie saw the future.

The visual made her stomach churn.

Leigh could locate a person using a personal possession. Aldon had learned Leigh was capable of doing so the moment he'd taken Sadie's blood.

No wonder he'd taken her captive.

Sadie was the only real friend Leigh had. As such, Aldon had known Leigh would come to rescue her. Then he'd have everything he needed to find Thomas and locate the zephyr.

Hell in a handbasket.

She looked at Ava as she made it to her feet. Trey did the same, shuffling back as he did. He stopped at her side and she reached for his hand. He wrapped his fingers around hers, his grip tight. She let the touch settle her before she walked toward Ava, extending her free hand.

There was more information to share, things Ava needed to know.

"Don't you fucking think about it!" Diskant yelled.

"Stop." Ava soothed the wild man with a simple touch, reaching out to Sadie as she did. "If she has something to show me, it's my right to see it."

"Him too." Sadie's gaze ventured to the Omega, her eyes flitting over his huge form. "Create a link. We'll seal the circle. He needs to know as well."

Diskant's snarl of warning didn't deter Sadie. She didn't stop until her palm met Ava's. Their minds merged—Sadie's, Trey's, Ava's and Diskant's. As usual, Sadie felt disoriented and off balance. The present time no longer mattered. They were stuck in a vortex of the mind, everyone's thoughts churning together. She concentrated and called on her magic, using it to settle those trapped in her head.

Clarity. Warmth. Reason. Purpose.

Yes, this was comforting. This was the center she needed to balance.

She felt the familiar, warming glow of her power and showed them what to expect, recalling pictures of Rainbow

City. The entire population had been destroyed in hours by a pestilence demon—one that had been conjured using a zephyr. Unseen, the demon had done its work. Bloodied bodies, eaten away as a virus ravaged them one by one. All it had taken was the presence of the beast, one who drew power from the sickness it inflicted.

Her strength started fading, the product of mentally sharing so much with so many.

There was so little time and so much to tell.

She did her work as quickly as possible, thinking of the images she'd been shown of the Fallen—vampires who embraced the dark side of their magic. Powerful, radiant and stunning, the Fallen were stronger than most of their supernatural counterparts. The last time they'd risen to power the world had faced the Third Pandemic. Millions had died, suffering what they thought to be the plague. If her kind hadn't intervened—assisted by those they usually considered enemies such as shifters, witches and warlockes—the taint would have spread.

"*Aldon isn't of the light. He'll kill us all,*" she conveyed telepathically, swaying as her magic dissipated. "*Vampires and Shepherds are the least of your concerns. If he gets what he's after everyone you love is doomed. There won't be a tomorrow to look forward to.*"

Her legs buckled but she never hit the ground. Solid arms scooped her up. She went willingly, content when she felt Trey's solid chest and capable arms holding her tight. She took comfort in his scent, letting him be the strong one for once. After today, none of them would be safe. Aldon had started the game, one he intended to finish.

There was nowhere to run and nowhere to hide.

It could very well be the end of days.

Trey tried to keep his shit together as he held Sadie. What he'd just seen—how Sadie had just fucking shared what she knew — rocked the ground beneath his feet. Diskant and Ava looked equally shaken. He could scent Ava's fear as it poured from her. The acrid smell of Diskant's rage scorched his nose.

"Get back to your posts and keep your eyes open." Diskant snapped out of it, barking the order to his guards. With a sideways look at Nathan he added, "Call Cade. Tell him to cancel the pack meeting. If he asks questions, don't give him answers. Tell him to close shop and get his ass over here." He turned his head, gazing at Trey. "As for you two. Bring her inside. It appears we do have a lot of shit to talk about."

Nathan returned to the Camaro, retrieving a phone from his jacket as he left. Diskant kept his arm around Ava as he led them to another fence that surrounded the house. He punched a code into a numerical lock system, opened the gate and ushered everyone inside. A set of back doors opened and Emory appeared, his mate Mary right behind him.

Thank fucking God.

As brothers, Trey and Emory had faced some issues. But now, with Emory mated, things had finally settled into place. Apprehension filled the air and Emory gave Trey a level stare. He met his brother's eyes and tried to communicate his need for backup, hoping his brother could read between the lines. He hadn't told Emory about Sadie, worried about his brother's reaction to his mating with a vampire.

At that moment it felt stupid to have kept something so important to himself.

"What's up?" Emory asked, standing so Mary remained protected behind him.

"Get back inside." Diskant motioned to Emory and Mary, indicating they should move with a wave. "It's not safe out here."

"Do you think they understand how important this is?"

It took Trey a second to comprehend Sadie was communicating with him telepathically, keeping the conversation between the two of them. He turned his full attention to her, peering down. Her brilliant blue eyes met his. He wasn't entirely sure how it worked, so he simply thought back to her.

"*Yes.*"

"*Good.*" She sounded so tired. He wanted to take her to bed, shield her in his arms and watch over her as she got the rest she obviously needed. Her lips curved slightly at the corners into a small, knowing smile. "*I'm not sleepy, just drained.*" There was laughter in the thought. "*I'll be back to fighting form in a little while.*"

"*I don't want you in fighting form.*"

The thought of her fighting for her life, facing Aldon on her own...

He growled and lifted his head to find everyone staring at him. He swiftly lowered his head, cursing himself. They didn't know he had been talking to Sadie. How could they? He probably appeared totally unhinged in their eyes, likely to go off at any second. Hopefully they thought the attitude was normal.

Newly mated males were known to be pissy.

Diskant urged Ava into the nearest recliner. "Get off your feet, Ava mine," he whispered, stroking her hair.

She didn't protest, settling into the plush furniture with a sigh. She'd gotten past the first trimester of pregnancy and her constant fatigue worried the Omega more often than not. It was the reason Diskant had returned the status of Alpha of the pack to Trey—so he could ensure Ava carried and delivered their child without any undue stress.

So much for that.

Trey took a seat on the sofa, keeping Sadie nestled against him. She sighed and rested her head beneath his chin. Her exhaustion beat at him. His brave little mate was more delicate than she thought. Good thing he'd found her. She wouldn't have to face the world alone. He'd keep her safe. Make her happy. No more fuckups. No more stupid mistakes brought on by his stubbornness and dedication to the pack. Since he'd come to Diskant, the cat was officially out of the bag. He wouldn't take back his claim on her—even if he could—no matter if it cost him everything.

Emory had taken Mary to the fireplace. She rolled her eyes when, once again, he placed her behind him. She wrapped her hand around his arm and stepped in beside him. The glare he gave her promised a future punishment but she didn't seem fazed. Instead she smiled at him, her doe-brown eyes brimming with love.

An invisible fist squeezed Trey's heart.

If Sadie had any love for him before, had he destroyed it? Had his dumb ass managed to ruin the only good thing he'd ever have in his life? He ran his hand over her head, enjoying the feel of her hair against his palm. It was going to be hell gaining her trust. Women had the memory of elephants. Even if she forgave, she'd never forget.

Fuck me.

"*Keep thinking such sweet things and I just might,*" Sadie purred in his head.

Son of a bitch. Fuck me twice.

"*Sneaking around in my head, are you?*" he thought back, wanting to give her ass a hard slap for the intrusion. Not because he minded—her awareness of how he felt would give the leverage he needed. His intentions didn't stem from anger or agitation. The thought of her perfectly rounded rear turning a nice shade of pink from a few well-aimed pats turned him on.

"Does anyone want to give me a clue about what's going on?" Emory asked briskly, studying Trey. "Why have you brought a vampire to our home?"

"She's mine, brother," Trey growled, warning the male to tread lightly.

"Yours?" Emory frowned and his nostrils flared as he scented the air. "She's a leech."

Trey felt Sadie tense against him, Emory's hateful words piercing her like daggers.

"Say that again and I'll rip you a new asshole." And he would, sure as shit. "I'm making it clear here and now. Vampire or not, she's my mate. Deal with it or get the fuck out."

"Zip it, diptwats," Diskant muttered, shaking his head. His eyes drifted to his mate. "Shut the fuck up. We've got other shit to think about."

"How so?" Emory might have seemed at ease but Trey knew better.

As a family member of Shepherds, Mary remained in a constant state of danger. Plus Emory wasn't stupid. Under normal circumstances Diskant would have forced Trey to leave with Sadie. Shifters and vampires didn't mate. Especially not with Alphas. Yet here the Omega was, welcoming Sadie to the fold. Emory recognized and understood that.

Smart man.

"Tell me everything," Emory ordered.

"Fuck, I don't even know where to start," Diskant conceded, lips molded into a scowl. "Ava's brother has put another target on our asses. We're dealing with some heavy shit." Moving from his mate, he started pacing. "We're going to have to arrange a meeting with the pack. It's not going to go well. First we'll have to get them to accept Trey's mating. Assuming they do, we're going to have to tell them what's about to happen to the city. They're not going to take the news lightly. Most of them will probably cut and run."

"What news?" Emory snapped and Mary shifted closer to his side. "Answer me."

"Remember the vampires that attacked Ava the night I found her?" Emory nodded and Diskant said, "They were sent by someone—a master vampire to be precise." He glanced at Sadie and Trey before he continued, "It's Aldon. He's into some deranged shit."

Emory's irises flashed amber as he nailed Trey with an accusing glare. "I thought you said we could trust him."

"I was wrong." Talk about an understatement. He'd been more than wrong about the vampire. He'd been stupid as hell. "He's been planning something big for months. I had no idea." He rested a hand on Sadie's thigh and gave it a squeeze. "If it wasn't for Sadie none of us would have known what was happening until it was too late. He'd have taken us down with a snap of his fingers."

"Isn't that convenient?" Emory's livid gaze intensified, irises becoming yellow. "Maybe you're too blind to see what's going on. Maybe she's trying to play you. That's what vampires do. Or have you forgotten? She's probably not even your mate. They use magic to trick people and you're wrapping yourself around her finger like a pussy-whipped pup." Emory gazed around the room. "Am I the only one who finds all of this a tad suspicious?"

"Emory," Diskant snarled, "Simon says shut the fuck up." Their Omega stopped pacing and faced Emory and Mary. "If you don't want to have faith in your brother then have it in me. Do you honestly think I'd have welcomed a vampire if I didn't have a good fucking reason? Do you honestly think I'd put Ava or Mary in harm's way? I'm going to tell you what's going on, there's just a lot of ground to cover. I'm trying to sort this shit out in my head."

Sadie tried to rise from Trey's lap. "I can show him."

"No," Trey snapped, planting his arm over her midsection. "You're too weak. You need to rest."

"It's not as hard to communicate with one person." She leveled him with a determined look. "We need to clear the air. This is the fastest way to do it." When he opened his mouth to argue she shook her head. "We've wasted enough time. We have to find Leigh."

God, he hated it when he didn't get his way. But she was right.

"Fine," he growled and stared at his brother. "But he comes to us. You stay right where you are."

"*Barbarian*," Sadie reprimanded him privately.

"*You're damn right*," he replied immediately. Fuck grabbing her by the hair and dragging her around. He was going to chain her ass to his side. "*You ain't seen nothing yet, baby.*"

Emory hesitated, his attention riveted to his mate. After several seconds he gave Mary a nod and moved away, walking slowly toward the couch. Mary seemed uncertain, gnawing at her lip, wrapping her arms around herself.

"What's she going to do?" Emory asked, cautious and jumpy. "Bite me?"

"You'll never be that lucky, fuckwad." The simple notion of Sadie feeding from Emory had Trey's wolf clamoring for his brother's blood. "She's going to touch you and share what she knows. Which is more than you deserve after the shit you just spouted."

Sadie lifted her hand when Emory stopped beside them. Emory didn't want to accept her touch—Trey could smell the detestation coming from his brother—yet he did just the same. He wasn't aware just how quickly Sadie could send another person shared thoughts and images, thinking it took minutes at the very least. He found himself surprised when she pulled away in seconds, appearing pleased. Emory, on the other hand, looked like he was going to toss his Cheerios.

"Fuck," Emory exhaled, taking a step back, eyes saucered. "Jesus."

"Now you know why I couldn't break it down to you like the ABCs," Diskant said, validated. "Not that easy to explain, is it?"

The double doors opened and Diskant, Emory and Trey growled in unison. The sounds lessened when Nathan stepped inside. The poor bastard looked like shit. He'd obviously been running his hands through his hair—the strands darted in all directions—and he was as wired as a wild animal in a cage. If they didn't find Leigh soon he was bound to look even worse.

"Cade's on his way," he informed them as he walked to the couch and rested Sadie's sword against Trey's leg. "Have you decided what we're going to do?"

"We're going to get our shit in order." Diskant's power as an Omega fell over the room as he spoke. "We need to find this girl who's so important and bring her here before we even think about addressing the pack."

Nathan took a step back and took a deep breath. As a Beta he was the most sensitive to strong emotions, especially when a shifter called on his or her beast. With Diskant being able to change into every single animal form, it pulled more energy from the man. Trey tried to compensate, calling on his own beast, directing waves of fortitude to his second-in-command. His wolf met Nathan's and strengthened it, giving it a measure of comfort. Nathan righted himself, his nod in Trey's direction his expression of gratitude.

"I don't know if she'll come," Sadie confessed, sounding sad.

"Oh she'll come," Diskant's voice lowered an octave. There was an underlying threat in his words. "She's placing every single person I'm in charge of in danger." He turned his gaze to Sadie. "I'll fight your nest and take her by force if I have to."

"You're not putting a fucking hand on her." Nathan stormed into the room, baring his teeth. "I don't care who or what you are. She's my mate. As such she's due protection from the pack. If you hurt her, you violate everything we stand for. I'll contact every single pack we're connected to. I'll tell them what you've done. They'll bring you down one by one."

"He won't hurt her, Nathan," Ava chimed and shuffled from her seat. Diskant moved to assist her immediately, his anger about Leigh swiftly turning to concern for his mate.

"She's only a girl," Ava whispered, using the hand Diskant offered her for balance. "She didn't ask for this."

"If you promise to give her your protection, I can find her," Sadie said. "There are only so many places she could be." Everything inside Trey rebelled at his mate's offer. She must have sensed his unease because she pulled away so he could see her face. "I'm not running. I'm presenting an option. None of you can cover as much ground as quickly as I can. Besides," her eyes lowered to his mouth and returned to meet his gaze, "you and I have to talk. There's a lot we need to discuss."

"Are you sure she'll come back?" Emory questioned, wary despite what Sadie had shown him. "Are you sure we can trust her?"

If you want to earn her respect — if you want everyone to believe in her — balls up.

"Yes," Trey responded as he stood, lifting them from the couch. "We can."

As soon as he was upright he let his mate go—his wolf howling in his head at the loss of contact—and took a step back. He retrieved her weapon and handed it to her. She accepted the sword like the warrior she was, gripping the sheath that covered the blade. He knew she was capable of defending herself—she'd practically saved their asses when they faced Aldon—but he couldn't prevent the instincts that demanded he prevent her departure. It was his duty to watch over her. Only a pussy would stand idly by as his mate ventured off without his assistance, guidance or protection.

Fuck. This was one of the hardest things he'd ever had to do.

Letting her leave, left with only the hope she'd return.

What if I can't trust her? What if I'm wrong?

"Come back to me." Even in his own head he sounded like a sappy, lovesick pup. "Don't make me hunt you down. I will if I have to. When I find you it won't be pretty. I mean it, Sadie."

His pride had been forgotten. He couldn't care less what the others thought.

If he lost face in front of those he trusted most, he'd get over it.

If he lost his female, he'd never survive.

Her eyes lingered on him as though she heard the thought. "I'll be back. Promise."

Gazing around the room, she slid her sword into the sheath that protected her weapon. "Don't wait up on me," she instructed. "The clock is ticking. Start making plans."

Then, before anyone could stop her, she gazed at Trey and disappeared.

Chapter Six

"You can't be serious." Leigh strangled the pillow in her arms, staring at Sadie as though she'd lost her mind. "I'm not going there. With a bunch of werewolves! Haven't you had enough of them already? Did you see how they act? They're like animals. You can't talk to them. They don't understand reason. You've lost your mind!"

"Leigh…"

"Don't 'Leigh' me," Leigh snapped. "You're crazy. Certifiable even."

Sadie clenched her fingers, trying to stay calm.

Finding the terrified vampire had been easier than Sadie had thought. Just to be safe, Sadie had phased to the home she shared with her coven, taking sanctuary inside her bedroom. Leigh had been there, seated on her bed, clutching one of her pillows. The young vampire had made an intelligent decision. Their sisters wouldn't ask Leigh questions about being in Sadie's space, and Leigh probably figured it was the first place Sadie would go once she escaped Aldon.

Speaking of which…

"I don't have time to explain, you're going to have to trust me."

The moment she'd landed and seen Leigh, she'd simply blurted the truth—they had to return to Trey and Nathan. And they had to do it now. She'd promised Trey she'd return and she was going to keep her word. She'd glimpsed so much from him—things she hadn't dared believe.

She had to know if his feelings were as true as he thought they were.

"You're not safe here." Sadie kept going, trying to persuade Leigh. "I have to show you something."

"Like what?" Leigh fidgeted on the mattress, her knuckles turning white as she fisted the corner of the pillow. "That I'm mated to a freaking werewolf? Do you want me to join the family?"

"Would that be so bad? Is the idea so repulsive?" A stupid question, if Sadie counted her own misgivings to Leigh in the past about having a werewolf lover and partner. "Not all of them are like Trey. Nathan is different. I've seen the way he reacts with people. He's got a big heart. He's a Beta because he has a genuine concern for others. He'd take care of you. When you disappeared he was worried sick. You should have seen him when I left. He's terrified for you, Leigh."

"I don't love him," Leigh grated through clenched teeth, lowering her head. "I can never love him. My heart belongs to someone else. It always will."

"What?" Sadie had known Leigh's wounds ran deep but she hadn't known the young woman loved someone from her past so deeply. "Who?"

"It doesn't matter." Leigh went from enraged to somber. "That time in my life is over."

Certainly Leigh had mentioned understanding love. She'd even said she'd been in love before her change from human to vampire. But she hadn't taken the matter further. Sadie should have asked questions about Leigh's past, tried to get answers. Instead she'd given the fledgling space, figuring they had plenty of time to discuss Leigh's issues.

Just another thing I didn't think about until it was too late.

She started reaching out to Leigh, wanting to share what she knew with her friend, when a floorboard creaked in the hallway. Turning on her heel, she came face-to-face with Geneva. The head of the coven stopped in the doorway, cocking her head to the side. Her disapproval was evident, her ever-present attitude kicked to full-blast.

"So you've finally decided to grace us with your presence," their coven mistress observed.

There was zero concern from the woman. None.

Geneva was a cold person. But this seemed...unnatural.

As usual, her thick brown hair had been pulled into a French twist that allowed multiple corkscrew curls to fall over her head and surround her face. Her strange, yellow-hued eyes always seemed to know more than they should. Sadie'd never paid attention to it before but she should have. Geneva had always been ahead of the curve, seeing things before anyone else. And she'd been so interested in Aldon—almost obsessed.

There had to be a reason for it.

What has the sneaky bitch been up to?

"What can I say?" Sadie crossed her arms over her chest, taking her usual back-to-business stance. "I've been busy tracking Aldon. That takes time."

Geneva arched one of her dark brows. "Have you had any success?"

Talk about a dilemma.

If she indicated she had succeeded in her work, Geneva would want more of Sadie's time. The head of the coven would demand a private audience with Sadie that could last for hours. As much as the opportunity appealed to Sadie, since she wanted to grill Geneva for information, she had to get Leigh to safety. A bit of clarity had certainly changed things. For the first time in centuries she didn't have faith in the people she'd once placed her trust in—women who vowed to put each other's well-being over any others.

She'd never have believed she couldn't rely on her very own coven.

"Nothing that would interest you," she answered, trying to seem bored.

Geneva's eyes darted to Leigh then returned to Sadie. "You've been gone a long time to return with nothing of interest." Her nostrils flared and her irises lightened near her pupils. She snorted to clear her nose. "You've been around shifters again. I caught the stink of it in the hall. I've let the question go unanswered long enough."

Sadie braced herself, trying to think of an answer to the inquiry she knew was coming.

"What have you been up to?" Geneva asked. "What have you been keeping from us?"

I should ask her the same question. "I've been working, like I said."

She kept the conversation all about business and directed her thoughts to her job and numerous hunts. It was against the rules of the coven to invade a housemate's thoughts but she didn't trust Geneva. Not now. She wasn't letting the vampire get a glimpse of her mind.

"I've been investigating," she added, giving Geneva a cursory glance. "That takes me to all kinds of places and puts me in contact with all kinds of people."

"Not people—a werewolf—and a male one at that. You've been close to this one in particular, on more than one occasion." Geneva inhaled deeply and didn't try to hide it. "His smell is so potent it's practically oozing from your skin. I detect his blood. I can smell his seed on you."

The leader of her coven locked her in place with a wave of her fingers. Sadie didn't have a chance to arm herself. Geneva's magic spread through the bedroom. How had she not seen this before? How had it escaped her attention? Geneva was bad fucking news.

"There's only one way that could be possible." Geneva seethed, her face warped into an ass backward scowl. "It's not bad enough you took him into your body. No better than a common bitch in heat. You drank from him, didn't you?"

Sadie's heart missed a beat and started to pound. *Oh shit.*

Geneva's magic was potent stuff. Paralysis rushed over her.

Soon she'd be caught and unable to phase. Things had just gotten serious.

"Leigh, phase out. Right now. You have to trust me. Please. Something's very wrong here."

Thank Goddess, Leigh didn't argue. "Where?"

"Meet me outside the warehouse where we found Trey. I'll explain everything. Go."

Leigh phased, breaking Geneva's attention just enough for Sadie to visualize the parking lot outside the building Trey had been trapped inside. Geneva's face—one that generally gave away nothing—contorted in rage. She tried to extend her magic, to keep Sadie caged in the bars of her magic. Sadie fought back, calling on the magic that was all her own. The two energies collided, bursting together.

"Bedding with wolves. You are a traitor to your blood. A disgrace to our kind."

"That may be," she hissed between clenched teeth, concentrating to phase. "But my intentions have always been honest. Everything I've done has been for the good of the coven. Can you say the same?"

She didn't give Geneva the opportunity to answer. Something was definitely not right. The coven had been betrayed, but not by Sadie. Whatever their leader had been up to, it wasn't good. Geneva had her own agenda. Perhaps she wanted Aldon removed but for reasons that benefited her and not the coven.

After the dust had settled and Leigh was safe, Sadie intended to return. Something of this magnitude couldn't go unquestioned. She had to protect the innocent women in her coven.

As the haughty and furious vampire reached for her—Geneva's yellow eyes glowing neon—Sadie called on the full power of her magic. Her reserves were weak but she had just enough to teleport from the room. The blinding white surrounded her, answering her summons. The world shifted and fell away as she phased, allowing her to slide out of Geneva's grasp, obliterating the vampire's hold on her.

But she saw Geneva's eyes as the vampire's mask fell away and revealed her true face.

Son of a bitch.

Geneva was not the woman she claimed to be. She never had been. Not only was Aldon a danger, so was the leader of a coven of vampires with numerous powers.

Sadie'd thought things could possibly get worse.

She arrived outside the warehouse. Shivering in the cool night air and facing Leigh who waited for her across the street, she realized she'd been wrong.

* * * * *

"You've gotten us into some serious stuff here, man," Diskant told Trey. "We've got enough to deal with without worrying about the end of the world."

Trey agreed but there'd been no way around it. "What would you have me do? Turn my back on my mate? Toss her aside like trash? You're mated. You know that's never going to happen. She's mine. I'm not letting her go."

"The pack isn't going to take it well," Emory said, glancing at Mary. "Remember how they reacted when they learned about my mating? And that was only a few months ago. If you throw something like this on them…" Emory shook his head, sympathetic to Trey for the first time since he'd arrived. "I don't know what they'll do."

"Some of them will leave." Diskant sighed and dry washed his hand over his face. Tossing his hand to his side, he said, "Other males will challenge Trey as Alpha. It's something we can't avoid. Unless we can convince them they place themselves at greater risks if we're divided."

"That'll take some serious convincing." Emory tugged Mary close, wrapping his arms around her. "We'll have to approach this cautiously."

"I'm afraid we might not have that kind of time," Trey snapped, thinking about the enemy they were facing. "You didn't see Aldon at full power. He was like a brick shithouse. He put me and Nathan on our asses with a wave of his fucking hand. If it hadn't been for Sadie he might have killed us."

"What do you suggest we do?" Diskant questioned. "Show them what your female's capable of? Even if you do that most of the werewolves will balk at the notion of accepting a vampire as their Lupa. Those who understand her kind will be afraid she'll try to make your wolf a familiar. And if by some miracle you can get them to give her a chance, your mate will have to fight for her position if any females decide to challenge her for the spot."

"They can't say shit once I claim her." Trey's throaty growl resonated through the room. "She's already taken my blood. Once we're mated no one can deny it. And she hasn't made me a familiar. I'd know if she had."

"She's not a human or shifter, Trey," Emory reminded him. "There's a reason we don't mate with vampires. Have you thought about that? The pack might follow you but not if they think you're under the influence of a vampire. Even if she hasn't made you a familiar, they might not believe it. You can't convince them if they don't want to believe."

There was that.

Being mated to Sadie meant she would be able to control his wolf if necessary but any mate could do that. Males and females needed the balance of their mates. It wasn't unheard of for the balance to shift from one to the other. Most shifters weren't certain how it worked when they mated vampires—as shifters avoided blood drinkers at all costs—but horror stories had been passed along for years.

It was dangerous business, mating to blood drinkers.

He intended to learn what hold Sadie would have over him, but he had to actually seal the deal in order to understand the eccentricities of their union.

Add it to my long list of shit to consider.

"Maybe I should step down." He glanced across the way to Emory. "Maybe it's time someone more capable filled my shoes."

"Oh yeah, that'd go over well," Emory laughed, years of bitterness openly on display. "The pack might have accepted Mary but that's only because Ava made them. And I've never wanted to lead the pack. Besides, you know how they feel about me. They still don't trust me not to lose my shit. They think I'm a basket case. Coo coo ca choo."

"You need to contact Kinsley," Ava said, looking to Diskant. "The pack might throw a tantrum but they'll listen if he can get the prides to back our decision. They know we need the help right now. I don't think they'll risk too much with everything that's happened. Finding a new place to call home will take time. They'll be alone until they transition."

The Omega's face showed his pride—and appreciation—for his female's insight. "You're right. I'll call him. Once he knows what's going on he'll be on board. He's the clearest head of the bunch."

Ava grinned. "Which is why they'll listen to him."

"There's something else, baby," Diskant said softly and kneeled at Ava's side. She'd returned to her seat as soon as Sadie had vanished. Nestled in the chair she seemed smaller, her swelling belly more pronounced. "This doesn't end by bringing Sadie and Leigh here. We're going to have to locate your brother. We can't have the amulet floating around. It's too dangerous."

"I know." The sadness in Ava's voice seemed to affect everyone in the room. "I agree."

Mary rushed from Emory's side and placed her hand on Ava's shoulder. "It'll be okay. We'll face whatever comes together. I'll be here, right beside you. I have to look after my godchild, after all."

"We have to establish a place here for Leigh." Nathan, who'd remained quiet up until then, added his two cents. "I don't know what's wrong with her but she's weak and fragile. A hard wind would knock her over. She'll need to feel welcome or she'll wither. She'll have to know she's wanted and needed here. She needs to feel secure."

"Mary and I can do that," Ava said, softening toward the Beta. "Don't worry. We'll make her feel at home. It's not like the house isn't big enough for all of us. We'll be safer if we stick together."

"You'll have to do the same for Sadie," Trey demanded, determined his female receive equal treatment. "Once she turns her back on her coven she won't have anywhere else to go."

"She saved my life, Trey." Ava's sincerity was evident. "I owe that woman. I'll do anything to help her. And somehow we're connected. I want to understand how she knows me so well. I need to know where I come from."

"I'll start preparing rooms," Mary said and patted Ava's shoulder. "There's more than enough space to give everyone privacy. This house is enormous."

"What about the station?" Trey asked, thinking about the firehouse that had become his home. "Someone has to stay on duty. If we abandon it Shepherds will know something's up."

"You're right," Diskant sighed. "That's why I asked Nathan to get Caden's ass here."

"Him?" Emory's eyes widened in surprise. He could scarcely believe what he was hearing. "You're going to ask the human of the pack to watch over our asses?"

"Not necessarily," Diskant corrected with a sly glance. "I'm simply going to ask him to move his shit into the place and keep things in order for a while. Any Shepherd who trespasses on Cade's watch will wish they'd been born with brains. He wants a piece of their asses just as much—if not more—than we do."

"Not if the information we recently received is true," Nathan said, head bowed, hands clenched into fists. He shook his head as though he needed to get in control of his emotions. "There's a good chance we've got a lead on the men who killed his wife. He's got first dibs. We swore we'd give him the information as soon as we received it. He'll want to go after them as soon as possible."

Shit.

Trey knew Nathan was right. Caden deserved his revenge. The man had lost everything he loved. Shepherds had attempted to lie to the human, telling him shifters were responsible for the death of his wife and unborn child. Cade had started hunting pelts afterward, slaying every shifter in sight. Then Ava had shown the bitter and heartbroken man the truth. It hadn't been an easy transition but once Cade had gotten jive to reality, he'd wanted the heads of the men who'd killed his family on a silver platter.

"Hopefully the pack meeting didn't get that far." Diskant ran his fingers through his hair, growling low in his throat. "They wouldn't have started without Trey. No matter how hard Cade pushed for information, they'd have kept their mouths shut."

The roar of a car engine in the distance snared everyone's attention. Nathan looked at Ava, who closed her eyes. After a moment she opened them and exhaled softly.

"It's Cade." She confirmed their suspicion. "He's almost here. And he's not in a very pleasant mood."

"He's never in a pleasant mood," Trey muttered.

"You got that right," Diskant grumbled his agreement.

Why should the man be? If it was Trey, he'd be pissed too.

Earlier that morning Caden had been promised information he'd been waiting weeks for, only to be pulled away from those who had the news he wanted to hear. He'd almost had vengeance in his hands. It was like taking a toy away from a lonely infant. If he were in the human's situation, he'd be pissed too.

"I'll get the rooms ready," Mary told them, leaving Ava's side. "I'll also have to get Rocky's kennel," she added, referring to the Boxer puppy Emory had given her that'd grown by leaps and bounds. "I don't think it's safe to let him roam outside."

She walked to Emory, lifted onto her toes to kiss him on the cheek and left the room.

A door slammed and heavy footsteps approached. Cade breezed into the house as if he owed the place—typical. He didn't look like a happy camper, scowling at them.

"You requested my presence, your majesty." He mock bowed to Diskant. "Well here I am." Glaring at Trey, he quipped, "As for you, don't ever ask me to cover for your ass again. I don't like being left high and dry and I don't like being promised answers when no one wants to talk. Next time take care of your own shit." Trey tried to talk but Cade waved him off. "Don't worry about me. You have your own problems. Do you have any idea how angry the pack was when I told them you weren't coming and had wasted their time? Smooth move, Ex-Lax."

"Caden," Ava acknowledged the man coolly. "It's always such a pleasure."

The man knew better than to confront Diskant's female and said nothing.

Good choice.

"It appears something more important has come up," Diskant informed the short-tempered male. "And before you start spouting off—I'm talking about 'it's the end of the world' kind of shit. You can't get the people you're after if that happens, can you? So mellow the hell out and use that thing between your ears called a brain for a change."

Since tensions were so high, Trey shouldn't have been surprised when Sadie and Leigh popped into the room. The world loved to nudge those teetering on the edge. Still, relief almost sent him to his knees. She'd returned, just as she promised. He rushed to his mate, only to stop midway when she shook her head. He froze and looked at her companion.

Leigh — God help her — looked petrified.

"What the fuck?" Cade yelled, eyes trained on the females, going for the gun at his side.

Nathan charged the human like a freight train and took Caden down. They fought for the weapon, squirming on the ground. Cade was more than able to handle himself but Nathan was fighting for his mate. It didn't take long for the Beta to rip the gun from Cade's hand and send it skittering across the floor.

"Don't you ever, ever, pull a gun on a woman in this house," Nathan snarled in Cade's face. The two men were almost nose-to-nose. "Especially mine. Everyone else might put up with your shit but I won't. I'll drop you where you stand. I will kill your worthless ass."

"Women," Cade replied menacingly, lifting his head so he and Nathan almost butted noses, "don't appear out of nowhere. Neither do shifters."

"It's because we're vampires, idiot." Sadie schooled him good and proper, her eyes ice white. She glowered at the men on the ground. "It's called phasing. Not that I'd expect a human to understand anything about that."

She vanished again, going from Leigh's side, reappearing crouched next to Cade and Nathan. She kneeled, getting into Cade's personal space. "Shifters don't have shit on us, mortal. You pull a gun on me and I'll be behind you before you can blink. I'll break your neck before you know what's happening to you. You'll go down faster than a five-dollar hooker."

"Have you lost your fucking minds?" Cade's gaze shot around the room. "Are all of you totally insane?"

Nathan gave the human a harsh shove and cautiously made it to his feet. Trey shifted closer, prepared to take the man down if need be. Cade moved slowly, keeping his attention on the Beta. Step by step Nathan backed his way to Leigh. The skittish vampire tried to move away from the werewolf but it didn't do her any good. Nathan grasped her arm and tugged her against him, forcing her to his side. Trey could relate. He wanted to do the same with Sadie. Seeing his female relying on her abilities and speed instead of turning to him for assistance gnawed at his pride.

"Vampires?" Cade huffed, clenching his fists. "Aren't your hairy asses enough for one house? You decided it would be good to add brides of Dracula to the mix?"

"Can I show him?" Sadie asked, her attention steeled on Cade. "It'll be faster than any of us trying to explain and he needs to know who and what he's dealing with. Plus I think your human needs a bit of enlightenment."

"Do it," Diskant directed curtly before Cade could bolt.

Fuck, Sadie was fast.

She had her fingers clasped around Caden's wrist before the man could try to escape, trapping him in her strong grasp. At first he tried to yank free. She held her ground. After a couple of seconds he stopped pulling away, his untrusting gaze homed on Sadie.

He looked full of wonder.

He also looked like he was going to retch.

"That's right, dumbass," she whispered, holding on tight. "Watch, listen and learn."

Caden relaxed, tight shoulders easing, the muscles in his arms going soft. Instead of leaning away from Sadie he moved closer. Trey's beast snarled at their closeness, demanding he do something about it. Enough time had passed. Cade—the asshole of all assholes—had all the information he needed and then some.

Trey went to snatch Sadie from Caden's range when she let go of the man.

His body collided with his mate's and he curled his arm around Sadie's waist, tugging her against him. At first she froze. Then she went soft. He felt her fatigue—a faint pulsing of exhaustion beating at him. Her ass nestled against his hips, the tantalizing globes settling perfectly around his cock. She felt just right, soft in all the right places.

Claim her.

Don't waste any more time.

"It's impossible." Cade sounded as dazed as he appeared. "Things like these...events like that...it can't be true."

"You know it is," Diskant said, and his sidelong glare at Cade made Trey uneasy. "Think about it."

Hesitantly, with gravity, Caden nodded.

Fucking bastards.

They were hiding something—Diskant and Cade.

What had the Omega shared with the human member of the pack?

What didn't he know that—as the Alpha of the pack—he should have?

If things were different he'd have pushed the issue, giving them hell until they told him what going on. But his inquisition would have to wait. Everyone in the room had to be on the same page. They had Leigh but Aldon was still on the loose. Until they had their safeguards in place they had to be united by their common interests.

"You're going to need to crash at the station for a while," Diskant told Cade. His irises stabilized, returning to their usual golden hue. "Trey'll have to stay here until we sort things out. After we talk to the pack and find out how many are willing to stand in the line of fire, I'll make sure to give you as many guards as I can."

"And the information you promised?" Cade asked.

Diskant growled, lips drawn back. "You'll get it."

"You need to call Kinsley." Everyone's eyes turned to Ava when she addressed the room, reiterating her earlier concern. "We'll need the prides with us on this. He's the only one who can convince them to help us."

Kinsley—a rare and respected sixth generation black panther—was one of the scarcest of the feline shifter races. The prides trusted him enough to listen to whatever the male had to say. The male was almost never wrong, seeing every curve before anyone else.

Ava was right.

Without the Alpha's assistance, the pack would have to guard the city alone. As it was, the few felines who'd agreed to monitor the station and guard Diskant's domicile did so grudgingly. Cats always looked out for their own best interests. Kinsley would have to flex some serious muscle to convince them to assist Trey. While Diskant could shift into any feline form—and remained their Omega—members of the pride didn't feel his approval warranted their inconvenience.

They turned to Kinsley in all matters.

He'd be the only one who could sway them on this.

"I have to warn the guards they'll be pulling double shifts." Diskant went to his female's side and took a knee. He was so large—and she was so fucking small—he dwarfed both his mate and the piece of furniture. "We have to make sure everything is secure here before we worry about anything else."

"Shit," Sadie whispered and pivoted so that she faced Trey. "I'll have to talk to Leigh. We're the only ones who can make sure magic won't penetrate the house." She peered over his shoulder, looking around the room. "You don't have any safety nets." She appeared exasperated. "Anyone with magic can get inside. Aldon took my blood, he might be able to track me."

Panic etched over her face as she closed her eyes and magic burst from her, the energy a sharp throb against his skin. She whispered something in Latin, evoking what could only be a spell. Her anxiety became his. His female was worried about something, so much so she was draining her already dwindling reserves. Her thoughts weren't clear but he could sense them.

She was worried about Aldon and something else she perceived as a threat.

"There," she sighed, opening her eyes. "It'll hold, but only for so long." Her gaze darted to Leigh. "We'll have to take care of the rest of the residence. No one can know where we are."

"Can you do that?"

Sadie had to turn her body to see Leigh. When she did, a frown marred the beauty of her face. "We can do it," Sadie replied softly, "but we'll have to be strong." With a sigh, she shook her head. "I'll have to talk to Leigh too. Shielding spells take up a lot of energy. She's too weak to help right now, so more than likely I'll have to provide for her. If I do, it'll take more time."

"Provide for her?"

Sadie's breasts teased his chest as she rotated around. She lifted onto her tiptoes, her mouth caressing the ridge of his ear. "Feed her."

His dick, already partially erect from the feel of her plush ass, hardened substantially. "Does that mean…"

"I'll need to recover." Fuck a duck, she didn't move, her lithe form flush against his. "Giving blood means taking blood."

It felt like all of the blood in his body went directly to his cock.

He'd give her all she needed to recover.

"You're already mine," he warned in a low growl, "but once I've put my mark on you it's a done deal. You won't be able to run, darlin'."

"Even if it means coming clean with your pack? I won't be swept away to a private place for you to fuck, Trey." The misery he'd caused had never been more apparent, her despair visible in her gaze. "I won't let you hurt me again."

"Diskant," he called out, keeping his eyes locked with the heartbroken female. He had a lot of damage to undo and a helluva lot of healing to start. "I'm taking my mate to our room. We've got unfinished business."

The Omega didn't fuss—not that Trey expected him to. Diskant knew the score, being mated himself. Shifters understood how it went. Once you found the one intended for you, nothing else mattered. The fighting, Aldon and all the rest could keep. Priorities went in a particular order. In this case, it was time he made his status in Sadie's life known.

She didn't trust him.

He didn't blame her.

But goddamn it, he was about to show her he wasn't the man she believed him to be.

Once he'd crossed this barrier, no one in the pack could argue the mating. They could resent it, demand he step down or try to make him leave the city. But they couldn't prevent what had already transpired. With or without their backing, he had to do what was best for him for a change. If he didn't he'd become the jaded, bitter and unfeeling asshole who existed but had stopped living, unaware of the beauty and grandeur around him.

"W-wait." She looked back as he dragged her from the room. "I haven't had time to talk to Leigh. She's scared. I need to explain…"

"It'll keep. Trust me. She's fine here. She's with Nathan. He won't let anyone hurt her." He waited until they vanished around the corner before he spun around and pinned her to the nearest wall. "I've waited too long for you."

"The shields, we need them—"

Thrusting his hips against her, he growled, "You need blood and I'm going to give it to you. But first I'm going to devour you, baby. I'm going to strike the match that makes you burn."

She lifted her mouth to his but he ripped his head away. His nose piloted him, directing him to where Mary had wandered through the gargantuan house. The female wasn't far away, just a few doors down. When he arrived at his destination he found Mary tossing additional pillows onto a bed. Emory's female stilled when she saw them in the entranceway, her chocolate-brown eyes becoming wide as saucers.

"I guess this'll be your room," Mary murmured and rushed toward them, her cheeks turning red. "I'll go see if anyone needs anything."

Trey moved aside to let Mary pass. The skittish woman didn't miss a step, fleeing from the area. With an arm around Sadie's middle, he carried his mate over the threshold and closed the door.

Finally, his wolf thrilled in his head, *the wait is over.*

It's time.

Chapter Seven

Sadie'd envisioned this moment—in so many different ways—but she'd never thought it would happen. Yet here she stood, caged in Trey's embrace. He dipped his head, dark strands of hair loose around his face. The desire in his eyes made her insides wilt. He looked like he wanted to eat her up and, given her sexual frustration, she was more than willing to let him.

"We don't have a lot of time." Although she hadn't forgotten how much he'd hurt her, she wanted this. "We have to hurry."

"That pisses me off, you know." He dipped his head and nuzzled her neck. "I don't want to rush. I want to explore every inch of your body. I'm going to find out what turns you on and gets you hot."

An electric pulse zinged down her spine. She wanted the same thing—to lick every crevice of his body, to see how he reacted when her tongue darted over his smooth skin. His temperature was much warmer than hers, his body like a miniature furnace. When she nibbled at his flesh her lips would be cool and soft. On the other hand, when his hard, wet tongue slid over her clit it would burn her up in all the right ways.

Back they went, step by step.

He removed her holster and tossed her sword to the ground. Her knees hit the edge of the mattress and they went down together. His weight bore her down, his larger size ramping up her desire. As a vampire, she rarely felt vulnerable. That had been fine in the past, when she'd taken control and got what she needed from casual encounters. In hindsight the sex had been lackluster. She'd always wanted to let someone else take charge and see to her pleasure. With Trey she wouldn't have to indicate what she wanted. Shifters were just as sexual as vampires. Only the males lived to dominate. They didn't give an inch.

He'd take control. And she'd love every minute of it.

"Fuck," he rasped, drifting down her body. "I want to see you."

Undressing was never sexy. Taking off boots and clothing was usually awkward and time-consuming. Thankfully they were both so keyed-up that removing her garments didn't prove a problem. He started at her feet, stripping off her boots and socks. She did her best to assist, squirming as she wriggled free of her leather pants. Her panties got caught in the mix, tugged away when Trey yanked her pants down her thighs and over her ankles. He cast the clothing aside and she lifted her torso from the bed, pulling her shirt over her head. Only her bra remained, shielding her breasts from view.

"Off," he growled, watching her, his irises a prismatic shade of gold.

He looks so sexy like this. A big, bad wolf.

She teased him, bowing her back as she reached behind her to unlatch the clasps. When the bra was loose she brought her hands around, holding the material in place. His gaze followed her movements, his tongue darting out to wet his lower lip. She cupped her breasts, rubbing the soft, lacy material over her skin. Her nipples tingled, the hard points aching with each brush of the cloth. Warmth flooded her pussy, her clit was practically pounding. She wanted to feel his lips on her nipples, to see how good he was with his mouth and tongue.

Trey met her eyes. "If you want to keep that bra, I suggest you ditch it."

Lifting her arms, she maneuvered the straps over her hands and tossed the flimsy material over her head. Trey growled. The ominous sound filled the room—dangerous, low and harsh. A thrill shot through her, a wave of fire cascading under her skin. This was what she'd waited for. Not some dream but the real deal. She tried to lower her arms but Trey stopped her, capturing her wrists in one of his large hands. His dark head lifted slowly as his gaze traveled the length of her torso.

When their eyes met again, his stare froze her in place.

Dear Goddess.

She'd wanted to be mastered and to relinquish control but she hadn't understood just how assertive Trey would be as a lover. A simple look—his eyes boring into hers—and she finally appreciated who and what he was. Not just a man, but an animal as well. He was about to take everything she had to give and then some. He wouldn't accept anything less than her best.

"Stay," he instructed, his golden irises vibrant. His face descended, coming closer. His breath caressed her mouth, warm against her skin. "Just," he whispered, breezing his lips over hers. "Like." He teased her lower lip with a flick of his tongue. "That."

Who the hell was she to argue?

She did as he asked, remaining in place. His lips curved, forming into a small, sly grin. Slowly he released her wrists, his fingers drifting over skin. If he'd wanted, he could have pinned her down and forced her compliance. As susceptible as she was in his presence, he could do just about anything he wanted. Vampires were faster but a werewolf made up for their lack of speed with strength. So it surprised her he kept his enthusiasm in check, careful as he touched her. If he was this hot when he was holding back, she couldn't wait to see what he'd be like when he let loose.

He lifted his big body from hers, studying her breasts. "You're perfect, baby." Lowering his head, he pressed his lips to her stomach. She quivered, her muscles going taut. "You smell so good, darlin'. I bet you're wet as hell. Good thing I'm finally going to get my taste."

He moved lightning-fast, sliding his hips down her body. With a quick maneuvering of his hands he placed her legs over his shoulders. She struggled to breathe, keeping her hands over her head, lifting up so she could see his face. He lowered himself to the ground, kneeling between her outstretched thighs. The heat of his breath brushed her exposed folds, making the skin seem hypersensitive. She'd decided to have her pubic hair removed via a nifty spell decades ago, after she'd discovered oral sex felt so much better when performed against bare skin. Now, waiting for Trey's attention, she knew it had been one of the smartest decisions she'd ever made in her life.

She nearly screamed in frustration as he rested the side of his face against her thigh. The stubble on his jaw felt like tiny bristles skimming over her flesh, prickly yet soft. He was so close. One shift of her hips—a tiny bit of movement—and his mouth would be where she wanted it.

"Trey." She exhaled his name, trembling as she waited for him to take things further.

"I've got a lot to make up for," he said softly, meeting her gaze. There was so much intensity etched in his features—so much longing. "I'm going to start here, Sadie. I'm going to give you what I should have a long time ago."

Her libido didn't care how he made things up to her, so long as he did something.

Shifting his weight, he got in position. He reached for her pussy and parted her labia with his thumbs. She heard him drawing a deep breath, taking in her scent. His lips hovered over her mound, making her painfully aware of her situation. He wasn't going to rush, even if she begged him to. This wasn't just about her, it was also about him. She'd harbored her fantasies. Of course he had his as well.

Some men loved going down on a woman.

From the looks of things, Trey was one of them.

The first lick along her crease was firm, his tongue going from the base of her pussy to her hammering clit. She arched her back and parted her legs, shoving her heels into his shoulders as her toes curled. His mouth wasn't just warm it was blistering hot, leaving behind a path of fiery tingles. Another lick followed the first, then another. He groaned when he lapped at her yet again, the heavy vibration nearly enough to make her come. She'd never been so excited, aware of how heavy her breasts felt, how swollen her clit had to be.

It wouldn't take much to send her soaring.

The tip of his tongue darted over her folds, skimming up and down. Then she felt it slide past and delve inside her. Her gums tingled and her fangs dropped. The euphoria she'd experienced shifted, her now-sharp canines reminding her of her bloodthirsty nature. She recalled how Trey had reacted to what she was in the past. He'd loathed her. Wanted to fuck her and send her away.

Shaking off the bad memory, she pressed her lips together, telling herself not to think but feel.

Enjoy the moment. Don't complicate things.

"Fuck, baby." His hands slid from her pussy and he cupped her ass. "You're so sweet."

Knowing shifters were within hearing distance she muffled her cries of delight, rotating her hips with each stroke of his tongue. His fingers clasped her bottom, his grip almost bruising. Blood pumped through her veins, the sound literally pounding in her head. She considered reaching down and grasping his hair, using her hold to guide his mouth to her clit. Sheer willpower kept her arms over her head. She bit her lip, fighting her vampire nature. Not only did she want to come, she wanted to drink from him while she did.

"That's it," he grated.

One hand moved from her ass. His hard and thick fingers skimmed over her folds. He brought them to the mouth of her sex, rotated them in a circle to get them wet and slid them inside. She bucked against his hand, wanting him to go deeper. He didn't rush, taking his time, sinking his fingers into her until he was third-knuckle deep. He knew precisely what to do, turning his wrist slightly, rubbing her vaginal walls. She shuddered when he hit her G-spot, parting her lips to take a deep breath. The tip of her fang caught the lower one as she did, breaking the skin.

Trey stilled and his head darted up.

She shuddered, frustrated that he'd stopped—until she realized why.

He stared at her mouth, focusing on where she'd injured herself. Her fangs weren't as large as a shifter's but they were still noticeable and different. She froze, mortified as she stepped back in time. At first—before he'd known what she was—Trey'd wanted her. He'd been so hard she could feel his cock trapped between their bodies, the enormous length substantial and damn impressive. She'd imagined riding him hard and easing the ache deep inside her. But that lust and desire had vanished the moment he'd put two and two together. He'd been repulsed and disgusted by her nature, staring at her like she'd grown a second head. What should have been beautiful quickly turned to scattered ash.

She could still hear the words he snarled in outrage and disbelief.

A goddamn vampire.

"Don't." His gruff voice brought her back to the present. "The shit you're thinking about doesn't matter."

"Doesn't it?"

"Not anymore." He thrust his fingers inside her, fucking her steadily with his hand. "You're mine, baby. I warned you. I'm going to put my mark on you for the entire fucking world to see."

She could have argued or told him to go to hell but her body's reaction overcame her doubt. She'd been twisted as tight as a corded rope, one more turn and she'd break and unwind. After all she'd been through, she deserved this small consolation. Maybe it was stupid to believe him but she wasn't going anywhere.

Not when she was so close.

Not when she wanted this so badly.

A little more... Just a little more...

His fingers returned to her G-spot, his touch hard and determined. She rode his hand, swept into the fire building in her stomach. Heat spread through her abdomen, a tendril of electricity venturing to her pussy. He bent his head, bringing his mouth to her slit. Then he trapped her clit between his lips—his tongue hard, warm and wet—and sucked. The suction against the bundle of nerves pushed her over the precipice. The world vanished, becoming a huge blur of white.

Yes.

She slammed her eyes closed, throwing her head back.

Spasms racked her body, her muscles flexing as she came. Euphoria and elation scorched her from the inside out, each flick of his tongue its own brand of fire. He kept sucking her clit, tapping the tip of his tongue over the delicate nub. His hand pumped, his fingers forcing her pussy to part and make room for their invasion. She held on to the sensations, riding out each wave, never wanting them to end. He didn't stop until the last ripple of pleasure had passed, leaving her a gasping, shivering mess on the bed.

His fingers slid from her pussy and she detested the loss, craving his nearness.

He rose, yanking his shirt over his head. His muscles flexed, displaying hard lines and smooth planes from his shoulders to his waist. She forced her body to function, shaking off the warm fog of climax enveloping her. She sat up and reached for his jeans, admiring the muscles that flexed between the V of his hips.

He'd had his taste. It was time for hers.

His fingers wrapped around her wrists, stopping her short of her goal. She gazed up at him, confused by the interruption. Removing his shirt had mussed his hair, the strands darting in all directions. Even so, he'd never looked more irresistible. He licked his lips, his irises a bright shade of amber.

"Not this time. I want you so bad I'll lose it before we've started."

He let her go and went for the buttons holding his pants in place. At the same time he toed off his shoes and kicked them aside. Her breath caught as he revealed himself. She could see how defined he was, able to distinguish each set of muscles from the next. He was absolute perfection from his head down to his feet. Before she could enjoy the visual, he bent to remove his jeans. She gritted her teeth, willing her bloodlust to settle, waiting for him to stand tall and proud before her.

The pants hit the floor and he righted himself.

She'd seen him before but she wasn't prepared for how stunning he was. His fully engorged cock strained toward his bellybutton, the thick, mushroom head a darker hue than the stalk. She'd been with her fair share of men but none of them compared.

Not to Trey Veznor.

He wrapped his fingers under the tip of his cock and squeezed. A glistening bead of pre-cum appeared in the slit. She wanted to lean forward and lick it away, teasing the hard, supple skin with flicks of her tongue. His thickness and length would be impossible to cover with her mouth, meaning she'd have to use her hands. The image of doing just that sent a tremor through her. She'd give him pleasure, swallowing every drop of his seed as he came. Then she'd send him over the edge a second time, sinking her fangs into the vein in his thigh.

"Give yourself to me, Sadie." A measure of desperation accompanied the request. "Lie back, open those pretty thighs and take me."

Apprehension struck, coiling its way to her heart.

She wanted to give him what he wanted—she yearned for it, in fact.

But fear clawed its way into her mind, a harsh remembrance of what had happened when she allowed herself to jump headfirst into something without weighing the consequences beforehand. He was the only one who could provide the blood she needed to survive, so he'd always own that part of her. But there was one thing she could control, no matter how small it seemed.

"Your mark won't scar," she confessed, telling him the truth. Unless she used a spell to allow it, he could bite her all he wanted and it would never matter. "You're not the one who makes that decision."

"It'll stay," he growled, releasing his cock. The swollen length bobbed toward his stomach, the heavy shaft upright and stiff as he leaned over her. "Do you know why?"

She shook her head, resting back on her elbows, shivering as he kneed her legs apart. His eyes were practically glowing, his lips drawn back just enough she could see his canines lengthen. She felt his wolf then, sensed the energy Trey put off. Something had changed, a shift she might not be able to see but could feel. The creature inside the man was even more threatening and powerful. It didn't merely want her, it *needed* her.

And it was about to do whatever it took to possess her.

"You haven't fully experienced the bond between us, baby. But you're about to. You'll see that no matter what you say—whether my mark stays on your skin or not—you belong to one man."

He reached down, guiding his cock to her cleft. He slid the tip through her wet folds, running it up and down. On the final pass he rested the tip against her pussy. Even as wet as she was, he had to work his way inside. She inhaled sharply as the wide head penetrated her. He released the base and lifted his head.

Oh shit.

Before she'd sensed the wolf. Now it stared at her through Trey's eyes.

She'd pushed the animal, even if she hadn't meant to.

Placing an arm beneath her, he shifted his weight and lifted her onto the mattress. The instant her back hit the bed he thrust, parting her like a breeze, the unyielding length of him spearing inside her in one swift motion. His sac hit her ass, her pussy aching as it stretched to accept him.

She'd wondered what he'd be like when he let loose and didn't hold back.

She was about to find out.

"Me," he growled, rolling his hips, grinding against her. "You belong to me."

Satin and silk. Warm and slick. So damn tight his balls were going to burst.

Sadie's pussy wrapped around him, so snug he didn't dare move.

The wolf had ridden him hard, determined to claim her. Her quip about his mark being her decision had set off the beast, uncaging the feral portion of him. Despite the truth of her statement, he knew every single male in his pack would scent his seed on her, meaning they'd stay the fuck away. She didn't have to accept a scar on her shoulder. She knew the truth. So would everyone else.

Fuck the mark. She's mine now.

No running away, Sadie. No more promises you can't keep.

Her gorgeous light-blue eyes studied him, full and delectable lips parted for his kiss. He looked at her tiny fangs, groaning as his balls tightened and cock pulsed. In his dreams those sharp little teeth did all sorts of things to his libido. He'd gotten a glimpse of how good it could be when she'd fed from him earlier, busting a nut before he could think clearly.

Would it be the same like this?

Would she hold off until he was ready?

Unable to remain still, he withdrew his cock, hissing as he retreated from the haven of her cunt. She gasped, shaking as if she were on ice, staring up at him. Her pupils dilated, making her icy blue irises more pronounced. Her blonde hair cascaded around her, the lush strands like gold against the dark comforter.

Damn.

He was one lucky son of a bitch. This female — his female — was hotter than hell.

Time was short but he'd wanted to make this encounter memorable. He wanted to hear her cries and watch her face as she came. If he had his way he'd take the entire night, until she'd milked his cock dry. Sadly that wasn't going to happen. The mating heat was on him, the wolf snarling in his head as it tried to gain control.

Bringing a hand to her side for leverage, he plunged into her.

Shit.

It wasn't going to be easy to hold back, not when he was ready to explode.

Cautiously, he settled into a smooth, deliberate rhythm. He moved in and out, hard and steady. He nearly lost it when she lifted her hips, moving in tandem with his firm, purposeful strokes. Each time he sank balls-deep he felt the softness of her cervix. She took all he had and asked for more.

Fuck it all, she deserved more than this.

She shouldn't have had to accept him as her mate in a stranger's home, fucking him on a guestroom bed. This should have happened in private, in their own fucking residence, where he could pepper the bed with rose petals as soft as her skin and as pink as her lips. She deserved his time and attention as he adored her for hours on end.

His eyes strayed to her breasts. The nipples in the centers of the creamy swells were a dark shade of pink, the areolas hard and puckered. For a moment he let his fantasies take over, picturing his dick trapped between the soft mounds. She'd tell him to come, massaging her breasts, flicking her tongue over the tip with each thrust of his cock.

His balls tightened, an orgasm threatening to consume him.

Keep it together. Don't fuck this up.

He took a stiff point into his mouth, basking in her sigh of pleasure. He tapped his tongue over the tiny pearl, groaning when she wrapped her legs around his waist. The change in position allowed him to go deeper, his dick gliding in and out of her pussy. Each time he lifted away she pulled back, timing it so their bodies came together in a fluid motion.

Moving from one breast to the next, he growled, "You're killing me."

Her hand drifted from his arm. He started to complain, wanting more of her touch, when he felt her fingers in his hair. *Fuck yeah.* The tips of her nails skimmed over his scalp, parting the strands. She urged him closer, applying pressure to the back of his head. Her soft mewls of contentment drifted to his ears. He increased the suction, working his tongue over the hard peak.

Perfect, baby. Enjoy it.

"Like that," she whispered, grinding her pussy onto his cock, rolling her pelvis. "Goddess, yes."

For fuck's sake.

He hadn't been this eager to blow since his teens. Pubescent hormones were bad but when you threw a wolf into the equation it seriously complicated the male sex drive. Over time he'd learned to hold himself back, to see to a female's needs.

If only things were that simple now.

As much as he longed to appease his mate, he wanted to claim her too. Maybe when the wolf wasn't snarling in his head he'd be able to pay proper attention. He felt the perspiration on his back and brow, the result of denying himself what he wanted most. His canines had revealed themselves a long while ago, the wolf's demand that he mark their female and cement their union. The animal had stopped playing nice.

The beast emerged, trying to overcome the man.

Ripping his mouth from Sadie's breast, he rose above her. He didn't bother going for soft or romantic, fucking her hard and fast. His balls were heavy, his sac tight. She shifted with each rock of his body, her breasts bouncing. He ground his teeth together, telling the wolf to back the fuck off. It didn't listen, taking over, transforming his nails into claws.

"Trey," Sadie murmured, latching on to his neck with her hand. She pulled him down, lifting her shoulders away from the bed. "This time I need…" Her fingers tensed on his nape. "I have to ask…"

Magic wafted from Sadie and hummed against his skin. It took a moment to understand what he was feeling and identify the demands of his mate. Her hunger confused his wolf, catching the animal off-guard. Anxiety poured from his beast, mingling with the concerns of the man.

Did she always drink like this? He'd already given her so much.

What if he couldn't provide for her? Would he be able to keep up?

"Yes." He lowered himself, balancing on one elbow, giving her plenty of room.

He turned his head to the side, presenting his neck. Even if it made him as weak as a kitten, he'd give her anything she asked for. It was his duty to nourish her, one of the primary responsibilities of a mated male.

"Go ahead, baby." He wanted to feel it, to come hard inside her. "Take what you need."

Her teeth sank deep, the white-hot ecstasy of her bite shooting through his body. He growled, his hips jerking in an uneven motion as he climaxed. His cock pulsed with each stream of semen, his seed flooding her womb. Even as it caused the punctures in his neck to protest, he turned his face toward her.

Mark her.

Now.

Aiming for her shoulder, he brought his lips back. His teeth broke through her flesh, gliding past her soft and giving skin. Her whimper was one of pain and pleasure. She didn't stop drinking, taking his blood to build her strength. He pumped his hips, stunned to find his cock remained stiff despite his climax. He wondered if a mating bond would be established as it did when shifters mated humans. She didn't cry out in pain and he didn't feel a shift in his wolf. He didn't experience the separation he'd been told about. It was like a different connection was established between them, bringing them closer together.

"Again." Sadie's thought echoed through his mind. *"More."*

He kept his teeth embedded in her skin, hammering his cock into her pussy with enough force to shake the mattress. His skin itched, his wolf so close at hand he balled his fists to keep from shifting.

Fucking hell. It had never been so difficult to remain in charge.

Over the years his beast had learned its place. As an Alpha he had to maintain the balance. Sometimes shifters were known to mate in their fur—when they were both in animal form—but he'd never been turned-on by the idea. Sadie likely wouldn't be either.

Back off, he snarled at the damn thing.

His strength ebbed, the muscles in his arms and legs growing weak. He tried to keep going, thrusting for all he was worth. His dick might be hard but he couldn't complete the act without stamina. He'd done this long enough to know he could go a double round if so inclined, without any serious issues. The tugs against his throat were a stern reminder of Sadie's demands. Taking so much had left him drained. He couldn't keep going if she continued. With his luck he'd end their first encounter with a whimper not a bang.

Like a fucking pussy.

"Not quite," Sadie's voice appeared in his head again. *"Not even close."*

A burst of magic seared through him, beginning at his neck and winding down his body. His lethargy vanished, a newfound energy suffusing his muscles. Pressure built in his sac and another climax crashed over him. He released her shoulder, stars flashing before his eyes. A sharp, electric current crackled up his back, shooting through his arms and legs. It felt as amazing as it felt awkward. He'd never come that many times so close in a row.

Son of a fucking bitch.

Her pussy flexed around his cock as she came, her moan throaty and deep. Her fangs slid from his neck, the swipes of her tongue tender over the wounds. She kept him close, her thighs tight around his waist as she pumped her hips. He kept up the pace, wanting to extend her release. She kept shaking, enjoying the pleasure he gave her. He wished it could last forever.

Eventually she went soft beneath him, her quiet exhalation one of satiation and bliss. His gaze drifted to her shoulder as he backed away from her.

As she'd warned, his mark had vanished. There wasn't as much as a scratch or bruise marring her porcelain skin. The wolf, who had found satisfaction in their pairing, didn't approve. A growl crept up his chest, a prickle of fury washing over him. His scent would serve as a threat to any shifter who crossed her path but he wanted his dominance openly displayed.

She was his.

No other would ever have her.

"It doesn't matter," he warned, staring his mate in the eye. She licked the corner of her mouth, collecting the last traces of his blood. "With or without the mark, you know who you belong to."

He expected a lot of things—for her to tell him to fuck off or inform him he didn't have a say in the matter—but he hadn't counted on her letting him go and stretching her arms over her head. She sighed, happy as a lark. Whereas he was livid, she was totally at ease. A smile tugged at her lips, her blue eyes darkening a shade.

"If you say so," she purred, arching her back like a contented cat. "Barbarian."

Before he could respond someone knocked on the door. He wanted to curse his shitty fortune. True, they'd had time for nothing more than a quickie. He'd done what he needed to do, marking Sadie with his scent, acknowledging what she meant to him. But he wanted more. It wasn't supposed to be like this—wild, crazy and rushed. He'd waited centuries for this woman. A romantic he wasn't but he'd imagined things differently. Didn't women like sweet words whispered in their ear?

Maybe you've found a woman who won't put up with your shit.

"Trey," Emory called through the door, "you might want to hurry it up."

He started to tell Emory to kiss his ass when Sadie paused. Her eyes went cloudy, as though she were listening to something Trey couldn't hear. In a split second her eyes became cognizant. She scrambled away from him, scurrying back from his body. It was like she couldn't get away from him fast enough. He frowned, confused at her behavior. She didn't waste time, jumping from the bed to collect her clothes.

"That girl—that vampire—you left out here is freaking the fuck out," Emory informed him, yelling loud enough for the entire house to hear. "Mary and Ava can't calm her down. You need to get your *mate*," he emphasized the word sarcastically, "out here right now."

"Shit," Sadie spat, tugging on her underwear. "I shouldn't have left her."

Rising from the bed, he yelled, "We're coming."

"Right now?" Emory quipped. "I'd hoped you'd gotten that far already."

Smartass.

"Emory?" he yelled, wanting to strangle his sibling.

"Yeah?"

"Fuck off!"

"Don't thank me. You're welcome, shithead," Emory snarled. "Don't blame the messenger."

The floor creaked as Emory walked away from the door. Trey didn't bother with his socks or shoes, sliding into his jeans. Sadie had gotten dressed in record time, working on her boots by the time he'd shrugged into his shirt. She started to rush for the door and he stopped her, grasping her elbow. At least he knew it wasn't personal. She was rushed but it had nothing to do with their mating. Her mind was evidently with her friend.

"You need to calm down."

"Easy for you to say," she hissed, narrowing her eyes. "That's *my* vampire out there, not yours."

Damn Emory. The bastard had to shoot off at the mouth and get Sadie riled. He smoothed her hair with his other hand, straightening the blonde strands tangled around her shoulder.

"If you don't act like you're in control, everyone'll think you're weak. You don't want that." He waited until the anger drained from her eyes to add, "Diskant doesn't trust the weak. He never has. You have to prove you can keep Leigh in check. Otherwise Nathan won't be able to do squat to keep her safe. Diskant will want her gone." He let the words sink in, giving Sadie a few seconds. "Do you understand?"

She broke eye contact, turning her head. "I understand."

The situation was all kinds of fucked up. His mate didn't have many choices. The weight and responsibility had to be killing her. If she didn't walk the line carefully, Leigh's fate wouldn't be up to her. Diskant would take any measure necessary to protect Ava and the pack, even if it meant taking the life of an innocent woman. If it wasn't for Nathan the Omega probably would have already eliminated the threat.

He cupped Sadie's face, trying to reassure her, skimming his thumbs across her cheeks. She turned her head and pressed a kiss to his palm. Such an innocent and sweet gesture that was sad in a way. He wanted to tell her everything was going to be okay but he wasn't going to lie. They'd finally found common ground. Telling her things to make her feel better—even if he had her best interests at heart—would destroy the tentative truce between them.

"I'll be with you," he said, struggling for the words. Proving himself worthy had never been so difficult. "If you need me...if you want me..."

Silence followed. Then—so softly he had to strain to hear—she replied, "Thank you."

It wasn't what he wanted but it was a start. He led her to the door and opened it. He waited until she'd stepped outside to follow. The die had been cast. From this moment forward, nothing was certain.

Yet, strangely enough, he experienced something he hadn't felt in a long time.

Hope.

Chapter Eight

Finally.

Magical defenses were in place, invisible shields where they needed to be.

Aldon couldn't find Sadie despite the blood he'd taken from her, even if he tried to use a spell. But the blood Trey had given her had been just enough to get the job done. It had taken every ounce of her magic to finish the deed. She couldn't keep going. Not like this. And she couldn't take more from Trey to regain what she'd lost. Not yet. Taking more was too dangerous.

That meant she wouldn't be able to provide for herself and Leigh.

She watched her friend, wondering how she should break the bad news.

"I'm beat," Leigh said, peeping through the blinds covering the window.

Sadie wanted to tell the young vampire she had no idea.

Instead of basking in the afterglow of her encounter with Trey, it had taken her nearly an hour to calm the fledgling down. Leigh had lodged herself in a corner in a bedroom, crouching between a dresser and the wall. Nathan had tried to calm her down but his presence only upset the girl. Sadie'd come to the rescue, asking everyone to leave in order to take charge of the situation. Trey and Nathan hadn't liked it but they'd relented. During their absence she'd managed to convince Leigh to put aside her fear, warning her Aldon would find them if she didn't. Sadie had given Leigh as much blood as the vampire would take, explained what they needed to do and shortly thereafter they'd gotten to work.

To Nathan and Trey's credit, the shifters had gone about their business. Although Sadie had seen them check in on them here and there as they moved through the house. The women—Ava and Mary—had made themselves scarce. Sadie wasn't sure if they were busy or didn't trust the crazed vampires in their home. Either way, she understood. Things weren't simple. Leigh had to understand that now more than ever.

I have to tell her. Sadie drew a deep breath. *Bring on the crazy.*

"We need to talk." She plopped down on the bed, glad to get off her feet.

Yet again her pride and confidence had gotten in her way. She'd thought she could do this. After all, she'd defended the coven for years. But the people in Diskant's home weren't her coven and Aldon wasn't an idle threat. In light of what she'd learned, she'd accepted she couldn't defend everyone on her own. Leigh had all a vampire could need—blood from a sister, power beyond a human's belief—but it wasn't enough. Not even close. With his abilities Aldon could crush through the girl's defenses and take them down one by one.

Leigh had to accept things had changed.

"About?" Leigh asked, continuing to look outside.

"What's at stake," she exhaled in a rush, frightened for the first time since she'd entered Disktant's domain. Trey's earlier warning returned to torment her. Diskant would kill Leigh if he had to. Sadie had to make sure that didn't happen. "You have to be prepared."

Leigh pivoted, a wave of dark hair spilling over her shoulder. "I don't understand. You said we only needed to cast the spell. We've done it," she stated, relief on her pale face. "We're safe."

Safe? If only.

Leigh's abilities surpassed Sadie's by leaps and bounds. As painful as it was to admit, the newborn vampire's magic was much more potent. It shouldn't have come as a shock when Leigh had memorized the spell Sadie had taught her, worked to create it and sealed off the place without breaking sweat. Even now—standing in front of Sadie with her face aglow—Leigh looked like she'd done little more than climb a hill. Meanwhile, even if Leigh wasn't aware of it, the magic had put Sadie on her ass. If it weren't for Sadie's determination to defend the compound—to defend Trey—she might have given up. Fortunately Leigh had taken over with ease, invoking the spell like a seasoned pro.

That was the bitch of it.

Leigh thought everything was gravy.

The naïve creature had no idea how strong she really was.

Be honest. Tell her the truth.

"Your magic is stronger then you realize. That comes with a cost."

A shadow of agony crossed the woman's face. "You think I don't know that?" Leigh snapped with a hint of bitterness. "I don't cast spells or use my abilities unless I have to. I wouldn't have now if it weren't so important. You know how I feel. I've told you why."

Leigh hated the magic, feeling it made her less human.

The poor thing—even though she knew better—held out hope that one day she'd return to her normal life. She denied herself blood, preferring to eat human food that did nothing for her body. It left the vampire thin, ghostly pale and constantly weak.

Sadie wanted to curse the world that had treated Leigh so cruelly.

One minute Leigh had been a human girl with hopes and dreams. The next she'd been changed by a vampire who'd left her to rot. No one knew why. Some rogues thought it was funny to create fledglings who didn't understand what they'd become. Leigh's case was strange though. Most creators—even dickhead rogues—usually returned to their progeny and established some sort of connection. Whoever had made Leigh would always be able to find her. A link formed between a vampire and its child, one that could only be broken in death. Why he hadn't shown himself — why he hadn't returned — was anyone's guess.

"You're going to have to get over the past." Sadie lifted her head to stare at her friend. "This spell — our spell — is nothing. Call it a blimp on the shit-o-dar. We're about to deal with some medieval stuff. You're going to have to come to terms with your part in this."

A surge of exhaustion rushed through her.

"Some choices are never easy." She kept going, hoping Leigh would listen. "You take what you're given or you die. You're going to have to accept more than you're willing to, even if you hate me for it."

Leigh's bitterness swiftly changed to suspicion. "What do you mean?"

"I can't feed you," she blurted, shaking her head to clear away cobwebs clouding her thoughts. She bowed her head, unable to bear the horror in Leigh's face. "I thought I could but I can't. I'm sorry."

"I can go a long time without blood. It shouldn't be an issue." There was resolve in Leigh's statement, as though she harbored a small bit of hope.

Hope for what?

A world gone to shit? A world in which everyone would burn?

"Diskant will kill you." She hated the gravity the words carried. It wasn't her job to threaten members of her coven — it never had been until this moment. "He'll tear you apart if he thinks you're a threat. If you want to live, you're going to have to accept I can't provide for you. Starving yourself isn't an option. This isn't the coven. You can't hide out and pretend you're not a vampire anymore." Telling her sister-in-magic something so brutally honest hurt Sadie more than Leigh would ever understand. She tried to keep a level head, attempting to convey her concerns. "You're going to have to take what you're given, even if that means accepting what you're not ready for. I wish it were different. I wish I could give you choices. I'm sorry you have to..."

Take Nathan's blood. Be Nathan's mate.

Sadie's chest ached at the thought. Forcing Leigh to accept Nathan — a man the woman didn't love — wasn't what she wanted for her friend.

Damn it.

Life wasn't simple. If Leigh wanted to survive, she had to think about the future.

Maybe it was Sadie's old age. She accepted that some things were decided by fate. Leigh had been born a mortal, putting her faith in a higher power. The truth was no one knew what happened for certain when a person died. And Nathan wouldn't let anything happen to Leigh. If Diskant threatened to harm her the Beta would take Leigh somewhere else — to another pack perhaps. Sadie would insist on traveling with them but she needed to know if something happened Leigh would have a protector.

"You can't make me drink. It's my choice."

"It used to be," Sadie conceded, speaking quietly. "That's no longer the case."

"No longer the case?"

"You need to able to defend yourself. You can't do that if you don't feed." Bracing herself for the earful she was about to receive, Sadie continued, "What if something happens to me? What would you do then? Your options are limited. The coven isn't secure. They have weaknesses. And Geneva's been hiding something. I'm not sure what it is but it's no good. You won't be happy there. You need someone to watch out for you, someone who would give his life to keep you safe."

The silence that followed was almost deafening.

"You think you can force me to take blood from Nathan?" Leigh finally asked, voice shaking. "That'll never happen."

The scheming bitch! Sadie caught Leigh's thought and followed it, delving into her friend's thoughts. *I can't believe I followed her here. I can't believe I trusted her! She's been lying to me the entire time. And why not? She's finally gotten what she wanted. She's mated to her werewolf. She'll turn on the coven and go on her merry little way. Oh God, she'll try to make me do the same thing. She'll force me to become just like her.*

Sadie accepted the vehemence directed at her but even as she did she knew she'd missed the mark big-time. A face flittered through Leigh's mind in her panic—of a young man, smiling and laughing. Sadie knew it had to be the man Leigh'd lost after she'd been changed. She'd never imagined Leigh was so affected by the love she'd left behind. Yet Sadie felt Leigh's hurt, the heartache lancing through her chest like a rusty knife. The terrified young woman would never give up her hope for her past life.

Shit.

Leigh thought she could change what had happened to her. The only reason she'd given up was because she had to. She actually believed there had to be a way to go back to the way things used to be. If magic existed, there had to be a way. She wanted to be who she used to be more than anything.

"I'm not doing this because of Trey." Sadie knew if she didn't get this right everything would turn to shit. She had to reason with Leigh and help her understand. "You came to find me, remember? None of this happened because I wanted it to." She knew she had to tell her the rest as well. "There's a reason Geneva took you in, Leigh. I didn't question it at first but I should have. I don't know what it is but there's some ass backward shit going down in the coven. I have a feeling Geneva's been planning something for months. That's why she tried to trap me at the house. She'll use you. You'll find yourself snared in her web if you're not careful."

She's playing you for a fool! Leigh's thoughts—much louder now—slammed into Sadie's head. *She's one of them now.*

"So it's Geneva we have to worry about, huh?" Leigh strode from the window as her private feelings crashed into Sadie's mind. "You might have fooled me once but it won't happen again. If you're going to lie, at least come up with something decent."

Will the coven welcome me back? Leigh wondered. *Will they turn me away? Where do rogue vampires go? Is there a place for us?*

Every single worry in Leigh's mind merged with Sadie's thoughts.

They'll destroy me for leaving in the first place. They'll make me suffer. It'll be worse than before. Will they make me feed? Will I kill? What if they turn me over to...to...the vampire who made me? Oh God. I can't go through that. Not ever again. What do I do? Where should I go?

"I'm not lying," Sadie said, trying to stay composed. "Geneva was ready to turn on me. That's why I told you to phase. She almost trapped me before I could escape. She used her magic against me. She took you into our home for a reason. She wants something from you."

"Like you don't!" Leigh screamed.

Sadie used the little energy she had left to raise her head and look at the girl.

Leigh's entire body was shaking, her eyes brimming with tears. "You brought me here," she sobbed, eyes swimming. "You brought me to him. You knew exactly what you were doing."

"I didn't bring you here for Nathan." Not intentionally, not with ulterior motives. Sadie would never have done such a thing. "I swear. It's not—"

"I'm not listening to you anymore," Leigh yelled while her thoughts tumbled together, making it impossible for Sadie to understand them. "You're a liar! You're all liars!"

Oh no. She's going to phase.

Somehow—someway—Sadie knew she had to reach Leigh before she did.

She stumbled from the bed and grasped Leigh's arm. Months of starvation had shown her she could push beyond fatigue. As tired as she was, she had enough energy to maintain her grip. But it wouldn't last, especially if Leigh decided to throw a spell in her direction. She couldn't reason with the youthful vampire, not right now. Leigh's mind was too chaotic, too fucking wounded.

"*Trey!*" Sadie called out mentally, banking on his ability to hear her. "*I need you. Come to me.*"

In her weakened state she wasn't sure if it was her demand or the passage of time that caused Trey and Nathan to appear so quickly. The door burst open and the men rushed inside. The shifters' gazes darted to the women—Trey's full of worry, Nathan's filled with alarm—prepared to take on enemies.

"*She's going to run.*" Sadie directed the thought to Trey. "*Stop her.*"

"Get your female," Trey snarled to Nathan. "Don't let her go!"

Sadie welcomed Trey's embrace, leaning against him, allowing him to hold her. Leigh fought Nathan, thrashing about to break free. When she couldn't, Leigh screamed. Sadie's heart broke for the woman as she cried, slapping at Nathan's chest.

Leigh didn't love Nathan. She yearned for someone else.

In another time and place, Sadie would have fought Nathan if he tried to stake a claim.

It wasn't fair. It wasn't right.

Life seldom was.

"No! Get away from me." Leigh's defeated cry seared Sadie's soul. "No!"

"Shh, baby," Trey soothed, wrapping his arms around her. It was then Sadie realized she was trembling violently. "I'm here."

He was there but at what cost?

Her attention drifted to Nathan and Leigh.

Nathan subdued the fragile vampire easily, trapping her small form against the wall. The Beta was cautious but determined, snaking his hands around Leigh's wrists. Even if Leigh tried to phase, she couldn't. The fledgling was strong but hadn't yet developed her powers. For the first time Sadie was glad Leigh hadn't fine-tuned her abilities. Leigh had no idea what kind of danger she was in. In her current mental state she couldn't be reasoned with. There was nothing left to do but take care of her, keeping her from inflicting harm on herself.

"Tell him not to let her go." She sagged against Trey, emotionally battered. "She's scared and hurt."

No, it was more than that.

The poor woman was maimed—her soul torn apart and bleeding out.

Weakness sapped the last of her strength.

She sank into Trey's arms, closing her eyes.

If Aldon tried to find them, he couldn't.

Even if she'd lost Leigh's trust forever, everyone was safe.

For now.

"Don't you dare let her go," Trey snapped, holding Sadie close. "If you do, she's gone. You feel me? Hold her tight. Do not let her loose."

Leigh howled at the order, kicking out at Nathan's shins, tears streaming down her face. When that didn't work she attempted to ram her knee into the Beta's crotch. Nathan moved out of the way, dodging the blow, then moved in close. That riled the banshee up even more. She thrashed so hard she caused the nightstand to shake—wailing all the while—and the tiny knickknacks on the top rattled.

Damn the woman.

She'd already made enough noise to raise the dead. If Diskant found out the unstable female had lost her shit a second time he'd kill her for sure.

"For fuck's sake," he hissed, wishing she'd shut the fuck up. "Keep her quiet."

How in the hell the Beta kept his level of control, Trey would never understand. Nathan calmly placed one of his hands over Leigh's mouth, keeping the other locked around her wrist. Using his much larger body to his advantage he pushed his weight into her and caged her against the wall. Leigh didn't give up, curving her fingers into balled fists.

"You want to tell me what set her off this time?" he whispered in Sadie's ear. "What happened? Why's she so angry?"

"It's a lot of things, actually," Sadie responded telepathically. *"Give me a minute to catch my breath. I'll talk to her."*

"I don't want you talking to her." And he didn't. Not one small iota. Right then he really pitied Nathan. A crackpot for a mate? How fair was that? "The bitch is fucking crazy."

"She is not a bitch. And she isn't crazy." Sadie tried to shove away from him. "Don't be a dick."

Whatever. The insane woman was Nathan's problem.

Satisfied Leigh wasn't going anywhere, Trey slid an arm beneath Sadie's ass, lifted her from the ground and went to shut the door. He stopped when he saw Ava standing right outside the room, her arms folded over her stomach.

His good humor faded. Sadie tensed against him, going impossibly still.

Shit.

"Ava." Sadie tried to wriggle free, letting him go. "It's not what it looks like."

"This is my home," Ava said, crossing the threshold. She lowered her arms and closed the door, eyes on Sadie. "You stay here, you abide by my rules. That one," Ava's gaze drifted to Leigh, her irises no longer blue but an eerie hue of green, "needs to learn her place."

Double shit.

Leigh had just brought out Ava's dark side.

Nathan whipped his head toward the Omega's mate, panic in his expression. "Ava—"

"Quiet." Ava cut the man short, striding toward the wall. "If I can't get the message through her head then Diskant will. Is that what you want?"

Sadie dropped her weight, ready to defend her friend. Trey caught her before she could break away, wrapping his arms around her waist. When she tried to yank free he sent a clear and direct thought to her. *Do it and Diskant will come in here, rip Leigh's head off and send you packing. Watch, listen and stay right where you fucking are.*

"You've suffered, I get it." Ava stopped a few feet away from Leigh, resting one of her small hands on her burgeoning tummy. "Life's a bitch like that. But you're not in Kansas anymore. There are no red slippers here. You can't click your heels and go back home. As far as Diskant's concerned, you're better off dead than alive. He doesn't think you're worth the trouble or the risk. And I'm not going to argue with him over it. Especially if you're going to act like this."

Trey wasn't sure if he should keep his arms around Sadie or bolt for Nathan. Both were furious, the tension in the room so thick you could cut it with a knife.

Ava didn't back down, gauging her opponent, standing calm before the storm. Ironically enough Leigh had finally gotten hold of herself. No longer did she fight against Nathan, her attention was riveted on Ava. Maybe if they were lucky for a fucking change the vampire finally grasped what kind of position she was in.

"This," Ava said, gazing down as she rubbed her belly, "is more important than anyone else in this room. I'll do whatever it takes to keep my son or daughter safe, even if it makes me a monster." Lifting her head, she whispered, "I feel for you. You've been dealt an unfair hand. If things were different I'd try to help you. But I won't risk my child. It's never going to happen. It's best you know that now."

"You don't know anything about me." Leigh's thought ricocheted through Trey's mind. His chin darted up, his senses on alert. Everyone's faces told him they'd heard her as well. "I want to leave," Leigh informed them. "Let me go."

"I've been listening to your thoughts since you arrived. I know everything about you," Ava informed Leigh, a frown tugging at the corners of her mouth. "Like where you come from. Who your parents were... We share that, actually. My parents died when I was young too." Ava joined gazes with Leigh. "I know everything you've thought about since you phased here. I know what you're afraid of. What you're trying to avoid. I know what you'd try to hide," Ava shook her head, "not what—*who*—you'd try to hide."

After a pause, Leigh's eyes widened. "You wouldn't."

"Oh yes, I would," Ava whispered, nodding. "Do I have you attention now?"

Tears seeped down Leigh's face. She closed her eyes and nodded.

What the fuck was Ava talking about?

What had Leigh so shaken?

"Good, you're finally listening," Ava said. "You're going to do what I say from here on in. You won't argue. You won't try to run. You'll do whatever you're told, whenever you're told. I'm warning you." Ava's irises changed from green to yellow. "If you cause us harm—if you vanish without a trace or stir up any shit—I'll hunt Brett down and kill him myself."

Leigh's eyes flared open and she screamed into Nathan's hand.

"*What the fuck?*" Sadie snarled in Trey's head, clawing at his arm. "She can't do that!"

"Can't she?" Trey didn't blame Ava for protecting her unborn child. In a smooth motion he captured Sadie's forearms and brought them to her breasts, trapping her hands, keeping her back pressed against his chest. "She's the Omega's mate. She can do whatever she wants."

"I'm going to tell Nathan to let you go now." Ava took several steps back, inching away from Leigh and Nathan. "I expect you to calm down, pull yourself together and behave while you're in my home. And a small word of caution? Don't do this again. There won't be any second chances."

Nathan cautiously removed his hand from Leigh's mouth. Across the distance Trey could see the Beta's fingers trembling in rage. Leigh slid to the ground and Nathan followed, whispering soft reassurances as he crouched before her. Sadie didn't stop struggling to get free, wriggling like a worm on a hook, her fury directed at Ava.

"You're pissed. I get it," Ava said, turning to Sadie. "But I meant what I said."

"I think I made a mistake saving you in that alley," Sadie snarled, her words laced with acid. "I should have left you bleeding out on the ground. I should have left that gaping hole in your fucking head."

"Maybe." Ava didn't take the bait, remaining neutral. "Maybe not."

"I won't let you hurt her."

"How exactly will you stop me? Do you think you can kill me and take your chances with the pack? For the sake of argument, say that happens. Where will you go? To your coven? Are you going to ask them for help? Do you think they'll give it to you?"

Ava raised a hand and snapped her fingers.

"That's right. You don't have a coven anymore." Lowering her arm, Ava whispered threateningly, "Leigh's not the only one I've been listening to. I've been monitoring your thoughts since you walked through my door. Don't underestimate me because I used to be human. I'm not a vampire and I'm not a shifter. I'm something in between. That makes me a lot more dangerous."

Without another word, Ava walked to the door and slipped from the room.

"Get your hands off me," Sadie roared as soon as Ava slipped out of sight.

Trey let her go, feeling numb. He watched from the sidelines as she shoved Nathan aside and went to her friend. Sadie held Leigh as the woman sobbed, running a comforting hand down her back. Nathan turned to Trey, obviously torn. The poor bastard didn't know what to do.

Welcome to the club.

The Omega's mate had prevented a catastrophe but her involvement came with a price. Not only were they faced with enemies at the gates, they now had them right inside the doors.

Damn you, Ava.

So much for a welcoming his mate and her friend with open arms.

Time for damage control.

Chapter Nine

"Open up. I mean it."

Sadie tried to ignore Trey's firm knock at the door.

He meant it? Really?

What-the-fuck ever.

Funny how adrenaline could take a vampire from dazed to strong. She'd felt wrung out until Ava had shown up, started some shit and left Leigh a total mess. Then Sadie's protective nature had kicked in, her determination to shield the young vampire kicking into overdrive. She'd managed to put Leigh on the bed and force the men from the room, screaming at them to go.

They'd argued, naturally, trying to stay right where they were.

Too bad she wasn't in a pleasant mood.

A nice little scuffle had ensued. The men were gifted, she'd give them that. They were strong and hearty. But she had centuries of practice on them. Turns out she only needed a bit of motivation to put them on their asses. Something she should have done from the start. She'd been stupid to put her trust in Trey. He'd turned on her once and—in classic asshole style—he'd done so again. She'd thanked him properly, of course, as she'd escorted the loser and his sidekick from the bedroom.

Nathan had retreated with a bloody nose.

Trey had been graced with a blow to the family jewels.

Served them right.

"That's your final warning, darlin'," Trey warned, his voice a steady growl. "I'm going to let myself in if you don't open this door right now."

"You want me?" she snapped, moving from the bed. Watching Leigh bawl like a baby had put her in a fighting mood. If Trey wanted some of that action, she was willing to oblige. "Here I come."

She sneered when she burst from the door, got a lock on his face and decked him in the chin. He staggered back, taken unaware, bringing his large hands up to cup his face. Energy dripped from her, the need to expend her anger into something else—someone else—so strong she couldn't deny it.

Hell, she didn't *want* to deny it.

"First," she huffed, advancing on him, "I'm going to kick your worthless ass. I'm going to work you up and down this hallway like a fucking mop. Then, when I think you've earned it, I'm going to cut off your balls and feed them to you."

He lifted his arms into a defensive pose as he moved, trying to get out of her range.

Dumbass. Didn't he know he she was faster? Apparently not.

She clipped his chin a second time and brought her leg around. A swift kick swept him off his feet. He hit the ground hard, landing with a loud thump. *Idiot.* She went for broke, launching her body over his. She let her fists guide her, setting her feet shoulder width apart and kneeling down, pummeling him for all she was worth.

He'd brought this on himself. He'd known the score. He was more than aware of what she'd do if he scorned her a second time. He hadn't listened. Nope. He'd taken Ava's side instead, falling in line like a good little puppy.

How do you like me now? She slammed her fist into his mouth. *Fucker.*

"Don't piss me off," he snarled, capturing one of her hands before it could connect with his jaw again. "You have a right to be mad but I'll only put up with so much."

He didn't just say that. Not after everything she'd given him.

"You'll only put up with so much? Sweet thing, I'm going to make you eat those words."

She moved faster than he could see, springing away from his grasp. Her only regret was she wasn't as fast as she should've been. In another time and place she'd have wiped the floor with his sorry ass. If she'd been able to feed on others she'd have taken blood from another source and beat the shit out of him like he truly deserved. Trey had no idea what she could do. He'd only seen her drained, not at full speed.

One day, I'll show him. Then he'll understand all I've sacrificed.

He came at her, arms extended. He thought he was going to catch her?

Ignoramus.

Her vision caught the movement, centuries of agonizing training kicking in. She shifted her weight, unaware she'd done so. His fingers swiped her arm but slipped away as she moved. He was more than foolish for taking her on. The egotistical shithead was out of his head.

Fool.

A simple glide and she sidestepped out of his reach a second time. She brought her arms to her chest, curling her fingers to taunt him. "Is that the best you've got?"

He thought he could bring it? If he kept up like this, she could go all night.

She caught a shadow in her peripheral vision.

Someone had decided to watch.

She didn't turn, eyes attuned to Trey. She'd make sure the dumbass served as a reminder of what she was—of who she'd been to her coven—a protector and vampire warrior in her own right. She hadn't survived all these years by being slow or stupid. A part of her hoped Ava was watching. Her beliefs wouldn't let Sadie harm the woman while she was pregnant but once Ava'd delivered her baby all bets were off. The horrible woman had hurt Leigh in the worst way imaginable. There was no excuse for that.

Aldon be damned.

Trey rushed her but she dodged carefully away. All she needed was an opening. She didn't want to kill him—that would kill her—but she could make him suffer. She'd draw this moment out and make it last, taking his blood even if it meant spilling it and not drinking it. It was no less than he deserved. He'd hurt her so many times in so many ways. Even after she'd given her body to him, offering herself on a plate served with a side of fuck-me-over-pretty-please.

She should have known that wouldn't be enough.

Men—whether they were shifters or not—always wanted more.

"I hate you!" she screamed, aiming a punch at his head. But she knew it was a lie. She didn't hate him, far from it. If only she could.

You're so fucking weak! Grow up.

She kept swinging, uncaring where the blows landed.

After all this time she was tired and emotionally exhausted. Without the welcome venom of outrage to give her strength she was ripped open and bleeding out. She couldn't keep going. Not anymore. Everything finally managed to catch up with her, taking her down several pegs. It shouldn't have bothered her so much. Eventually everyone had a breaking point. She just hadn't thought Trey would be the reason she'd finally found hers.

There was no choice but to accept her fate.

She'd made the decisions to bring her to this point in time.

Damn it. Damn him.

At that point it was only about hurt and despair, loss and fury. She wasn't in control anymore, left to the mercy of the man she wanted to pummel. He would reduce her to nothing. Even worse? With a bit of praise or sweetness she'd let him. What good was immortality if it left her so weak? What was the point of living if this was all she had to look forward to?

The walls fell away, leaving her naked and painfully aware of herself.

He could see her now — scarred, battered and bruised.

Who gives a shit? He doesn't care. Why should you?

"Hate you," she breathed, pumping her fist into his chest, trying to convince herself it was true. "So much."

"I know." Trey didn't fight, accepting each slam of her knuckles into his hard pectorals. "I don't blame you. Let it out. Let it go."

Let it go?

All the pain she'd locked up unleashed, her misery swinging wide open. Her knuckles ached, the muscles in her arms felt heavy as she tried to lift them. She kept swinging, breathing past the agony. Her target was the invisible phantom that kept her from finding any measure of happiness. The shadow of her heart offered a glimpse of what she wanted most only to take it away time and time again. Goddess, she couldn't let him win. Not like this, due to her lack of emotional integrity. He'd taken too much. She couldn't give him this too. Not if she expected to look at herself in the mirror. Her pride was on the line.

How could he respect her if she didn't respect herself?

"I'm sorry. I wish you knew how much." He caught her hands, holding them tenderly. She held her breath, trying to find the strength to pull away. "Turn all that hate into something else. You don't have to be the strong one anymore. You don't have to be afraid. I'm here. I'll keep you safe. You have me."

"Have you?" Anger, warm and welcome, revived her. Yanking free, she yelled, "How could I? I never had you."

"You've always had me. I was too stupid to admit it."

"You son of a bitch!"

She took another swing and he took her down, capturing her in his embrace, using his size and strength against her. She screamed, letting herself go, accepting the inevitable. He had her now. The fight was over. To make sure Leigh survived she had to surrender. Her life wasn't the only one at stake. And — even if she loathed it — she wanted Trey. She always had.

He knew it too. He'd always known.

That was her ultimate degradation.

"How did I come to this?" Goddess, she sounded pitiful. "I'm a fool."

"No you're not." He snaked his fingers into the hair at her nape. Pulling her head back, he forced her to look at him. "Don't ever say that again."

It was hard to see him now, her vision blurred by tears.

For a moment she thought she gleaned sympathy and dread in his expression.

"Foolish," she repeated, running on empty.

"Never," he rebuked her. "Never, Sadie."

But she was. Eventually he'd know it as well.

She broke down, crumbling in on herself.

There was nowhere go. No safe place to run.

She'd finally hit rock bottom.

And it was all her fault.

It felt as though something unlatched in Trey's chest. He watched Sadie's face blaze triumphant in rage only to scatter to ashes in defeat. She cried, her tears like ragged blades ripping into his soul. He wanted to give her what she wanted but he didn't know how. She'd said she hated him and he believed her.

Why shouldn't she? He'd given her no reason not to.

"Let her cry it out." Diskant emerged from the shadows. "It's what she needs."

"Is it?" Trey asked quietly, trying to hold his mate and figure out what the fuck to do. Diskant was one of his oldest friends and the Omega was mated. Perhaps he did understand. Needing some kind of answer, he started babbling, "I've failed her every single time she's turned to me for something. I thought she'd understand how important she is after I claimed her. I thought she would understand how I feel."

"She's a woman," Diskant replied as though it explained everything. "They're prone to mood swings. Trust me." He stepped into the light, a scowl on his face. "I know what Ava did. I understand her reasoning, even if her actions were harsh. I came to apologize." He looked at Sadie, furrowing his brows. "I think it's a bit too late for that."

Trey felt like lashing out but kept his temper in check. "She told you what she did?"

"Not exactly," Diskant answered and peered over his shoulder. After a moment, his attention returned to Sadie. "The connection I have with Ava... It's changed."

For the first time Diskant was revealing what Trey suspected—that Ava and Diskant communicated in some telepathic form. They'd tried to hide it but Trey was around them too much not to notice. Everyone knew Ava could hear the thoughts of humans. Many suspected she could enter the minds of shifters too. Now Trey knew for certain. Ava had a powerful ability. No wonder Diskant always knew so much. He remembered her telling Diskant she'd been listening to Sadie's thoughts as they'd approached the house.

That was how she'd sensed their arrival.

She'd been eavesdropping.

"She told you what she was doing and you didn't tell her to stop?"

"She didn't tell me shit," Diskant spat, angry. "The only reason I'm sharing this is your mate is the same. We're both in the same fucking boat." He huffed, shuffling his feet. "Ava doesn't know her mental shields have weakened in the last few weeks. I can hear her even when she tries to block me out." His jaw clenched, shoulders tense. He studied Sadie differently, glowing yellow eyes combing over her form. "I didn't know you'd be paying us a visit. When your mate is in better shape we'll have to find out how much she knows about Ava. We need to understand what's going on."

"You think she'll tell you? Now? After what Ava's done?" A growl crept up Trey's throat. "If Sadie knew what Ava had planned do you honestly think she'd have left Leigh here? Do you truly believe she'd have come to us and not taken the woman somewhere else? Ava just fucked everything sideways. She's done damage that might not be repairable."

"Ava didn't want to confront the woman," Diskant chided. "Not until she broke down a second time." Diskant's vibrant gaze swept to Trey. "Not cool, by the way."

"Not cool? Are you serious? You're coming at me with not fucking cool?" Trey cracked his neck, trying not to succumb to the fury of his wolf. "I'll tell you what's not cool. Your female threatened a woman she promised to welcome to her home. She threatened Leigh and gave her no way out. How'd you think Sadie would react? My female isn't a weak-minded bitch. She doesn't want to rock a jock or whine for attention. She's a fighter. Ava lit a match that started a fucking fire."

"Be that as it may, we've got shit to sort." Diskant shifted his weight, taking a step closer. "You're in no frame of mind to think through things clearly. Good thing you have me."

"Oh fearless Yoda," Trey snapped, broken as Sadie cried. "Guide me."

Show me the fucking way, you son of a bitch.

Ava had fucked things up in the most colossal way. Before her interference things had been peachy keen. Leigh had lost it but Sadie could have calmed the vampire down. Now? Trey knew he was fucked, fucked and fucked. Sadie hated him. She'd said so very clearly. All of her hurt and pain had come at him hard and fast, the impact slamming into him full force.

How did I manage to fuck her up so badly?

How do I repair the damage?

"We have to prioritize. Bitching at each other like a couple of pissy old women won't accomplish squat. You need to screw your head on tight and listen up." Diskant kept his outward exterior calm, despite the fact Trey could feel the man's tension. "If we want to survive this we have to put things in order. Handle yourself. You're acting like an ass."

"I'm listening." And he was, but it took all of his willpower not to sweep Sadie off her feet and carry her away. He bit back his fury because Diskant was right. "Start talking."

"I thought we should make Leigh leave. She might be safer somewhere else." Diskant smirked when Trey snarled. "I said I thought. Past tense."

"And now?"

"The pack is our primary concern." Any hint of amusement in Diskant disappeared. "If we can gain their support then we're on the right track." He met Trey's eyes, intent etched in his distinct features. "We have to have their support. Do you feel me? If we don't, nothing else will matter."

Anger bled away, replaced by a cold bitch-slap of reality.

Shit. Diskant was right. Again.

Without the pack, they'd be fucked.

As an Alpha, Trey needed his brothers and sisters for strength. It went without saying Diskant did as well. As an Omega Diskant fed off the power of others. Once it was gone Diskant became a mere shifter. Certainly he could still shape into any form but he lost the edge that gave him substance. Trey would too without a pack standing behind him.

Their lives—even if they sometimes sucked—consisted of a constant checks and balances system.

"Tell me what you're thinking."

"We'll hold a meeting and announce your newly mated status," Diskant responded. Oddly enough the Omega sounded cautious, like he was about to say something he knew Trey wouldn't want to hear. "You can introduce them to Sadie, give them whatever story you choose and make it clear nothing's changed. You have to convince them that the mating changes nothing. You're still their Alpha and you'll put their needs above yours."

"Where's the catch?" There was one, Trey knew.

"You're going to tell them she hasn't bitten you. And you're going to make damn sure they believe you too. You're going to tell them you've taken the vampire as a mate but you'll never let her feed from you. Not ever. You can't become a familiar if she takes blood from another source. They can't fear her in that capacity."

Trey couldn't believe what he was hearing. He'd given Sadie his word. He'd sworn he'd accept their mating before the pack. That meant accepting all of her—eating habits included.

"Did Ava hit you with the stupid stick? They'll know she's taken blood from me."

Diskant growled—the sound a combination of the cat, wolf and bear that resided inside the Omega. "Keeping them on our side is our primary concern."

"We won't build the foundation from a lie." If they did, they'd pay in the future. "They need to understand what's at stake. They have to accept Sadie isn't a danger. Who she feeds from isn't important. Her loyalty is what they should be worried about."

"Listen to me, goddamn it."

No. Not this time.

He'd been born long before Diskant. The Omega was smart and loved the shifter races but Diskant had no idea of how the pack reacted to a lot of things. They'd never buy such a shit story. They'd know Trey was lying. Especially those who were mated themselves. Bedroom sessions always got out of hand. There was no way Sadie wouldn't get a bite or nip in when they got horizontal. *Shifters* bit each other during sex for fuck's sake.

"No," he growled, shaking his head, rejecting the plan. "We'll deal with it another way."

"We have Shepherds at our back and fucking vampires at our front." Diskant advanced, no longer giving polite suggestions. "You will convince the pack the mating wasn't of your choosing. They can't know you've been keeping this from them. You'll tell them you were just as shocked as they are but it is what it is. If they discover you haven't been honest and have kept her a secret they'll hang you out to dry. This is about more than you or your mate, by the way. In case it's slipped your fucking notice we're trying to prevent genocide."

Damn it.

Trey wanted to clock his friend in the face and tell him to fuck off.

Maybe he could get the pack comfortable with the idea of having Sadie around. After all, they'd accepted a Shepherd and human. Shitty things came in threes. Obviously his number was up. There was no exit strategy. No way to make things safe for everyone.

"I talked to Kinsley." Diskant informed him.

"And?"

"He's on board."

It took a minute for the words to sink in. Fucking-A.

Kinsley MacGregor—the Alpha who influenced all the feline shifters—would be an ace in the hole. With his backing the Alphas from the prides would fall in line. Trey frowned, holding Sadie a little tighter. Unless the man decided to cut and run on a whim. Feline shifters were solitary creatures, looking out for their interests before anyone else's.

"You sure?"

"I am." There was zero doubt in the reply.

"What's he bringing to the party?"

"Centuries of knowledge."

Like that explains anything. "Enlighten me."

"This happens every few hundred centuries."

"The world goes to shit?"

"Shifters mate with vampires." Diskant gazed over his shoulder again, making sure no one was listening in. After several seconds he looked at Trey. "It's not uncommon when the world gets off-balance."

Off-balance? I'll take understatement of the fucking millennium Alex.

"Her heart," Trey motioned to Sadie, relieved that she'd quieted, "is broken because of me. I was so concerned about what the pack would think I treated her like dirt. She's suffered enough. I won't turn my back on her and lie about how things are. Excuse me if I don't give a shit about things being off balance."

"She's smart. Give her a chance to be part of this." When Trey opened his mouth to speak Diskant snarled, "Your female has existed for a long time without you. She's earned the right to voice her opinion in the matter."

Something clicked, a lock sliding into place. "You trust her."

"Ava trusts her. Don't ask me why. I don't have an answer."

Ava trusted Sadie. Really trusted her. "And you trust your mate?"

"What do you think?" Diskant asked, agitated and out of patience. "If Ava thinks Sadie has the power to heal the pack, why should I argue? She got them to accept Mary."

"She announced her pregnancy." Trey broached the topic with caution. Diskant remained anxious when it came to Ava's condition, which was understandable. But it made the man more dangerous than usual. "You're an Omega. She's your mate. It's good news."

"Then maybe you should get your mate in the family way."

An invisible fist clenched Trey's heart and squeezed.

Family way. Sons and daughters.

My sons. My daughters.

As far as he knew he and Sadie would never have children. No boys, no girls. Vampires and shifters didn't produce offspring. How had he forgotten that? How had it slipped his mind? He visualized little girls with Sadie's hair and eyes, or little boys with his features. Did Sadie want children? Did it break her heart to think they'd never have any?

Will she hate me even more for taking what she wants from her yet again?

Trey released Sadie, rising to his feet. The wolf in him wanted to see Diskant bleed for the insult. His mate slid against the wall, crying softly. Diskant froze, his eyes going wide as though he'd gotten jive to what he'd just spouted.

"I didn't mean—"

Trey put all of his weight into his swing, gaining momentum as he turned. He clocked Diskant in the jaw, sending the Omega to his knees. "Mean what, you selfish son of a bitch!"

"Careful, pup." Diskant recovered, breezing his knuckles over his lip as his gaze darted to Trey's face. "Don't piss me off."

"Then don't piss me off," Trey countered, adrenaline pumping through his system. "I'm tired of your bullshit."

"Stop." Sadie's softly spoken request pulled the men short. They turned toward her as she said, "You don't have to argue. We'll tell them what they need to hear."

Trey hated how defeated she sounded. "Like hell."

"You can't help the pack without their support. It's the only way." Both men watched as Sadie made it to her feet. "I'll do it, but I have a condition." Her reddened eyes drifted to Trey, ice-blue irises condemning. "Once this is over, it's over," she stated briskly, as though she were trying to detach herself from the situation. "You'll feed me when I need it but this..." Shaking her blonde head, she exhaled, exhaustion outlined in her posture. "I'm done."

He wanted to hit something—hard. "No."

"We don't have time to argue," she said, skittering from his touch when he reached out for her. "There are more important things to think about."

That's where she was wrong. As far as Trey was concerned she was the most important thing in the world. Without her he'd become a hollow shell, his entire life empty and lost. He couldn't protect the pack like that. He wouldn't want to exist if there was nothing to look forward to. Over time he'd not only fail his mate, he'd fail everyone around him.

"We're going to face the pack," he reached her in two steps, roping an arm around her waist, "together." She tried to worm her way free and he yanked her to his body, holding her lithe form against his. "No more running, Sadie. No more promises you can't keep."

"Trey," Diskant reprimanded sharply. "Think about what you're doing."

"I have."

For months he'd agonized over what was best for the pack, going over each scenario as he tried to think of a way to introduce Sadie to them. He'd spoken to Nathan many times, hoping to resolve the situation without bloodshed or violence. It wasn't going to be easy, regardless of his choice.

"This is the only way. I'm not letting her go and I'm not pretending she doesn't mean everything to me. They can take it or leave it."

Diskant's beasts rose, sending energy from the man. "You selfish son of a bitch."

"Pot calling the kettle black?" Trey ran his hand down Sadie's back, his fingers drifting through her hair. "It wasn't so long ago that you left the city to protect Ava. You handed the pack over and didn't look back. You chose her over everyone else."

"It's not the same." Diskant formed his hands into tight fists.

"Because of her condition?" Trey took a step back and relaxed his grip on Sadie, ready to shove her to safety if Diskant charged. "Do you really think that justifies your decision?"

"I should break your fucking neck." Diskant lifted one of his hands and pointed at Trey. The Omega's eyes changed colors, morphing from yellow to green. "You've forgotten your goddamned place."

"That's quite enough." Ava appeared at the opposite end of the hallway, glaring at Trey and Diskant. "We'll never accomplish anything if you two keep fighting."

"Pinkie," Diskant warned in a low growl, "I told you to get some rest."

"I'll rest when I'm dead," she retorted.

"Damn it, woman." Diskant strode toward her. "I'm going to tie your ass to the bed."

Ava let Diskant's threat pass without notice. "Kinsley will be here soon," she informed them, her attention drifting to Trey and Sadie. "He wants to discuss the situation before he talks to the prides. If you need to clear the air, I suggest you use what little time you have before he gets here."

Trey glanced around, trying to decide where to go. They needed to talk. Privately and unbothered. His mate needed to understand how strongly he felt about matters. He tightened the arm around Sadie's waist and started toward a small bathroom across the way.

It was then that he noticed Nathan.

The Beta—who had remained silent throughout Trey's fight with Diskant—moved to make room for Trey to pass. Trey hesitated, watching Nathan walk a few feet down the hall. The man stopped outside Leigh's door, shifting his feet, studying the barrier standing between him and his mate. Sadly the door was the least of Nathan's concerns. The true wall erected between him and Leigh was far more obtrusive. Nathan extended his hand, fingers hovering over the knob. After a moment, he bowed his head and let his arm drift to his side.

Poor bastard.

Anyone could see Nathan's desolation and sadness. Gloom surrounded the male, shrouding him in uncertainty and confusion. His nature wouldn't him to allow him to leave Leigh uncared for but his ability to sense emotion must've told him that his presence still wasn't welcome. He turned away but didn't leave. Resting his shoulders against the door, Nathan sank down and took a seat, protecting his female in the only way he could.

The visual tore through Trey.

If he didn't smooth things over with Sadie he could suffer the same fate.

Determined, he lifted his female's feet from the ground and rushed to the bathroom. He went inside, closed the door and carried Sadie to the sink. There wasn't a lot of space. The area consisted of the toilet and a sliver of counter space. Sadie's lack of emotion perturbed him. She hadn't shown signs of sorrow or anger. Instead she seemed resigned, accepting whatever she was given.

Time to push her buttons.

She gasped when he let her go and spun her around. She braced herself with her hands, meeting his gaze in the mirror. Her blonde hair swept over her shoulders, offsetting her wide blue eyes. He shoved his hips forward, trapping his hardening cock between the globes of her ass. Although he'd always desire his female, his needs extended beyond simple physicality. He wanted her to know he'd meant what he'd said. He couldn't exist without this woman. More than that, he refused to live without her.

"Do you want me?" he asked hoarsely, muscles shaking.

"I…" She broke eye contact and tried to lower her head. "I shouldn't."

He didn't let her avoid him or the question, capturing her chin in his hand, making her look at him. "Don't think about the bullshit. Forget about everyone else but us. Tell me the truth." Bringing his head to her ear, he looked her in the eye and repeated, "Do. You. Want. Me?"

"It's not that simple, mutt." Her eyes flashed, fury radiating from the icy depths.

"Why?" He grinned, thrilled that her fire had returned.

"I can want you, but that doesn't mean I love you."

"You don't have to tell me you love me. I already know. I've known for a long time."

Those three little words coming from her would mean the world to him. But they weren't necessary. Because he already knew how she felt. She claimed she hated him and he believed her, because the malice came from resentment. It was entirely possible to loathe a person you loved. The complexities of her feelings were a mixture of adoration and hate, neither complete without the other.

"You arrogant prick," she snarled, her eyes filled with outrage. "Egotistical asshole."

He nipped at her throat, ready to up the ante. His sense of smell told him she was angry but she was also turned-on. Her arousal drifted to his nose, the fragrance succulent and sweet. Bringing his hands around her waist, he plucked the button to her pants. He quickly lowered the zipper and moved back to tug the material down her thighs. As soon as her ass was bared to his gaze he made quick work of his jeans, working the button and zipper loose and bringing the material to his knees.

When she tried to slide free he caught her, cupping her breasts in his hands.

"We're going to face the pack together. I'm not hiding anymore and neither are you." He gave the soft mounds a squeeze and pressed his swollen cock to her ass. "But if you want me, you're going to have to fight for me. Even if the pack accepts our mating, females have the right to challenge you for the position. It's not going to be easy. You'll have to take them down to earn your place." He rubbed his fingers over her nipples and she groaned. "Will you fight for me, baby?"

"I'm not sure." She trembled beneath him, her wounded gaze relaying her need for reassurance. "Are you worth fighting for?"

Was he? Not really.

He'd let the ball drop over and over again. He'd hurt her. Left her wounded and bleeding out. Then he'd been an asshole, asserting his claim on her, rejecting Diskant's notion that Sadie should be able to voice her opinion on matters. Thus far she hadn't had much of a say in things.

No more.

He let her go and brought a hand to the base of his pulsing cock. His sac tightened and a drop of semen leaked from the tip. Bending his knees, he got in place. Her wet heat beckoned, her pussy slick and ready. He guided the head into her channel, grinding his teeth as her cunt accepted his entry and wrapped around him inch by maddening inch.

Fully lodged within her, he stopped.

"I have an idea. This time around you'll make the choice. I'll prove I'm worth the risk." Resting his head on her shoulder, he murmured thickly, "How about I show you what I can give you? You decide if I'm worth fighting for."

Chapter Ten

Sadie knew she shouldn't give in. She didn't need to make things easy for Trey. She was supposed to maintain some semblance of pride, show him she was more than capable of existing in a world that didn't include him.

Unfortunately the heart wanted what the heart wanted.

All the resistance in the world wouldn't do her a bit of good. She could try to suffocate her feelings, locking them away so no one could see them. An illusion would be created but she'd know the truth. Like a magician using trickery to deceive an audience, her efforts would be a façade.

You can't lie to yourself.

She wanted to give him the chance he kept asking for. When she'd lashed out at him earlier she'd been devastated by Ava's harsh treatment of Leigh. Her friend's suffering had her acting without logical thought. She'd unleashed her anger in the only way she could, taking her frustration out on Trey. Afterward—when she listened to Diskant and Trey's argument—she understood and accepted what Ava had done. Nothing would be easy from here on out. With danger from the Shepherds, the threat of Aldon and the possibility the pack might rebel or turn their backs on Trey and Diskant, everyone had no choice but to keep a lid on things at home.

Trey's cock jerked, his hard, hot thickness spreading her wide. As they were, leaning against the counter, she could feel his weight bearing her down. She loved the way he felt, his large form like a shield around her. She lifted her head, gazing into the mirror. He kept his chin on her shoulder but his eyes were raised, his irises a beautiful shade of gold.

Would she fight for him? Could she?

She thought about the woman who'd tried to get his attention months ago. She'd been so angry and possessive. Using a veil to remain invisible, she'd slapped the woman's drink, dousing the werewolf bitch in alcohol. Trey'd found it humorous. The woman who'd borne the brunt of Sadie's wrath hadn't been as amiable. She'd felt powerful then, proclaiming her hold on Trey even if he hadn't been aware of it.

Just thinking about another woman touching him, whispering to him, holding him...

A tremor shook her from the inside out.

Of course she'd fight for him.

At this point she'd do anything he asked of her.

She hated entering his mind and absorbing his thoughts. Doing so was the ultimate invasion of privacy. But she couldn't help herself. She slid easily into his head, gathering information. She'd gained a glimpse of his resolve, his determination to win her over. He wanted her to trust him even though he knew he'd hurt her. Each time she'd eased into his head she'd gotten to hear the things she wanted most. But she'd been terrified to accept what she found as truth. The last time she'd let her guard down he'd betrayed her in the worst way possible.

If it happened again—if she endured heartbreak for another time—she'd be done for.

He kept his eyes on hers and eased his cock from her pussy. She wrapped her fingers around the edge of the small counter, clenching the marbled surface. Goddess help her, she couldn't look away. The intensity in his gaze—the way he stared at her as though she was the most precious thing in the world—made her eyes burn with tears she refused to shed. He paused, just barely lodged inside her.

"Show me." Her request came across like a plea but she didn't care. "Make me believe."

He returned as gently as he'd left her, tender as his cock eased its way back inside. With a tilt of his chin he swept her hair from her neck. He didn't stop watching her, kissing her nape. This time he didn't take her with force. He moved cautiously, drawing out the moment until he was totally sheathed within her. His breath was warm against her throat, his lips soft as he breezed them over her skin.

If he was trying to seduce her, he was doing a hell of a job. She trembled with excitement and anticipation. A familiar tingle settled in her gums. She didn't try to fight her body's reaction, parting her lips as her fangs lengthened. Strangely enough, she didn't have the overriding urge to bite him. Rather she wanted to let him tease her, was eager to see how long he could keep up with this new and unexpected game.

"I'll give you everything I am. I'll be whatever you need," he vowed, moving his hips back, leaving her feeling empty as his cock slid from her depths. "I won't let you have regrets." His mouth swept from her neck to her cheek. "I'll move heaven and earth for you if that's what it takes."

"Heaven and earth, huh?" It was difficult to speak and even harder to think, especially like this, with their bodies joined and skin touching. "That's not going to be easy."

"If that's what it takes," he repeated. "I never said it'd be easy."

"Even if you have to leave everything you've ever known behind?"

Having him so close and saying such sweet things made her head spin. This was what she'd dreamed about as a young woman who'd never been in love. The magic of a stolen moment with a lover she wanted to wake up with each day. The wonder of finding the one person who would make her life complete.

"I didn't think I could but I was wrong." He grasped her hip and pulled her back as he moved, filling her again, keeping things slow. "When I thought I'd lost you…" His voice cracked and he cleared his throat. "I tried to convince myself I couldn't have you because of what would happen if I did. I put the importance of the pack above everything, like I always have. I'd lived that way for so long that when I found you I didn't do what I should have. There's no excuse for my behavior."

"You were drunk." Yes she was giving him a get out of jail free card, but she was tired of fighting him, or thinking about the events that had divided them for so long. "I thought you might fall flat on your face."

"That's true but it doesn't matter. I'm not that man anymore. I'm not going back to an empty bed, thinking about you, wishing you were right there in my arms."

"This isn't just about us." Goddess, she hated admitting that. She wanted him so much she was almost tempted to say to hell with the rest of the world. He glided back into her, the thickness of his cock nudging her G-spot. "We have to think about everyone else." She couldn't believe she could formulate words, not with the fire building in her belly. "Maybe Diskant's right."

"No, he's not." Rubbing his cheek against hers, he asked, "Do you know why?"

She shook her head, biting down softly on her lip.

"We're at war, Sadie." He increased the pace, pumping his length in and out of her pussy. She rocked back, meeting his thrusts. "Our enemies will return. We'll have to face them head-on. I've seen what you can do. I know what you're capable of. You can protect the pack in a way I can't. You can give them a gift beyond measure. If you show them that—if you pledge your loyalty to them and to me—they'll have no choice but to accept our mating. Diskant will back my decision. They'll trust his judgment. They might not like it at first but they're not stupid. They know the danger we're in. They know what'll happen if we're not stronger than the people who want to kill us. And they know just how much Diskant stands to lose if he's wrong."

"I won't let you hurt me again." She made sure he saw the warning in her gaze, making her intentions clear. He had to know she wouldn't stand for any more bullshit. "If you want this, you need to know I'm not running. If I fight for you, you'll have to fight for me too. And your protection has to be extended to Leigh. You'll have to give me your word you won't let anything happen to her."

He stopped, his cock buried inside her. Letting go of the counter, she rested her fingers over the hand he'd placed on her hip. His fingers tightened over her flesh, his grip firm.

"I give you my word. Accept my mark. Stand beside me when I face the pack."

Uncertainty and a healthy dose of fear almost destroyed the intimacy — almost. She pushed the emotions aside, reckless and tired of hiding how she felt because she was terrified of the unknown. Once he gave her his mark, he couldn't turn her away. She knew enough about shifters to recognize the mark carried weight. The pack would loathe her for having it but she didn't give a shit. She was a vampire without a coven, a woman without a place to call home. In the last day she'd learned those she thought she could trust were far more dangerous than a man who'd done something foolish in the heat of the moment.

Give him what he wants.

Take what he's offering.

She released his hand and reached for her hair, moving it away from throat. He eased back, giving her room. Once she'd tucked the heavy locks over her other shoulder she reached for him. Wrapping her fingers around his nape, she guided his mouth to her neck. He lifted his hand from her hip and pulled her shirt clear, giving him plenty of room to sink his teeth into her skin.

Giving herself over, she whispered the spell that would slow her rate of healing.

It wouldn't last forever—no more than an hour—but he didn't need that long.

She didn't turn away, focusing on the canines in his mouth that elongated and broadened. A rush of magic swept through her, sending a small wave of heat over her skin. In an instant she felt the difference. He felt larger inside her, his presence more formidable. She remained an immortal but she was weaker like this, nowhere near as strong.

"There's no going back," she whispered, voice quaking. "You'll never be rid of me."

"Good," he growled, irises brightening near his pupils. "That's exactly what I want."

Angling his head, he got in position.

Then he dipped his head and sank his teeth into her flesh.

He was an asshole, biting harder than necessary. Her blood coated his tongue. Metallic, warm and sweet. He chose the slope of her neck, where the delicate arch of her throat met the sleekness of her shoulder. Unless she wore a shirt that covered the area, everyone would see the mark on her skin. That's what he wanted. Everyone would know the mating had taken place, he'd given her his brand and she'd accepted it.

Up until then he'd been excruciatingly gentle, taking his time as he fucked her, trying to convey how much she meant to him. One day soon he was going to take it further, making love to her as she deserved. The wolf, however, had other ideas. The damn thing roared in victory the instant Sadie moved her hair free of her neck. It rode him hard, wanting to own every single inch of her inside and out. He plunged into her pussy, groaning as her cunt clasped his cock.

He knew then he'd almost lost the only chance of happiness and fulfillment he'd have ever known. The connection he'd felt the first time they'd come together returned. His beast basked in the feeling, reaching out to its mate. Trey kept up the pace, slamming into her slick heat. She bowed her back to allow him to penetrate deeper, keeping her neck bared to him.

Peering up, he took in the beauty of her face.

Her eyes had drifted closed, her long lashes fanning her cheeks. Her skin had taken a rosy hue, her tiny fangs peeking out from her parted lips. She rocked with each plunge of his hips, taking every inch of his cock, her breasts bobbing with the motion. She was wet and tight, her pussy latching on to him like a fisting second skin. Releasing her shirt, he lowered his hand, skimming his fingers down her stomach and stopping when the tips rested just over her mound. Finding her swollen clit, he rubbed his middle finger over the hard little bead.

He wanted them to come together, gaining the release they both needed at the same time. Her vaginal walls gripped him and he heard her sharp intake of breath. Using pressure, he worked the hard nub with his finger and increased the intensity of his thrusts. Her hair swayed, sliding free of her shoulder. Snaking his other arm around her waist, he slammed into her.

He was so close, teetering on the edge.

His sac drew taut, a heavy tingle building at the base of his spine.

Come for me, darlin'. Come for me.

Moving his hand from her hip, he offered her his wrist. She wound her fingers around his forearm, her lips whispering over his skin. He knew the minute she slid her fangs into his skin he'd lose any control he had over his body. He trapped her clit between his thumb and fingers, pinching softly as he manipulated the bundle of nerves. Her pussy clenched so tight he had to slam his eyes closed and concentrate, determined not to climax before she did.

His best efforts weren't worth shit, not when her tiny teeth scored his skin.

He came so hard he saw spots, tiny speckles clouding his vision. Sadie moaned, the sound muffled as she drank. His knees nearly buckled when her cunt squeezed down on his cock, milking him as Sadie found her release right along with him. She didn't take as much she had before, gently drawing on his skin. He kept up the pace, encouraged by the wolf inside him. The animal had finally gained the ultimate satisfaction, claiming the woman destined for it.

She pulled her fangs from his wrist and flicked her tongue over the punctures, slowly nursing the wounds. He slowed his thrusts, cautious as he unclenched his jaw and eased his teeth from her shoulder. Immediately his eyes swept down, his attention focused on the evidence of his bite. Her skin hadn't mended—two ragged tears along with smaller breaks in her pale flesh—but the bleeding was minimal.

He ran his lips over the indentions.

Finally. It's done. She's mine.

"Don't sound so smug." Sadie looked up from his wrist, meeting his eyes in the mirror. "You might have bitten off more than you can chew." A smile tugged at the corners of her full lips. "You don't really know me. Not yet. We could be great in the sack and have the best chemistry in the world but be totally incompatible when it comes to everything else."

He felt a smile of his own forming. "Bullshit."

"Bullshit?" she repeated, tilting her head, blue eyes playful.

"If you've been reading my thoughts as long as I think you have you know exactly how compatible we are." He'd felt her presence months ago. Back then he'd thought she'd been a figment of his imagination. Then he'd discovered she was very, very real. "In fact, it's about time you start leveling the playing field. It's only fair I know everything about you too."

"What do you want to know?" She pushed her ass back, rocking on his softening cock.

"Everything, naturally," he said. "But I'll start with your last name."

"Hmm." She sighed when he stroked her arm. "Dumus."

"Sadie Dumus?" he repeated, as though he as testing the word.

"That's right."

"No middle name?"

"No," she exhaled softly.

He stretched his arms past his mate and turned on the sink. Then he retrieved the hand towel on a nearby rack. He wet an edge of the cloth with warm water and took a step back. His seed had seeped from her pussy, coating the side of her thigh. He wiped it away, taking care as he cleansed her legs and swept the towel over her labia. She shuddered but remained in place, allowing him to care for her.

"Next time I'm going to draw you a hot bath, give you all the bubbles you can handle and massage you from head to toe."

"Promises, promises." There was humor in the retort but he noted the seriousness that had crept into her face. She reached down to pull up her pants and dropped her head. "We have a lot to do before we can relax."

Damn. In the heat of the moment he'd forgotten about everything else. Nothing had mattered but the two of them. He'd needed to find balance with his mate in order to take the necessary steps to face what was sure to come.

"Kinsley is here." She tried to straighten her shirt despite the fact the neck had been stretched to hell. "Ava just warned me. She said we need to cut our bathroom break short."

Fuckedy, fuck, fuck. He quickly tucked his dick away and yanked up his jeans.

He didn't want to rush outside and end the moment. He wanted to stay right where he was, talking to Sadie like a lover. This was the first time she'd been truly mischievous, speaking to him with happiness in her voice. He wanted it to last, learning what made her laugh, discovering all the little things that made her smile.

Besides, as soon as they left the room he'd have to get ready to kiss ass.

Kinsley had always been Diskant's confidant, not Trey's. They needed the man's support but Trey wasn't gung-ho about turning to him for help. Kinsley's assistance—as much as they needed it—would undoubtedly come with a cost.

Sadie started to slide away from the counter and he stopped her. He turned her around, bringing them face-to-face. They were about to meet the world outside, but not before he gave her a kiss that would make her toes curl.

Dipping his head, he pressed his lips to hers. She opened for him, her tongue darting out to stroke his. He wasn't easy or tender, kissing her hard and deep. She groaned, wrapping her arms around him. He grasped her ass with both hands, squeezing the soft mounds. He didn't want to come up for air but he knew he had to.

Once again they were stealing a moment of borrowed time.

"Soon, baby," he swore, heart pounding, gazing into her eyes. "I'm not going to settle for this shit. I'm going to give you everything you need. No more half-assed fucking in a hurry."

"Now don't go saying something like that that." Drawing her hand down his chest, she lifted on to her tiptoes and kissed his cheek. As she leaned away, she grinned. "I'll have you know I'm quite fond of half-assed fucking in a hurry."

He was so shocked by the sincerity in the statement he didn't try to stop her when she glided away, striding with her head held high for the door. He tossed the towel into the small hamper on the side of the counter, shaking his head as he moved to follow her. Once again she'd upped the ante, taking their mating up another notch.

So she liked quickies? Fan-fucking-tastic.

He couldn't wait to show her that she'd love nice and slow even more.

Chapter Eleven

Fabulous. Another fucking mystery.

Sadie stayed close to Trey but she kept her gaze on the enormous male seated across from Diskant and Ava. Kinsley had dressed in black leather that matched his shoulder-length hair, his piercing emerald green eyes giving away nothing. Another feline shifter had accompanied him, standing quietly at his back. She'd seen Kinsley at Club Liminality on a few occasions—a place that catered to all things supernatural, which also happened to be the place Ava had worked as a bartender once upon a time. The owner of Liminality—Brett McGovern, who also happened to be a fucking warlocke—didn't tolerate any bullshit. It was a safe place to venture so long as a person approached situations carefully. Due to that, she'd never gotten up close or personal with Kinsley.

Now she wished she had.

He had a mental block of some kind going on. Like Ava's, only different.

Instead of nothingness when she tried to slide into Kinsley's head, she found herself directed to weird thoughts. One minute she'd see a bright, sunny sky. The next an image of a child eating ice-cream would flash through her head. Since she didn't want him to know for certain she was monitoring his mind, she couldn't ask if he was fucking with her or if he was really that fucked up in the head.

What the hell? Has the entire world flipped upside down?

For a split second she wondered if Kinsley had been reading her mind.

He looked straight at her, his unwavering stare coming across almost amused. Breaking eye contact, Sadie glanced at

Ava. If she wanted she could ask Ava if she noticed something weird about Kinsley's thoughts. But she didn't know if Ava would be honest or not. They hadn't established any sort of trust.

"*It's not just you.*" Ava's thought answered Sadie's question. The petite female didn't turn to Sadie but continued telepathically, "*I've only been able to get a clear line into Kinsley's thoughts a couple of times, but that was when he wasn't paying attention. It didn't last more than a second or two. I think he can sense when someone enters his head. He's able to keep people out.*"

Was that so? Interesting.

"Your best bet is to find Ava's brother," Kinsley said, his rich Scottish brogue accenting his words. Returning his attention to Diskant, he kept talking. "If the amulet is as powerful as you say, you won't have to worry about anyone or anything once you have it."

"We're working on that," Diskant replied, placing a hand on Ava's leg. "For now we have to deal with issues in the pack."

"There is that." Kinsley lips quirked. "Do you want my advice?"

"I wouldn't have asked you to come here if I didn't."

"Don't tell them about Aldon. Let them know about the mating but don't tell them how serious shit is right now." Kinsley's gaze drifted to Mary and he winked. "You've already lost a quarter of your pack to stupidity. If you lose anyone else you're going to have to pack up and find another city to call home."

Shit. Sadie was stupefied. *They'd lost that many people?*

She knew many members of the pack—especially those who were mated and had children—had left after Emory'd mated with Mary. As a Shepherd, Mary was considered an enemy of shifters the world over. It didn't matter that the woman was nothing like her relatives. Her presence alone made the werewolves in Trey's pack uneasy.

And now they have to deal with me.

"There's another option." She knew it was going to piss Trey off but she said, "We don't have to tell them anything about me. You can give them enough information about Aldon and Leigh to get their support. That's far more important."

"Sadie, darlin'," Trey growled and snagged her by the waist. "Shut the hell up."

In another time or place, she might have been annoyed. It wasn't everyday she let someone insult her. But she knew Trey wasn't trying to be an asshole. She sensed his frustration. He wasn't going to let her step down and take a place in the shadows. Moving forward meant doing the right thing by her.

He'd marked her. He'd claimed her. It was a done deal.

She caught herself before she lifted her hand to the scar on her neck. The healing process had started, mending the tissue. Everyone had noticed it. She'd tried not to blush or react to their stares but each time she'd seen someone gazing at it she instinctively tried to cover it.

Like now.

Everyone was staring at them, curious to see how the newly mated couple interacted.

"I'll shut the hell up when you start thinking straight." She snorted, trying to play it cool. "My way makes sense."

"Your way," he drawled in a raspy timbre, "ain't happening."

Sadie started to reply when Ava said, "Don't bother arguing. They're all Neanderthals."

"Not me," Kinsley remarked, thickening his accent. His gaze swept over the women in the room, a gleam in his emerald eyes. "I'm all charm."

"Yo, Casanova," Diskant snarled, eyes narrowed. "Put your ego in check. Get back on track."

"Fine." Kinsley shrugged and reclined in the oversized chair, nonchalant and seemingly unaffected at the annoyance in Diskant's request. "My official opinion is you tell the pack about the mating and keep the rest to yourself. Otherwise you'll cause panic. Work out a plan and track down Ava's brother." He lifted his eyes to Trey. "Aldon's not an idiot. Eventually he's going to come here. I suggest you move the girl you're hiding and take her somewhere else. In the meantime I'll talk to my eyes and ears in the area. They might be able to provide additional information. I'll also speak to the pride Alphas and let them know they need to tighten security."

"And if they ask questions?" Trey asked.

"Shepherds might have been quiet for a while but they're not gone for good," Kinsley said, menace creeping into his voice. "You let me worry about my people."

Sadie tried to keep her reaction to Kinsley's advice under wraps. Everything he offered made perfect sense but she didn't want to think about sending Leigh away. How would Leigh react if she was placed in the company of strangers? And who in the world could keep her safe?

There wasn't a coven Sadie trusted to do the job. Not anymore.

She inched closer to Trey, taking a small measure of comfort at his closeness. He seemed to understand, increasing the tightness of the arm around her midsection. Wasn't it strange? A couple of days ago she'd almost died. She'd sworn she'd hate him for what he'd done. Then—before she could fully wrap her head around it—she'd found herself in his bed, accepting his mark and standing by his side.

Funny how things turned out.

Unbelievable.

"Whatever you say." Diskant sounded incredibly tired. "I think I know of a place we can move our guest. I'll have to make a few calls."

"Nathan won't let her leave without him," Trey interjected quietly, soothing Sadie by breezing his lips over her temple. With her settled, he said, "That means the pack will have double the shit to deal with. They might be fine with kicking my ass out but they won't want to lose Nathan. He's the primary person they've all been able to trust."

"Then tell them a simplified version of the truth," Kinsley suggested. "They'll understand if he's found his mate and needs time away to initiate the union. You don't have to tell them who or what his mate is. Not yet, anyway. Sometimes small truths are blessings in disguise. The issue is," Kinsley broke his relaxed posture, leaning forward to rest his elbows on his knees, "who can you trust to take Nathan's place? You'll need a Beta who can keep everyone calm."

Silence followed, a heavy apprehension filling the air.

Trey shifted his feet, his body bumping Sadie's. She reached out to him with her senses, telling herself she wasn't going to intrude on his thoughts. She had to start trusting his reasoning and stop second-guessing things. Tension wafted from him, slamming into her in waves. He had an answer to the dilemma but something caused him to hesitate.

"Everyone knows Zach was next in line for the position," Kinsley said softly. "It can't hurt to ask him."

"No." Ava looked horrified. Diskant tried to enfold her in his arms but she shook him off. "He's been through too much. You'll push him over the edge."

"It might be what he needs, Pinkie." Diskant's reprimand was gently given. "There's a reason he didn't follow Katie after she died."

"*Katie?*" Sadie thought to Trey.

"*Zach's mate.*" Even in her head she could feel Trey's grief. "*She was inside Dougan's Bar when it exploded.*"

Sadie's heart bottomed out. *Oh Goddess.*

She'd been standing outside the bar when the explosion had taken place. At the time she'd been watching Trey as she usually did—hidden by shadows, aching for a man she could never have. He'd left with the pack to face zealots who'd threatened the city. Shepherds had planned an attack, deceiving the shifters. With many of the men gone, a lone man had entered the werewolf bar with a bomb strapped to his chest.

Ava and Nathan were the only two who made it out alive.

Sadie had come across them in an alley. After she'd killed the Shepherds who were ready to attack the fallen woman and shifter she'd come to their aid. It was then that Sadie had used her healing magic and blood to give Ava the strength she'd needed to live. Diskant had arrived shortly after and almost killed Sadie, mistaking her for the enemy. She'd managed to get away before the damage became lethal. He'd been so fierce, eager to rip her head from her shoulders.

"I thought you couldn't survive without your mate." Her knowledge wasn't totally limited and she was almost certain shifters didn't last long once they lost their partners. "How's he still alive?"

"She was human. Zach hadn't fully sealed their bloodbond." There was something else he wanted to say. This time he spoke the thought aloud. "He's determined to see every Shepherd dead. The pack is all he has. They could give him something else to live for. It might be what he needs to heal."

"He's been to hell and back but he's not given up. I think he's a solid choice," Kinsley informed Trey. "But you'll have to tell him everything. You can't leave anything out." Turning to Diskant, Kinsley kept going. "If you have a safe location for the other female I suggest you move her as soon as possible. There's no need to add fuel to the fire. Get her out of the city and take Aldon out of the equation. Shepherds haven't struck again yet but they will. This has to be sorted as quickly as possible."

"I'll need to make a few calls," Diskant said, sliding his hand up and down Ava's back. She was still shaken and it showed. "More than one person owes me a favor."

"Then do it." Kinsley rose in a swift, seamless motion. "I'll get things started on my end." He walked over to Ava and knelt, looking her in the eye. "It's going to be all right, lass," he murmured, giving her a smile. "You just take care of that wee one. Let us worry about the rest."

When Kinsley stood, Trey let Sadie go and walked to the cat shifter. "Thank you."

"Don't thank me." Kinsley reached out to shake Trey's hand. "If I need help in the future, you'll pay me back. That's not negotiable."

"Whatever you say," Trey replied and thought to himself, *fucking cats.*

Sadie wanted to chuckle but she forced her face to remain expressionless, witnessing the exchange as though she hadn't heard a thing. The man who'd stood behind Kinsley had gone to leave, stopping just beside the entranceway to the large room. It was then that Sadie noticed Nathan. He'd been lingering just outside, listening to the conversation. He didn't look happy. In fact, Sadie was certain he wanted to beat the hell out of something.

"Sadie," the Beta said, studying Diskant, "Leigh is asking for you."

Shit. "I'm on it."

She didn't want to leave but she knew she had to. She wasn't sure why she looked at Trey for his approval but she did. She'd expected him to nod or tell her to go ahead. He stunned her silly by striding away from Kinsley, snaking an arm around her and giving her a hard, thrilling kiss. She nearly sagged, wanting to take things to another level. Somehow she managed not to open her mouth and tease his lips with her tongue.

"I'll be right here, baby," he whispered. She inhaled his scent, shivering at the heat of his body against hers. "When you're finished come back to me."

She felt like a shameless hussy who didn't give a shit what anyone thought. "Okay."

It felt as though she'd lost a part of herself as she walked away from him. Nathan gave her a sideways glance as she darted past him. She increased the pace, hurrying to Leigh's room. She had to do damage control, get Leigh sorted out and take charge. That's what the young vampire would need right now. Anything else would spook her more than she already had been.

With a deep breath for courage, she opened the door and stepped inside the bedroom.

* * * * *

Trey had wanted to bolt after Sadie. Each time she left him he wanted to bring her back to his side. To distract himself, he'd put his focus on Nathan. Leigh's rejection had shattered the male. The Beta looked beaten and emotionally worn down. Even so, Leigh was the man's mate. Nathan would do anything for her. She could hate him more than anything in the world and he'd still lay down his life for her. Diskant wouldn't be making any calls without Nathan's approval. That much was clear.

Poor son of a bitch.

"I have a serious matter that needs my attention," Kinsley stated, pulling Trey's gaze from Nathan. "You need to set things up within the next twenty-four hours. After that I'll be on a leave of absence. I'm not sure how long I'll be gone."

"What?" Diskant snapped in disbelief. "You've got to be shitting me. Can't it wait?"

"No." Kinsley's mood switched, going from calm to aggressive. "I've helped you as much as I can. Those are my terms. Take them or leave them."

It was rude to interrupt but Trey didn't give a shit.

Fuck manners.

"You told Diskant this has happened before." Trey hurried to ask the questions he needed answers for. "How do you know that?"

"I just do. I know a lot of things." Kinsley took a step back from Diskant, although he kept his attention on the Omega. "There are shifters on the West Coast with vampire mates. Most shifters prefer not to talk about it. You have to learn when and where to ask the right questions. Timing and location are everything."

That made sense. Even if a pack accepted a vampire due to a mating, they weren't likely to advertise it. And Kinsley had been around longer than any of them. If anyone knew what was what it was Mr. MacGregor.

"What was the fallout?" Trey asked. There had to have been some. He wanted to be prepared.

"I don't know the story for every situation but I can tell you about one in particular. Some members of the pack left after their Alpha mated with a vampire, but most stayed."

"An Alpha?" Trey couldn't believe it. News like that would travel, even if a pack tried to keep it quiet. A normal pack member might have issues introducing a vampire mate to his group but an Alpha was—at least Trey thought—unheard of.

"You're wondering how they've kept it a secret. It's understandable." Kinsley nodded at Diskant, gave Ava another smile and turned to Trey. "They struck a bargain. Everyone swore to stay silent on the matter. The Alpha's scent covered the female so it threw most shifters off her scent. Even if they thought something was off, they didn't know what it was for sure. And there's something else."

Kinsley strode from Diskant to Trey. The big male came close, standing mere inches away. He met Trey's gaze, relating the importance of what he was about to share.

"The Alpha agreed that if his female ever used their mated connection against the pack, they had his blessing to kill them both. He gave them serious leverage in order to gain their trust. You'll need to do the same. Face your kin. Tell them what you're willing to sacrifice in order to keep what's yours. Have Diskant give his word that he'll hunt the two of you down if things go sour. They know he'll do it if he has to."

Fuck. It'd never happen.

"I can't do that." He wouldn't let anyone harm Sadie, no matter what she did.

"You can and will." Kinsley's eyes shifted to the shifter who'd accompanied him. The man gave Kinsley a nod and walked from the room. "You can't have your cake and eat it too," Kinsley said softly. For a moment, Trey though he saw a glimmer of pain in the man's eyes. "I understand there are things you want to do and then there are things you have to do. You're going to have to make your priorities clear. The pack won't respect you if you don't."

"They might not respect me anyway."

Even if Trey came to them with sincerity, the shifters in his pack could turn their backs on him, shunning him completely. He'd always been part of a pack. The thought of being on the outside looking in devastated him. And even if they didn't want his help, they needed it. Shepherds would return and unleash their own brand of hell. Shifters would suffer mercilessly before they were killed.

Kinsley stepped to the side, dismissing Trey as he started to walk away.

"Then give them a reason to. The ball's in your court."

Trey remained in the same spot, mulling over Kinsley's advice. In the meantime Kinsley exited the room, his footsteps fading as he left the house.

Could he actually promise something like that to his pack? Effectively putting a target on Sadie's back? He knew she couldn't survive without him, so even if he offered his own life it would end hers as well. Which was better? A quick death? Or a slow, miserable one?

"Ava, baby," Diskant whispered. "Would you get Cade?"

"Of course I will." There was an enormous amount of love in the words, Ava's adoration evident. She padded over to Diskant and kissed him on the cheek. "He's in the kitchen. I'll make everyone something to eat while I'm there."

Nathan hovered in the doorway and watched Ava leave. Once she'd gone he moved to the center of the room and looked at Diskant.

"If you have any respect for me," he said, "you'll let me make decisions when it comes to Leigh. I'm not letting her leave without me. Where she goes, I go."

"I'm thinking she needs a bit of space from you." Diskant wasn't cruel, only honest. "I know it's not easy but you need to give her room to breathe."

Nathan's low growl hummed through the room. "I can't protect her if I'm not with her."

"I sent Cade to help someone a while back. The people who asked for our aid owe me a favor. If they'll take Leigh, they can protect her. Believe me when I say they have more firepower than we'll ever have." Diskant's face softened, his compassion shining through. "You can accompany Leigh if she goes. But I'm warning you that these people don't care much for shifters. You're going to have to back off a little. Give your female time to heal. You'll smother her if you're not careful and she'll resent you for it."

"You called?" Cade snarked as he graced everyone with his presence.

"We have to move Leigh. It's too dangerous to keep her here. If I can swing it we're going to keep her hidden by the enclave in New Orleans."

Maybe his eyes were deceiving him but Trey thought he glimpsed a flash of nervousness in Cade's gaze. As he usually did, Cade quickly masked his emotions. The man didn't want anyone to know how he felt—good or bad.

"What does that have to do with me?"

"I'll need you to take Leigh there and make sure she's settled. As soon as you get back I'll get the information you want. You'll be free to go and do your thing. I'm giving you my word. You can break from the pack completely or you can return. It's entirely up to you."

Trey's head bolted up and he stared at Diskant in confusion. They'd planned to have Cade stay at the firehouse to calm the pack's possible angst. Apparently Diskant felt it was necessary to change their strategy. Which begged the question—who would protect the city? The pack needed an Alpha or Beta nearby in order to feel safe.

"All right," Cade said, nodding. The man was so eager to get the job done he was almost brimming with anticipation. He was about to get the revenge he'd wanted for so long. "When do we leave?"

"I'm not sure. Soon, hopefully," Diskant replied, peering over at Nathan. "Come with me. We'll need to sort out the details."

The Omega and Beta swept from the room, leaving Cade and Trey alone.

In the last few months the men had developed a strange kind of bond. It might be stretching it but Trey felt like the man actually considered Trey a friend. On a rare occasion they exchanged jokes and barbs. Beneath his rough exterior Cade was still a man with a huge heart. Trey knew that better than anyone. After Mary had come along Cade had backed her up more than once. He'd taken the wounded woman under his wing, ready to take on anyone in the pack to protect her, even if Mary and Emory hadn't known it.

"It's finally happening," Trey said. "You're going to get what you want."

"That's the thing." Cade didn't look at Trey, keeping his eyes forward. "I'm not sure…now that the moment's here…" Cade shook his head. "It doesn't matter." The smile he gave Trey was forced. "Let's not talk about me. Are you going to be okay? Without me watching your back you're liable to get your ass kicked."

"I might," Trey admitted. "But then again I might not."

"I wouldn't worry too much." Cade cracked his neck and sighed. "I've seen what that woman of yours can do. If the shit hits the fan, take cover behind her. I'm sure she'll demolish whatever comes at you."

"Fuck that." He'd never cower behind a female. "If anyone takes cover it'll be her."

Trey took a moment to really look at Cade. Something was bothering the male.

"What's eating your goat?" Cade tried to blow him off but Trey wouldn't relent, prodding, "Talk to me."

"There's nothing to talk about."

"Bullshit."

Cade narrowed his eyes, finally gazing at Trey. "Are we having a girly moment?"

"If you want to call it that." *So far, so good.* Cade might look angry but he was being sarcastic. A positive sign. "You're going to be leaving. No sense in keeping what you need to say bottled up."

Cade averted his gaze. "It's not easy to put what I'm thinking into words."

"Are you worried you won't be able to do it?" Trey knew Cade wanted to kill the people who'd murdered his family, but wanting and doing were two different things. "Are you having second thoughts?"

"Fuck no," Cade snarled, staring Trey in the eye. "When I find them, they're dead."

"Then what's the problem?"

The hatred washed from Cade's face, his brows smoothing out. "When it's done, I have to decide what comes after. I've wanted this for so long, I haven't thought about what comes next."

"You go on living." Trey rested a hand on Cade's shoulder. "You owe it to the memory of your family. Your wife wouldn't have wanted any of this for you."

A small laugh escaped Cade. "Andrea would beat my ass." With a sigh, he confessed, "After she died, I took comfort in thinking she was watching over me. Then I started hoping she wasn't. I didn't want her to see the things I did. I never want her to know what kind of man I've become." There was a slight hesitation before Cade said, "Not too long ago I met someone. I didn't think it was possible but for a little while I was able to think about something else."

"That's not a bad thing." Trey tried to think of who Cade might have met outside the pack. He couldn't tell if Cade was talking about a man or a woman. Taking a chance, he asked, "Who is she?"

"That," Cade straightened his shoulders and put on his hard-ass façade again, "is none of your fucking business."

Trey had his answer. It was a female.

There wasn't any sense in pushing. Cade wasn't saying anything else. Trey accepted what he'd been given, pulling his hand away. "I feel sorry for her, whoever she is. You are an enormous pain in the ass."

"Should we go find your majesty and see if he needs us?"

Cade was finished. No more talking. Back to business.

"I suppose we should."

As they exited the room Trey let Cade take the lead. He watched him closely, wondering how things would pan out. Once upon a time he'd wanted the human to stay the hell away from the pack. Now he loathed the idea of Cade leaving. Maybe it was for the best. The tortured soul had to defeat his demons. If he didn't he'd never find any measure of peace.

He tried to picture the woman who'd broken Caden Stone's stupor.

She'd have to be feisty and strong-willed. The females in the pack had taken to Cade because they sensed the dominance in him. A weaker woman would likely run in the other direction.

The last twenty-four hours he'd wished for a lot of things—safety for Sadie, a way to defend his pack, the promise of a brighter tomorrow—so he wasn't surprised when he sent another request to whatever it was that decided the future. If fate would be kind enough he hoped Cade would find his way back to the female who'd impacted his life even if only for a short period of time.

If anyone deserved a second chance, it was the human who'd lost everything.

Chapter Twelve

Before Sadie ventured on a hunt, she often took time to prepare. Usually she phased to one of the private apartments she rented throughout the world, meditated and used her surroundings to get into the right state of mind. She'd thought she'd be able to do that this time around but the minute she'd appeared inside her New York hideaway she'd known she'd been wrong.

It wasn't possible to ease into a relaxed state.

Not when she kept thinking about Trey.

She hurried into the bedroom. The air was stale, the dust tickling her nose. She hadn't ventured to the apartment in months and it showed. Rushing past the bed to the closet, she snatched an overnight bag from the floor. She didn't bother looking at what she retrieved, shoving garments inside the pouch. She wanted a shower in the worst way. In order to have one she had to haul ass. She'd promised Trey she wouldn't take long.

Goddess, things are happening too fast.

She reenacted the previous hour's events in her head.

Before she'd left she'd had to talk to Leigh. The conversation had gone better than Sadie'd expected. Leigh had finally calmed down and willingly talked things through. Sadie had known it was due to Leigh's fear for the mortal man she'd once loved but Sadie didn't mention that. They'd focused on the facts, keeping things in perspective. Leigh hadn't mentioned Nathan and neither had Sadie.

They'd cross that bridge soon enough.

Once Leigh had been dealt with, she'd used her senses to find Trey.

Everyone had holed up in a large office, listening as Diskant told them what he wanted to do. An enclave in Louisiana had agreed to take Leigh. Nathan and Cade were accompanying her to North Carolina, where they'd meet their contact. Once there the men would sever all communication. It was safest in the event Aldon could read their thoughts and figure out precisely where they were hiding.

Then there was the issue with the pack.

Diskant had spoken briefly with Zach. Although Diskant hadn't been able to share all the details over the phone, the man had agreed to help in any capacity the Omega wanted. Diskant wasn't sure if Zach would continue to offer his support when he knew everything but Diskant decided to wait and see what happened before he planned his next move. First and foremost he had to think about how the pack would react to Trey's mating.

The thought brought Sadie back to the present.

She took a deep breath and turned her head, gazing out a window. The sun was setting, soon the pack would arrive. She had to hurry back. The decision had been made. Trey was going to step out with Sadie by his side. He'd tell them he'd mated with her and give any males the opportunity to challenge him for his position as Alpha. If that happened it came down to whether Trey won or lost. If it didn't the females would have the chance to take Sadie down a peg.

Or—worst case—the pack might attack and take them both out.

Diskant couldn't be certain it wouldn't happen. He had power over the pack's beasts but there were a lot of people to influence. Sadie knew Ava could assist him but Sadie wasn't entirely sure the woman had the strength. Ava was clearly powerful, easing in and out of minds at will. But she was also pregnant and anxious. In order to manipulate thoughts you needed a clear head, without emotions muddling things.

Maybe knowing they can kill you will make them happy.

She'd been calm when Diskant had gone over that part but Trey had shifted uneasily beside her, the arm he'd placed around her midsection tightening. He hadn't liked the idea at all. She'd calmed him with a gentle caress, sliding her fingers over his hand. He hadn't spoken up but she knew he wasn't happy. How could he be? If the roles were reversed she'd never have allowed anyone to threaten him.

Speaking of threatening...

She'd taken a lot of time to think about Geneva and the coven.

They weren't her priority or problem anymore but something about what had transpired nagged at her. Geneva had been so intent on Aldon, almost like his death was more of a mission. It wasn't just about him as a danger. For Geneva it had to be personal. At least Sadie'd gotten Leigh out. She had no idea what Geneva had in store but she did know Leigh didn't need to take any part in it.

Thinking about all the blood she had on her hands—blood Geneva had put there—made Sadie sick. She'd killed many people for the coven in the past. What if some of them hadn't done anything wrong? What if she'd done as she'd been instructed because she hadn't known any better?

She snagged a couple of sheathed daggers for good measure and tossed them into the bag. Then she picked up a pair of boots. She carried them into the bedroom, retrieved fresh underwear from her drawer and jolted for the bathroom as she stuffed them into the carrier. She managed to move everything to one arm in order to toss soap, shampoo and other necessities on top of her clothing. Her eyes drifted to the shower.

Goddess, she felt dirty. One hot, steamy fix was all she needed.

The problem was she wanted all six-foot-plus inches of Trey in that shower with her. She wanted to tease him beneath the strong pulses of the water, using her tongue as she slid his cock to the back of her throat. Just imagining the pleasure on his face got her hot and bothered. Instantly her nipples pebbled and her pussy spasmed. She'd thought that once she'd had him her lust would relent but she'd been wrong. She wanted him more than ever.

To hell with it.

She called on her magic, pulling more energy in order to bring the objects along with her. It bled over her, white-hot and burning. She accepted the bite of energy, knowing she needed it. She wasn't able to phase with another person but she'd mastered the art of carrying a sword and other things if necessary. In a blink she phased back to the bedroom Ava had given them.

Trey stood in the center of the room, his head darting up when she appeared.

"That took long enough," he snarled, advancing on her.

Dropping her belongings to the floor, she reached for him. "I wasn't even gone five minutes."

"One minute is too long."

He kissed her, his tongue delving past her lips.

Yes. This was what she wanted.

She placed her arms on his shoulders and stepped backward. Somehow she guided him into the bathroom. Thankfully Ava had thought ahead, giving them one of the larger rooms. With Trey around, Sadie'd probably need it. When they weren't in bed they'd be washing away the evidence of their play. They were already like a pair of rabbits, jumping on each other every chance they could.

"You're feeling dirty, aren't you?" Trey whispered, his words a heavy growl. "I like it when you feel dirty, darlin'. It gets me harder than hell." He clasped his fingers around her wrist and brought her hand to his crotch. His cock was thick and stiff, straining against his jeans. "Do you feel what you do to me?" His lips brushed past her mouth and he nipped at her neck. "I want to be inside you so bad, baby. I want to feel that hot, wet pussy of yours all around me."

"A dirty talker, are you?" She moaned and arched her back, pushing her breasts to his chest. She liked a man who spoke his mind. Some women might have been offended by the coarse language but she wasn't. She liked hearing how much she excited him. It was its own kind of turn-on.

"For the most part, but I can be romantic when the mood calls for it."

She released his cock and brought her hands up, fisting her fingers in his hair. He lifted his head and their eyes met. She loved his irises, how they shifted color from light to dark. Right now they were a beautiful shade of gold, the color stark against his tanned skin.

"I'm not in the mood for romantic. Are you?"

"Hell no." He went at her clothing, tearing the shirt from her back. "I want to fuck you so hard you won't be able to walk straight. I'm going to make sure you're so sore you won't be able to stop thinking about me and what I've done to you."

"Barbarian," she teased. "Isn't the mark enough?"

"No, it's not." He stopped undoing her pants and gazed at her. "I want every single thing you have to offer. I won't stop until you're mine in every way. All of you, darlin'. I'm going to have all of you."

Her heartbeat accelerated, breaths coming hard and fast. She knew what he meant. He wasn't going to simply fuck her. That would be too easy. He wanted to completely master her, taking her in a way she wouldn't be able to forget. The thought of his cock in her ass got her even wetter. Her clit throbbed, her pussy so slick she felt the moisture drenching her panties. She was no novice to anal sex. Although it wasn't entirely without pleasure, it had never been her thing either.

She had a feeling Trey was about to change all that.

"What are you waiting for?"

Her leather pants suffered for the question. Trey showed them the same courtesy he had her shirt. He was careful enough not to hurt her but he didn't give a shit about the material. She stood there, letting him work. She'd never had a man this eager for her. Ripping at her clothing, so wild all he could think about was sinking his length inside her. As he finished undressing her, she searched the room. To her relief she saw the nearby shelf had everything they needed.

"Ditch your clothes." She bit her lip when he snarled, trying not to laugh. "I'll meet you in the shower."

He didn't like the idea — the way he glowered at her made it clear — but he didn't waste a moment arguing. She used the seconds she had to get the water running, collect the shampoo, soap and baby oil. When she had them resting on the edge of the tub she stepped over the rim and shoved the curtain aside. She stepped into the spray, soaking her head. The hot water felt like heaven against her skin, cleaning away everything from the past few weeks. She felt Trey behind her, was aware of his large body as he clutched her hips and brought her back. His cock glided between the globes of her ass, the shaft hard and unrelenting.

"Turn around, baby."

He lifted her right leg as she did as he said, resting her foot on the edge of the tub. She stared at his body, appreciating the corded muscles, taking in the tattooed skin that traveled from his shoulder to his wrist. A tribal design, a combination of animals merged together. The other arm wasn't as carefully adorned, a swirling design resting over his upper biceps. Her people prayed to the Goddess of Healing but she wondered who'd been responsible for Trey's creation. Whoever it was had achieved perfection. His features, dark hair and glowing skin were absolutely flawless.

He sank to his knees and brought his lips to her cleft. "You smell so fucking good." His tongue teased her clit, swirling around the sensitive nub. "I'm going to eat you up."

"Do it." Dirty talk was well and good but the actual thing was even better. "Do it now."

She threw her head back, grasping at the shower curtain and wall. He decided not to torment her, swiping his tongue from the mouth of her pussy to the tip of her clitoris. She curled her toes around the edge of the tub, trying to keep her balance. The man was a fucking artist with his mouth, painting designs only he could see. He lapped at her slit and pressed two thick fingers inside her, stopping when his hand was flush against her sex. She thrust her hips forward, grinding her clit against his thumb.

"Fuck yes. Just like that," he encouraged against her tingly flesh, licking at her every couple of words. "Ride my hand. Take what you want."

It was easier to ignore the pressure in her gums. The sight didn't bother Trey and it was her nature. She simply allowed her fangs to drop, immersed in raw sensation. She undulated against him, groaning when his fingers hit the sweet spot inside her. The water drifted down her skin, steaming the air around them. Stray strands of hair tickled her back, sweeping toward her buttocks as she swayed back and forth.

"Perfect," Trey rasped. She lowered her head, watching as he laved his tongue over her pussy. The visual ramped up the tension, fueling the heat. "Exactly like that. Come for me, baby."

His lips surrounded her clit and he sucked—hard.

The pressure in her abdomen bubbled over like shaken champagne. She whimpered, allowing the climax to wash over her. She was grateful he was there to hold her because the one leg keeping her up wobbled, her muscles going weak. He didn't stop loving her with his mouth or fingers, using his free arm to help her stand. He cupped her ass, keeping her stable until she found her balance. Still he kept going, wringing every last bit of ecstasy from her.

It's his turn.

Shaky and out of breath, she lowered her foot and started to sink to her knees to reciprocate. He stopped her, slipping his fingers from her wet depths.

"Not yet," he murmured, licking his fingers clean. "I want to take care of you this time."

Talk about shifting gears.

He'd gotten her revved up only to slow her down.

She almost fought him over it, ready for more. His chest rubbed against hers, sending a prickle of electricity through her nipples. Then she felt his hands easing over her back, aiding the water in cleansing her skin. He massaged the muscles of her lower back, his large, capable hands working miracles. She could practically feel those talented fingers skimming over her body, tracing across every soft contour.

She kept that in mind when he retrieved the soap and washcloth she'd placed on the edge of the tub. He did what she'd hoped for, starting at her feet, working his way up. He paid careful attention to the apex of her thighs, soothing the skin with gentle swipes of the cloth. Once he'd finished he abandoned the cloth and used his hands. Sudsing her up with his palms, cupping the weight of her breasts when he reached her chest.

"Does that feel good?" he asked, running his thumbs over her nipples.

Did it ever. She closed her eyes, humming, "Mm-hmm." She never wanted him to stop touching her.

"Let's see how you like this."

A bottle snapped open, the sound cracking through the room. She waited, keeping her eyes shut. She heard him close the container and felt him return. He brushed against her, his enormous frame straining above hers. The water spray changed, hitting her in the lower back. His hands went to the top of her head. He massaged floral-scented shampoo into her scalp, rubbing his fingers against her skin.

And she'd thought him washing her body felt good? *Damn.*

"Go soft for me." He worked his way down the long strands, washing her hair. "Relax."

If she relaxed any more, she'd go to sleep.

Wouldn't that be a total waste? Stay awake. Just enjoy.

She let him do his thing, living in the moment. All of her worries vanished. There was only Trey. His soft touch. The warmth of his voice. The way he made her feel. If tomorrow never came she could die happy. She'd been given a taste of what she wanted, which turned out to be something far more than she'd ever expected.

"Time to rinse."

He stretched over her again and adjusted the stream of water. It hit her on the top of her head and she craned her neck, letting the lather wash from the locks and down her back. Trey swept his hands over her head, making sure all the soap was gone. She trembled when he turned her but she'd known what was coming. He'd gotten her relaxed for a reason. He didn't give a shit about reciprocation because in the end he was going to take what he wanted.

She placed her hands above the faucets, resting her palms against the tile. Trey manipulated the showerhead so the water rushed to the side, the heat from the spray keeping them warm. He reached down and squeezed her ass, using subtle pressure to part her cheeks.

"You look so fucking hot, Sadie." The admission was full of possessiveness and lust. "I've dreamed of taking you like this."

Funny. So had she. "Make the dream a reality."

His snarl wasn't nice—it was a promise to deliver what she'd asked for and more. He left her and she heard another bottle open with a snick. She didn't tense up, waiting for what would happen next. One of these days she was going to taste him. For now, if he wanted this so badly, she'd give it to him.

And she'd love every moment of it because it was real.

She'd stopped dreaming a long time ago.

Knowing how good reality could be, she never wanted to go back.

Trey forced himself to slow down, ordering the wolf back into its cage. His female had offered him the one thing shifters desired most, the ultimate act of submission. But he knew to approach things with care, to make the encounter enjoyable for her. She'd known what he was alluding to earlier. He'd seen it in her eyes when he'd tried to warn her. She'd made sure to retrieve things to make it easier for them too. Next to the soap and shampoo rested a bottle of baby oil. It would take care of things, pave the way.

He thought about how tight she'd be and his cock jerked.

Sadie hadn't shared her age but Trey knew she'd ventured around the earth and wasn't new to life's adventures. She might even be older than his five hundred and twelve years. A part of him hoped not, wishing her to be younger. Sexuality stirred in every creature, including vampires and werewolves, when the right time came. He didn't like thinking she'd taken many lovers in her life.

Who are you to judge? You're not exactly a saint.

Fuck it all.

The only man she'd take into her bed from this moment forward was him.

She'd never need the affection of another.

Since they were in the shower, he placed the bottle over her lower back and let it drip onto her skin. The silky fluid streaked over her pale flesh, traveling down the curve of her buttocks. He slid his fingers through the slippery puddle, getting them good and slick. Then he reached down, placing his fingers between the globes of her ass. He searched for the tiny rosette hidden between them and stroked the pucker with the tips of his fingers. His wolf snarled in his head, wanting to fuck her as badly as he did.

"Easy, baby," he said, working his way into her carefully.

He kept his hand level, making sure he didn't go too fast. She made things easier by bearing down. His fingers slid into her ass, gliding past the second knuckle. He pulled back and poured more oil over her. Only when she was soaking wet did he return, working the lubricant into her ass.

"More," she demanded, rocking back.

Fuck. His balls drew up and a spike shot down his cock.

If she didn't stop he wouldn't even make it inside her. He'd shoot his load before they'd even passed second base. Scissoring his fingers, he stretched the delicate area. She was tight but ready, her channel nice and wet by the oil. There wouldn't be any force when he entered her. She'd part like a whisper, giving him the room he needed.

He removed his fingers and stroked his dick, covering the entire length with the lube. When his cock was equally slick he fisted the base and placed the thick, mushroomed head against her entrance. He closed his eyes, fighting the wolf for control, drawing a steadying breath. The animal clawed the inside of his skin, begging to get out. He told the asshole creature to shut the hell up. Most men weren't this lucky. Some were mated to human women who refused to consider such a thing. While mating a female shifter—who usually had the same deviant desires—made things easier for males to experience anal sex, it was never a guarantee.

Taking a woman in the ass was the ultimate thrill.

He was the luckiest man in the world.

"Do you want me?" He pressed against the tiny hole, making sure he didn't penetrate her. For this he wanted her consent. Knowing she was right there with him. It wasn't worth it to him to have the moment if it didn't mean anything to his female. They had to experience this together.

"You know I do." She gazed at him over her shoulder. "I want you in any way I can have you."

Christ. His heart slammed in his chest. *She means it.*

He'd told her that he knew she loved him. In his own way he did.

But now he saw it clearly through her eyes.

She truly would take him in any way she had to. That was how devoted she was. No wonder his betrayal had cut her so deeply. She'd pretty much offered him her heart and watched as he tossed it to the ground and stomped on it like an asshole.

He returned her stare, wanting to see her eyes when he breached her. He was wide enough that it took more pressure than he'd have liked to get inside. He hissed when the head slipped past the ring of muscle and lodged in her ass, the constrictive walls hugging the tip.

Sadie lowered her chin, gazing at him with desire and adoration. He almost lost it.

Count to ten. Think of unicorns. Do NOT fucking come.

"What's wrong?" she purred, probably because she'd heard the thought.

The wolf—already eager and aggressive—broke free. "Not a damn thing."

Grasping her hips, he planted his feet. One hard thrust and he slammed his cock in her ass, burying himself from tip to hilt. She accepted him but the teasing playfulness on her face vanished. She gasped. Her eyes widened and her lips parted. Good. If she kept trying to provoke him he wouldn't be so cautious. He'd act like a fucking idiot, ramming into her like a sloppy teenager. There wouldn't be any care, only mindless horniness that wouldn't do her any favors.

Thinking on that, he reached around and thrummed her clit.

Her breath caught and her ass flexed around his dick. She was so damn snug he was afraid to move. She felt so good around him, like a warm, fisting glove teasing his prick. Fuck. He'd be lucky if he made it five minutes. Plucking her clit, he backed away. Her flesh parted, making way, enfolding him even as he withdrew. When only the head remained within her, he plunged back inside. His balls slapped her pussy, sending Sadie onto her toes.

"Hold on," he warned, ready to unleash his beast.

She didn't turn away, keeping her eyes on him as he moved. Her still-wet hair clung to her back and shoulders, a few pieces sticking to the side of her face. With each thrust he rubbed her clit, applying just enough pressure. He could scent her arousal and knew she was close. He wanted to feel her ass clamping down on him and know she was swept into a climax as he succumbed to the pleasure only she could give him.

There'll never be another.

No other woman will ever compare.

He watched her mouth, studying her fangs. Either she'd gotten enough from him or she was gaining more control. She seemed to be attuned to the sex more than her need for blood. Or maybe it was because each time they'd been intimate they'd been rushed. He wanted to find out everything about her. After he faced the pack, he intended to spend eternity figuring out the mystery that was Sadie Dumus.

"There it is." He gritted his teeth and tried not to think about how good she felt. "There you go."

She whimpered, rocking back against him. He rotated the tips of his fingers over her clit, moving faster and faster. Her blue eyes brightened, turning nearly white. He pumped harder into her, aware she was right on the brink. Just a little bit more and she'd fly. He wound her up, drawing her tighter.

Right there, baby. Let go.

With a strangled cry she came, her ass squeezing him tight. He let himself go, releasing a roar of relief and triumph. His seed jetted into her ass, his balls emptying wave after wave of semen. He hammered into her, unable to stop. His attention swept to her mark, the wolf like a snake beneath his flesh. It slithered inside him, howling its own shout of possession. The animal would kill anyone who threatened its bond with its mate, regardless of the penalty.

"Trey," Sadie moaned, going soft.

He stopped the motions against her clit, slowed down and wrapped his arm around her. She rested her weight against him, bowing her head as she took deep breaths. He kept moving, not wanting the connection to sever. He'd finally found his place. After all his trials and tribulations he'd found home. His cock softened and he reluctantly pulled away. The head popped free, leaving her open and vulnerable.

"You okay?" he asked, fighting for breath of his own.

She nodded and lifted her torso so she wasn't bent at the waist. He reached above them to return the streams of water to their bodies. Her sigh was one of relief and satisfaction. A smile spread across his face, happiness radiating over him like the rays of the sun.

This was as good as life could get. Here, with her.

"Just rest." He ran his hand down the length of her back, fingers drifting over the delicate arch of her spine. He rested his thumbs in the dimples in her lower back and made a mental note to touch them next time he fucked her like this. "I'm going to clean you up."

Another surprise—she didn't protest or try to deny him. In fact when he retrieved the washcloth she parted her thighs. He cleaned away his semen, lovingly caressing her thigh and lower back as he did. Knowing her ass was sensitive, he made sure to be tender, washing the area carefully. He made sure she was cared for before he cleaned himself, swiping at his cock.

Tossing the cloth aside, he returned to her.

She pivoted from the wall and faced him, a curious and shy expression on her face. He wasn't sure what put it there but he liked it. He wanted her to feel comfortable around him, even when she was exposed and uncertain. She needed to know she didn't always have to be ferocious or deadly. Not with him. When they were alone she was always free and safe to let her guard down.

An instinct he was born with told him to hold her. She needed it as much as he did.

He opened his arms and she stepped into them. They swayed in the shower, cocooned by the hot steam. He didn't want to pull the curtain aside and face the world but they couldn't hide forever. Emotions tugged at his heart, telling him he needed to share how he felt.

This had to be what people had told him about.

This has to be how Emory and Diskant felt about their mates.

He'd never been in love before but he couldn't imagine anything that was more intense.

"You don't have to say it," she whispered, her lips drifting over his neck, repeating his earlier words. "I already know."

He held his breath when her tongue danced over his skin, anticipating her bite. His cock remained soft but he knew he'd come the instant she bit him. He felt drained from what she'd taken earlier but he didn't have it in him to tell her no. With a soft kiss to his pulse, she drew away. His confusion must have shown because she immediately rested a hand on his chest, her palm directly over his heart.

"Next time." Tilting her head to peer up at him, she said, "You need to be strong for what's coming."

Just like that, everything came rushing back.

His growl came naturally. "I know I said you'd have to fight for me but I'm not sure that's best. We have a little time left. We can think of something else."

"Trey." This close, he could see how full and dark her lashes were. "I'd tell you if I didn't think I could handle myself. I'm not worried for me. I'm worried for you."

"Don't be." The last thing she needed to worry about was him. "Worst case scenario? They'll make me leave. Everything considered it might not be a bad thing. We wouldn't be tied down. We could go wherever we want."

"And you'd be miserable." Her fingers whispered over his chest. "I know you need them. They're all you've ever known. And that's understandable. It's who you are. It's what's in your blood. I'll do my best to prove myself. If Diskant thinks we can do it—if you believe you can do it— then we will."

"I don't deserve you." The words came right out, uncensored.

"I didn't think you did either but I'm starting to warm up to the idea." She shook her head when he tried to respond. "No more words. Let's just be for a while."

She lifted to the tips of her toes and he bent his head. Their lips met, soft and sweet. He cradled her to him and she slid her hands around his neck. Once again she was right. Nothing had ever been better. Their mating was like a key sliding into a lock. Doors opened, the world changed. Everything faded away but the woman in his arms, her skin warm and slippery from the water. Her mouth opened and he swept his tongue over her lower lip, asking for more.

"I'll give you more, don't worry," she whispered in his mind. *"Once we settle accounts we'll have all the time in the world."*

He couldn't prevent the fears that raced through his head. If something happened to her he wouldn't be able to survive the loss. If she was aware of what he was thinking she didn't let on, deepening the kiss.

And that was a good thing.

He didn't want her to see him trying to imagine a world without her in it.

Chapter Thirteen

Diskant Black had seen a lot of serious shit in his life, from battles to blood feuds. As an Omega—with the ability to sense other beasts and control most shifters—not much surprised him. Then his mate had come along, flipped him on his head and pretty much caused the world to start spinning in the opposite fucking direction. Like dominos, things had tumbled and fallen one by one. He'd thought he'd finally gotten things worked out when Sadie'd showed up with her friend in tow.

Trey and Nathan. Mated to fucking vampires.

He raked his fingers through his hair, glaring at the phone.

Craig Newlander had agreed to help, but as always the bastard was asking questions. It was the truce Diskant had made with the head of the Villati—a group of humans who researched and chronicled information on all things supernatural. Each and every time he'd had to reach out to Craig, Diskant's skin had crawled. He didn't like the man, not one fucking bit.

Heaviness weighed on his shoulders.

Nathan would want to know what was going on, and he'd given his word to give the male a say in things. Diskant wasn't sure how Nathan would take the news. In a few hours he'd have to depart with Leigh. Craig had played phone tag with the enclave but eventually the fucker had come through. The enclave said they could protect Leigh. Craig even indicated they were curious about the woman when they'd learned of her circumstances. Of course Diskant had kept her ability a secret, saying only that she'd been changed against her will and needed a safe place from others like her.

His eyes closed, the images that Sadie'd shown him flashing through his head.

Fear. Horror. Devastation. Loss.

Leigh had suffered in ways he didn't want to ponder too heavily. He only wished he could convey it to Nathan in a way that wouldn't destroy the man. The Beta was unstable enough. Much more and he'd lose control over his wolf. If and when that happened, Nathan would likely destroy any chance he had with his female.

Opening his lids, Diskant reclined in his chair.

The office usually calmed him. It was a quiet place where he could think things through. Now the space seemed almost constrictive, the walls closing in on him while he waited for the pack to arrive. He had no idea how they'd react to Sadie. After what had happened with Mary they'd probably get the fuck out of town. Without the numbers he needed to form a proper guard, he couldn't give his mate or child safety.

That didn't work for him. At all.

Take Pinkie to Alaska. Wish everyone your best and get the fuck out.

"Nothing's going to happen to me, you know."

He turned toward his female's voice, smiling when he saw her form in the doorway. She still managed to get under his skin. Rounding and pregnant with his child, she was even more radiant. He blonde hair had grown slightly, the pink strands a lighter shade since she'd stopped worrying about the color as often. Her enormous midnight-blue eyes took him in, seeing everything.

"Come here." He spun the chair around and sat up, making room for her on his lap. "Let me hold you, baby."

"If anyone gets too riled, I'll calm them down," she told him, resting her weight against his chest, tucking her head to her chin. "The world is changing. The pack's going to have to accept that. In order to survive you have to adapt."

Ava meant well. Due to the fact she raided his mind whenever she felt like it she knew everything about the pack. But she hadn't been born a shifter. She might see the pack and be a part of them but in a way she'd never fully understand them.

"That'll be easier said than done. There's a chance they're going to leave, Pinkie. If they do you're going to have to accept we can't stay here. It's not safe. We'll have to go."

"I don't want to move to Alaska," she grumbled and he felt the anger stirring inside her. "I like it here. This is home."

"You can finally meet my family." Optimism was a right good thing, especially if it could soothe his female's violate temper. "They can't wait to see you."

"If they want to see me they can come here," she countered. Even cuddled up in an innocent-looking ball the woman was all fire. "I didn't threaten a woman today only to back down when the fire gets hot."

He caught the catch in her voice. She was still upset.

Goddamn it.

He held her close, trying to alleviate her guilt. Although Ava was a formidable woman, she wasn't without compassion. She'd felt horrible about what she'd done to Leigh. When she'd faced the woman she'd pretended to be calm. Diskant knew she hadn't been. He'd sensed how upset she was the instant she left the bedroom, rushing from Leigh and Sadie. He'd reacted, going in search of her. When he'd found her in the kitchen she'd been shaking like a leaf and wringing her hands.

"You probably saved her life." He'd already told her that but it bore repeating. "She couldn't have left here alone. She wouldn't have made it very far." Skimming his fingers over her arm, he consoled, "And then there's Nathan. Imagine what it would have done to him if his mate had vanished. At least now they have a chance."

"Maybe you're right." His gaze went to her hand. She stroked her growing belly, talking quietly. "I just wish I didn't have to do it. You know, I thought carrying this baby would be the hardest thing I'd have to do this year." She snorted, shaking her blonde head. "I guess I was wrong."

"Ava mine," he whispered, resting his hand over hers. Taking her fury was one thing. He couldn't stand her sadness. "Don't make me bend your sexy little ass over this desk and take off my belt. I don't like it when you throw pity parties."

"As I recall, you were throwing the party. Not me. I was an unexpected guest."

Minx.

Lifting his hand from her stomach, he cupped her face. He drew her chin upward until their eyes locked. She was so tiny—so fucking fragile. He studied her, his gaze drinking her in. She was the most beautiful creature he'd ever seen.

And she was his.

He knew he'd been given a gift beyond measure. That's what made their current predicament so goddamn shitty. He couldn't let her go to Alaska without him but he didn't want her to stay either.

Those expressive blue eyes flashed in a silent warning. "I'm not going anywhere."

There she went, reading his mind again.

"Will you never do what you're told?" he asked her telepathically, without realizing he'd done so. By now it was second nature. *"Do you always have to be so damn obstinate?"*

"Obstinate my ass." Despite the rebuke her voice tendered, her brows unfurling. "You know how I am. You might as well give up the idea of keeping me barefoot and pregnant."

A cough drew Diskant and Ava's attention to the door.

Nathan stood just inside the frame, studying them. Ava sat a little straighter, allowing Diskant to assist her. A pang of remorse slithered through Diskant, working its way through his gut. Seeing them together—close and intimate—had to break something inside Nathan. It wasn't fair but when it came to mating, things rarely were.

"Come in." Diskant motioned to the chair situated on the other side of the desk.

Nathan's eyes darted to Ava. Hatred tainted the Beta's glare.

Diskant had to tamp down his inclination to put the man in his place, reminding himself that Nathan had been through hell. In any other situation he'd have taken anyone who showed Ava disrespect to the ground and offered their balls to her on a stick.

"*Easy, big boy,*" Ava thought to him, patting his arm. "*I'm not offended.*"

"You'll have to leave with Cade tonight," Diskant informed Nathan as the Beta took a seat. "But instead of heading to North Carolina you'll be meeting someone in Virginia." With a little shift, Diskant managed to ease his arm from Ava and retrieve a piece of paper. He tossed it toward Nathan and said, "That's the number for your contact. Don't call it until you're well out of town. We don't need to take a chance anyone will be able to track you."

Nathan reached for the paper. "Do we leave before or after the pack arrives?"

"Actually, I need you to get everything together and go as soon as possible." As soon as the sun set the pack would gather. It was best if Leigh had gone by then as an added precaution. The wolves might be eager for blood and two vampires would raise their hackles more than one. "You need to tell Cade to suit up."

Nathan's hazel eyes drifted to Ava again, only this time they were pained. "Tell me. I know you can hear her thoughts. What's going on in her head? I need to know what to do."

"Let Cade take the lead," Ava answered softly, the sympathy in her voice melting Diskant's heart. "He's human and she'll gravitate toward that. She needs time to move on with her life. She's been through a lot but she's stronger than she thinks. Give her space and she'll come to you."

"What about the human she mentioned?" There was misery in Nathan's question, as well as a desperate need to hear something positive. "She loves him."

"She does, but that doesn't change anything. He's human. She's not. She's accepted she can't go back. She just has to find a way to move forward."

Diskant's wolf reached out to the Beta, attempting to ease the man's beast. At first Nathan fought it. Then he relaxed. The surrender bothered Diskant more than he wanted to admit. Like this, Nathan wasn't much good to anyone. He was already looking for ways to ease his anguish. Not good when a person relied on the animal inside of them for protection, needing survival instincts to stay alive.

"Give him time." Ava's thought penetrated his mind. *"He thought Leigh would come back and they'd finish what they'd started. He needs time to sort through everything. He's still in shock."*

"I'll tell Cade." Nathan looked and seemed calmer as he rose from his seat. "What do you want us to drive?"

"Take the van out back," Diskant replied, opening one of the drawers on the desk. He found what he was looking for and tossed the keys over. "It'll draw less attention."

Nathan left without another word but Diskant knew the male's thoughts. Ava had entered the man's mind, taking the information she wanted. She relayed everything to Diskant, letting him ease into Nathan's head as well. The Beta was upset and terrified he'd fuck things up but with Diskant's assistance he'd finally put a handle on things.

"The issue's going to be Cade," Ava whispered, speaking softly so no one else would hear. She did that sometimes, talking aloud when she didn't have to. Diskant figured it stemmed from years of doing so. "He's got a lot going on in that head of his."

"Like the woman you told me about?" From what Ava had said she'd told him the human member of the pack thought about a female from time to time. "What was her name again?"

"Destiny," Ava responded absentmindedly.

He tried to relax but it wasn't possible.

The woman who'd snared Cade's attention wasn't just a woman.

She was a fucking conjurer.

Diskant had asked Cade to accompany the witch to New Orleans as a favor to Craig Newlander. She'd had guards but needed extra help to travel to the enclave that wanted to protect her. Considering most supernatural creatures wanted her dead, only human protection would do. That was why Diskant had sent Cade — the king of all assholes — to do the job. He'd never thought anything more would come of it.

Add another fucking problem to the list.

Having two vampires in the pack would be tough but it was possible. None of them would accept a conjurer. If vampires were considered dangerous then conjurers — with the ability to manipulate so many different things — were a fucking catastrophe.

"You won't have to worry about that for a while." Ava's energy washed over him, her mind warm as she dove into his head, pulling him away from darkness. "As soon as you give Caden the information he needs he's going to go. I'm not sure if he'll ever be back. Even he doesn't know for certain. He's confused and can't focus on the future."

"I guess we'll deal with it when we have to." God knew he wasn't up for anything else. They had enough shit to clean up. Again Diskant remembered how fortunate he was to have Ava as a mate. She brought so much to the pack. They had no idea how lucky they were. "Is there anything else I need to know?"

"There is one thing." She turned in his lap so she could see him. Placing his hand on her stomach, she gazed into his eyes. Love shone in the shimmering blue orbs—love directed right at him. "I heard the baby today."

He stopped breathing, becoming completely still.

The world suddenly seemed too big and dangerous.

Ava had been hoping this might happen. She'd started eavesdropping on pregnant women as soon she found out she was expecting. After the first trimester—and especially into the second—she'd found she could detect an unborn baby's thoughts. A fetus's impressions were muddled and unclear, more like feelings than words. But she'd found them. She'd hoped like hell she could do the same with the child growing under her heart but she hadn't been certain.

Forcing his shoulders to relax, he asked anxiously, "What did you hear?"

"It wasn't so much what I heard, it's what I felt."

He waited, his heart thudding in his chest.

What had she felt? Was something wrong?

"Nothing's wrong. At least not in the way you think." She leaned close, feathering her lips over his. Then—just when he thought he'd have to strangle the rest from her—she said, "It's a girl."

Chapter Fourteen

Shifters were here, moving all around the house.

Sadie inspected each thought, trying to lock on to the minds of the pack. It wasn't easy. She'd been instructed to remain inside. Diskant wanted to speak to everyone first, addressing the issue of Nathan's departure and Zach's new position as Beta of the pack.

Zach. Now that one was a pisser.

She'd sensed the male's arrival an hour earlier. When she'd eavesdropped on his conversation with Diskant she'd been shocked to discover he didn't really give a shit that Trey had mated a vampire. The poor man had actually felt jealous of his Alpha. He longed for the mate he'd lost—Katie. Sadie's heart belonged to him in that moment. Trey had told her how Zach's female had died but she'd felt Zach's pain when he pictured Katie's face, seeing the brightness of the fallen woman's smile.

The visual brought her a strange amount of strength.

That woman had died because her pack hadn't seen the Shepherds coming. With Sadie around they could detect the intentions of strangers. True she might not have been able to prevent what had happened but there was a chance she might've changed things. If they accepted her, she'd do everything she could to keep them safe. Innocent people wouldn't die.

Hopefully they'll listen. If I bust my ass I might be able to convince them.

She found herself reaching out with her mind, searching for Trey. He'd accompanied Diskant outside. The men knew the pack would sense their tension and thought it best to offer a united front. She found that Trey, in turn, was thinking about her. He tried to keep his attention on the pack and they hadn't noticed — to his knowledge — his lapses. But he ached for her. Knowing she was just inside but out of sight drove him crazy.

The memory of him in the shower — about to tell her he loved her — felt like coming home. She almost let him do it but she wanted the declaration to be sincere. She hadn't said the words herself and she wouldn't until it was time. The same applied to him. Besides, the words didn't change anything. Technically it was nothing more than a verbal acknowledgment. She wanted to hear him say it but not before he was ready. Maybe it would happen after they made love, or before he left on some silly errand.

Wasn't that how reality worked?

Loosen up. You're not doing yourself any favors.

Swinging her arms, she tried to steel her nerves and stretch her muscles.

She was grateful she'd stashed a sleeveless shirt at her apartment. The garment gave everyone a bird's-eye view of her neck and let her move freely. There was a good chance she was going to have to fight for her place in the pack. The females didn't intimidate her but she'd have to face anyone who stepped up. It could be more than one fight. She had to be cautious, using her resources only when necessary.

"They're a tough crowd."

Sadie stopped flinging her arms across her chest and looked up. Mary had joined her. She'd thought everyone had gone outside but she'd obviously been wrong. Alone, Sadie finally got a good look at the young woman. And she truly was young. No more than twenty-three or twenty-four years old. Her blonde hair was a shade darker than Ava's and long, reaching past her shoulders.

"Is that why you're not out there?" she asked. Maybe it wasn't a fair question but since Mary had been glued to Emory's side it seemed the most likely cause.

"That's exactly why I'm not out there." Mary sighed and crossed her arms, rubbing her hands over her biceps. "They don't need a reminder that I exist. Believe me."

"But they accepted you."

"In a way." Mary shrugged. "But I'm not like you. I can't earn their respect."

She didn't like how conquered the girl seemed. "And that's important, isn't it?"

"It is for you," she said sharply, as though she caught the glimmer of empathy. "I'm the enemy but they can kill me. You, on the other hand, are a threat. You'd better tread softly and grow eyes in the back of your head."

Then—sliding into Mary's head—Sadie recognized the source of her apathy. It was harsh, bitter and resentful. Mary didn't like Sadie being at the house. She'd been willing to give things a chance but had quickly changed her mind. In Mary's mind the sooner Sadie got the hell away from her home the better.

A vampire was too dangerous.

Especially around pregnant women.

"You think I'm a danger to Ava?" she snapped. The notion really pissed Sadie off. "You think I'd harm a pregnant woman and her fucking child?"

"I don't know who you are or what you'd do. I'm just warning you," Mary said, taking a step closer. "Diskant won't let you slide if you fuck up and neither will anyone else. You haven't shown anyone but Trey that we might gain more than we'll lose by keeping you around."

It was official. Between Ava and Mary the bitch quota in the house had been filled.

"Well since you put it that way," with a practiced motion, Sadie drew her sword from the sheath at her back, "I guess I'll make sure to leave an impression."

"You don't frighten me." Mary didn't flinch when she met Sadie's level stare. "I've seen things you can't possibly imagine. The threat of hell loses its charm if you've actually lived there."

Sadie didn't bother reading Mary—if she wanted to she could see what the woman had experienced—taking her statement as a slice of advice. She didn't really care to see any more horrific things today, not if she had a choice. Watching Leigh being driven away had pretty much put a do-not-fuck-with-me-anymore damper on Sadie's evening. Mary's sudden appearance and harsh warning were sufficient. The woman only wanted to say her piece.

Mary had made her point. She didn't have to say anything else.

Voices rose outside and Mary no longer seemed important.

Sadie spun around, gazing at the doors that led to the back of the property. The pack had met at the barn. There was a decent amount of distance placed between her and them. Yet—from the sounds of it—they weren't very happy.

"I think you're about to make your curtain call." When Sadie looked at Mary she found the woman no longer seemed angry. There was a sliver of remorse in the words. "Good luck."

It's no different than battle, Sadie told herself. *Prepare for what you can't see. Anticipate your enemy's movements and attack before they happen.*

If only it were that simple.

Everything rested on her shoulders. If she messed up everyone would suffer.

Footsteps approached and she froze, anxious to see who'd come to the house. The door opened and Trey's head peered around the edge. His dark hair scattered around his shoulders, the black leather coat he'd put on stretching over the bulk of his muscles. When his eyes settled on her they changed colors, going from gold to amber. The lines around his mouth smoothed, making him appear years younger.

"It's time."

Exhaling through her nose, she returned the sword to its proper place.

This might be the hardest challenge she'd ever faced but she'd never backed down from anyone or anything. There was no way in hell she was starting now when Trey needed her. Sometimes people had to bite and claw their way to the top. She wasn't above fighting dirty if that's what it took to win.

She shook her shoulders loose one last time, clearing her head.

Walking to the man she'd risk everything for, she said, "I'm ready."

Trey couldn't believe his eyes. This was the woman he knew, an Amazon fucking warrior like no other. There was hum surrounding her, the air almost electrified. If she had any concerns about what was about to happen it didn't show. On the surface she looked totally confident and alert. He hoped she didn't play poker because he had a feeling she'd kick his ass.

There was no way to read her.

"Sadie?" He stopped her before she could step outside. He had to make sure she was okay. "Talk to me."

She kissed him quickly, her mouth rough against his. Just as fast she yanked away and looked at him. Again, he couldn't tell what she was thinking.

"This is the way I have to be," she informed him, not cold but brusque as she continued, "If you want me to do this properly you're going to have to accept this is how I am. Until this is done this is the woman you'll see."

"Diskant told them about Nathan. They took that well." He started filling her in on the details, holding the door open so she could step into the dark night. "They took my news well too but we told them to hold their applause until they met you."

"You're not going to tell them about Aldon?" she asked, falling in beside him as he led the way.

"No," he answered, reaching for her hand.

She wrapped her fingers in his but she didn't relax. He felt the tension radiating from her. God help anyone who tried to play a prank on her when she was like this. She'd probably chop their head off and leave them for dead. He tried to consider it a good thing. Like this, no one would get the drop on her. At least she was ready to show the pack who she was, declaring her position in his life.

He punched in the code for the lock and opened the gate that led them toward the barn. Once they were on their way he took her hand again. "Is there anything you need to know before we do this?"

"Do you expect any fights to break out?" She still hadn't lost her edge. If anything she seemed even more focused. "Did you sense any potential opponents?"

"No, but I didn't give them the good news."

Trey knew the moment the pack picked up her scent. They turned one by one, nostrils flaring. His night vision allowed him to see everything clearly. Sadie didn't falter, soldiering forward. It would take a few seconds for them to detect something was off. Once they did...

Growls carried on the wind, merging together in a dangerous chorus.

"I told you to hear me out," Diskant snarled, trying to attract their attention. "Don't react without thinking. There's too much at stake."

"What is she?" a female standing next to the barn demanded.

"She's not a human," a male bellowed.

Trey studied the pack, his gaze darting over their faces.

Some of them knew what Sadie was but they hadn't spoken up. Others had never seen a vampire. Usually shifters and leeches didn't run in the same circles. Aldon had been the only one many of them had ever encountered. Their sense of smell detected something different but their eyes couldn't gauge the threat. Without seeing a vampire's barely noticeable fangs a shifter could never be sure. They might have an idea but not an absolute certainty. He wondered if maybe he could have tried to hide what Sadie was. The pack might have been fooled.

He pushed the notion aside.

Eventually they'd have figured it out and he had nothing to hide.

If this was going to happen, it had to be clear from the start.

"I'm your Alpha's mate," Sadie answered unexpectedly, stopping him several feet from the pack. "I've accepted his mark and the responsibilities that come along with it. I know what's expected of me and I'm equal to the task. If any of you want to challenge me for the position feel free."

"I want to know what she is, not who she is." Another female stepped forward, addressing Trey. "We have a right to know."

"If you'd be so kind as to look at me," Diskant's low growl silenced the crowd, "I'll be happy to answer any questions."

The pack didn't like it. Distrust and edginess was written all over them.

They did as they were instructed, facing the Omega. Trey studied Diskant, noting how angry the male had become. As the leader of the shifters of New York, Diskant wasn't accustomed to people questioning his authority. Usually if any of the pack reacted this way—especially since Diskant was a born werewolf and had been raised with many of them—he'd stomp serious ass and ask important questions later.

"I'd like to remind you that I have as much to lose as any of you. My mate is expecting. I'd never risk her or the life of our child. This issue isn't the most pressing danger we have to face. In case you've forgotten the Shepherds haven't fled. They've only slithered away to lick their wounds. They'll come back and when they do we have to be ready. We don't have time to fight amongst ourselves."

"If we don't have time to fight," a familiar voice spat, "tell us what she is."

Sadie's fingers tightened around Trey's. He wondered what had broken through what appeared to be an impenetrable shield around his female. His mate's gaze was riveted on the member of his pack who'd spoken, a woman who'd tried to weasel her way into Trey's bed on more than one occasion. Brandi was backed by her closest friends, her bestie Andrea glued to her side.

That fucking bitch.

Trey was certain Sadie hadn't meant for him to hear the thought. Her mental shields had to be slipping and he was growing attuned to what she was thinking. Or perhaps their connection was growing stronger. Either way he was able to feel her outrage and his wolf rose in response. It felt Sadie's distress and wanted to alleviate it.

No, damn it.

They'd think she'd made him her familiar if he didn't get a grip. Nothing in this world would convince them to accept her into the pack. The wolves would turn on them and kill them or run them off the property. If things got out of hand now a scuffle would ensue for sure.

"She's the woman who's going to help us protect the pack," Ava called out.

Before she could keep going Andrea added her two cents. "She's not a woman. She's something else. She's definitely not human. She reeks of something."

"It's called death." Sadie let Trey go and walked toward the group. "I've been called a harbinger before."

"Don't." He thought to her. He didn't want to see her trampled by the pack.

"I've got this." Her response was firm, her determination unshakable.

He thought she'd go for her sword but she didn't. Instead his female faced the werewolves in front of her head-on with her weapons put away.

"If you have a problem with the position I'm about to take," Sadie repeated, coming to stop a couple of feet from the women, "you're welcome to challenge me for it."

"I suppose that's easy to say." Brandi waved at Sadie's back. "Since you're armed."

"This?" Sadie slid the strap from her shoulder and glanced down at her sword. With a shrug she cast the weapon to the ground. "I don't need that. Not to take care of you."

The prickly hum of energy around everyone shifted, tension quickly suffusing the air. Everyone in the pack reveled in the possibility of a fight, their animals practically begging them for it. While they were partially human, they were also partially beast.

Brandi sized Sadie up before she started removing her jacket.

This wasn't how it was supposed to go.

"I have to show them what I can do. You'll never get through to them otherwise," Sadie thought to him. *"And you'll never be my familiar. I'd never perform the ritual to make it happen. But I don't have time to explain that and neither do you. Don't you dare move. Stay right where you are and watch."*

Before he could argue, Brandi unleashed her claws. He couldn't breathe, his feet weighted by invisible sand. The shifter female went at Sadie, fangs bared. Without pause Sadie met the woman head-on and slammed her fist in the center of Brandi's face.

The fight had started.

There was nothing he could do to stop it.

Chapter Fifteen

Stupid fucking bitch.

Sadie followed her first punch with a second, landing a solid blow to her opponent's flared nostrils. Blood gushed, winding down to Brandi's mouth.

Fantastic. Even better than she'd expected.

Not even two seconds in and she'd taken the lead. She hadn't used her speed yet — and wouldn't — unless she had to. The ignorant thundercunt from hell didn't know who she was messing with. When it came to women — regardless of species — some things remained the same. Even if Diskant could manage to get most of the werewolves in the pack to listen, these bitches would cause a stink.

A constant stream of doubt and negativity could very well turn the tables.

Fuck it all if she let that happen.

She hadn't expected the pack to surround them but they did. The wolves were so close they forced the women closer together. There was nowhere to run and little room to maneuver. She tuned everyone out, watching I'm-too-stupid-to-live Brandi shake off the lovetaps to her nose. Sadie's instincts kicked in, a prickle of awareness sharpening her vision and hearing. She reached out with her mind, listening for what Brandi was going to do next.

There wasn't much logical thought. The woman was all rage.

Sadie paid rapt attention to the woman's wolf, who wanted to spill Sadie's blood. The animal had started breaking free, trying to take control. She wondered if Brandi might actually shift. If she did it would change the game significantly. On two legs Brandi wasn't much of a threat. Standing on four paws she'd be a lethal opponent.

The deranged woman charged and Sadie whipped to the side. Brandi soared past her, barreling toward the people blocking her path. In a second she gained her balance and turned. There wasn't any sense in trying to drain the crazed female. Werewolves were stronger than vampires. In order to end the fight Sadie knew she'd have to engage the bitch and take her down. Using her natural abilities, she could do it easily. But was it the smart thing to do? Would she take one obstacle down only to face another?

Her temples pounded, her hands forming into fists.

It was such a thin red line to walk.

If she revealed her hand too soon the wolves around her might pounce.

"*Do it.*" Trey's order was loud in her head. "*Take her down.*"

She wasn't sure how he'd heard her thoughts and didn't have time to question it. The certainty in the command told her he meant it. He knew the pack better than she did. If he thought it was best to take Brandi down quickly there was a reason. Her entire body pulsed with energy, her magic rising. She didn't try to push it away, allowing the power to suffuse her.

Come at me again. She lifted her hands, taunting her prey. *Bring it.*

Brandi rushed her again, claws bared, fangs on display. Sadie stood still, knowing she had to make her move decisively. Time slowed down, seconds stretching out like hours. Sadie could see everything—the wind blowing through Brandi's hair, her pupils dilating, her claws growing longer. It only took three enormous steps and Brandi was within Sadie's reach.

Sadie reared back, putting all of her power into her swing.

Her fist made solid contact with Brandi's jaw, the impact enough to break bone.

The female flew back several feet and staggered. Sadie watched as Brandi toppled, landing on her back. Brandi didn't move, knocked flat on her ass and down for the count. Blood seeped from her nose and mouth, dribbling down the side of her face into her hair. Everyone standing around them gasped and veered back. Sadie kept her guard up, sensing there might be more women who wanted to see if they could do better.

"Is there anyone else?" she screamed, limbs shaking from the adrenaline coursing through her. "If so say it now!"

Murmurs came from the crowd and she felt the heaviness of their stares. She picked out random thoughts, darting from one mind to the next. Some were shocked. Others were impressed. A majority thought she was strong enough to be an Alpha's mate but still wanted to know what in the hell she was.

The group parted at her back but she didn't move. She knew it was Trey approaching her. Their connection had become so strong she could literally feel his fury. She might have won but he did not like seeing her fighting. The entire time he'd been terrified. He wanted her safe and felt it was his job to settle the score when it came to physical matters.

"You heard her," Trey announced and slid an arm around her middle. "The same goes for me. If you want to fight for my spot say so."

Of course it wasn't going to be that easy.

None of the wolves trusted her, even though she'd faced a challenger and came out on top. Several of the males sized Trey up but didn't speak, weighing the pros and cons of taking the man on. Sadie trembled, telling herself she'd have to find a way not to interfere if such a thing happened. If she tried to fight Trey's battles he'd never be respected as an Alpha.

This is such a load of crap.

"My mate has given up everything to be here," Trey informed the pack. "She has turned her back on everything she knows. You should be asking her why she thinks she's capable of doing the job and judge her on her merits, not by what she is."

But the question remained and it always would.

No matter what anyone said the pack demanded an answer.

She decided to show them. In a flash she phased from Trey to Diskant and Ava. It took the pack several seconds to find her. Once they did, they knew. Anyone who'd heard about her kind was aware of their strange method of travel. Ava moved next to her, so close their arms were inches apart. Diskant had already taken a couple of steps from the barn so that he stood slightly in front of them.

"A vampire?" someone asked, horror written all over his face.

"Yes, a vampire," Diskant confirmed, nodding. "One who has—as your Alpha told you—risked everything to come here."

"She can control him!" a woman shrieked.

"She could kill us all!" another woman cried out.

"I won't," Sadie replied, calling out, "I'd never do such a thing."

"Yes you would," someone screamed. "It's your nature."

"I've reached a bargain with your Alpha," Diskant shouted, keeping his shoulders back, arms resting at his sides. "If any such thing happens I will hunt them down and destroy them. They can run but they'll never hide. I'll spread the word to every single pack until they've been located and killed."

Sadie's stomach twisted. Thinking of the horde coming after her wasn't pleasant at all. But the possibility of something happening to Trey—that they would hunt him and put him down like a dog—constricted her chest. Breathing wasn't easy. She had to fight to inhale, forcing herself to remain composed.

Her gaze drifted to Trey and she wanted him to get away from the wolves and come to her side. Fear was like a spider creeping over her skin. She had to keep her hands—limp and unthreatening—at her sides instead of rubbing away the sensation.

"I don't know if it's a good idea to stay here anymore." A big male stepped forward, addressing the group. "With everything that's happened maybe it would be best for everyone to disband and find homes with other packs."

"I agree." Another equally large man backed the speaker up. "We've already lost too much. You can't ask us to keep trusting you when you bring Shepherds and vampires into the mix. There's only so much we'll accept."

No one wanted to challenge Trey. They knew better.

"That's your choice but I'd ask you to think about the dangers you'll face by leaving." Diskant's unwavering control impressed Sadie. Aside from annoyance with the pack he'd managed to keep weak emotion out of the conversation. "Shepherds just hit our city but they've been attacking others for years. You won't be able to avoid them as well in rural areas. They'll hunt you down. Here they're not as free to move around unnoticed."

"I think I'll take my chances." Andrea growled, scowling at Sadie. The angry werewolf looked at the people around her. "How can any of you even consider staying? You have a human mated to our Omega, a Shepherd mated to the Alpha's brother, and now our Alpha has taken a vampire as his mate. Think about how much this could cost all of us. Is it worth the risk to your families?"

"She's right," Brandi snarled and joined her friend. Blood coated her nose and chin. "This is fucked. I'm packing my bags. To hell with this shit."

A ripple of agreement soon followed, the wolves talking among themselves.

The alarm Sadie had for Trey changed, turning into panic for Ava, Diskant, Mary and Emory. With everyone gone they'd have to leave as well. That put them in a precarious position. She wasn't sure what to do or say. Fighting hadn't gotten the job done. Talking hadn't worked either. Diskant had given the pack a generous promise in order to keep Trey around but none of the wolves were having it.

Sadie tried to do a headcount.

There were maybe fifty people in the group. Not all of the pack members had been able to make it, as they were guarding areas in the city. If even a quarter of the wolves decided to leave there was a good chance the pack would scatter and go somewhere else.

Think of something fast. It can't end like this.

She tried to work out different scenarios, trying to find a potential fix. Then an unexpected scream echoed from the house, conveying raw terror. Everyone's heads turned, their eyes focused on the source of the sound.

Mary.

Sadie knew none of them could make it to the woman as fast as she could. She phased again, traveling to her weapon. She grasped her sword and phased to the living room of Diskant's residence. As soon as she landed she ripped the blade from its casing.

It was a smart decision.

Aldon stood across from Mary, who cowered in the corner of the room. Mary had a hand covering one side of her face.

The bastard fucking hit her.

Aldon spun, facing Sadie. "Where's your friend? Take me to her."

"The hell I will. I have to say," Sadie whispered, griping the hilt of her weapon, unadulterated vehemence thundering in her veins. "You are one stupid son of a bitch."

She caught his movement before he pounced.

Lifting her blade, she lashed out at her enemy.

"Mary!" Emory roared and rushed toward the house.

"Stay here," Trey ordered the pack, following his brother.

The wolf had risen instinctively, the harsh feel of fur brushing under his skin an indication he'd better move fast. If he didn't the animal would take over. He heard Diskant talking over the chaotic group, his voice rising over theirs as they shouted in confusion and uncertainty. Emory didn't bother with the gate, barreling into it with his shoulder. The metal bent and parted, making way.

Another scream—this time from behind him—drew Trey short.

He whipped around, shocked to see Aldon appear right next to Ava and Diskant. Then Sadie was there, going at the dangerous leech with all she was worth.

Fuck.

He reversed course, rushing toward the battle. Diskant swiped Ava up and moved her away while the pack backed the hell up. The growls the pack made were angry but weak. They didn't have faith in those who'd vowed to protect them. Without that safeguard none of them knew what to do. So they stood back, watching Sadie and Aldon exchange blows.

Trey's feet carried him over the distance, the world blurring by. He was almost in reach of Sadie, nearly able to touch her. Lashing out with a clawed hand, he aimed at the back of Aldon's head. As he swung the male vanished. Trey pulled back, barely missing Sadie. Her ice blue eyes darted over the crowd and her nostrils flared. Then she was gone.

Damn it.

Members of the pack, unable to do anything else, crouched into defensive positions. They were under attack but didn't understand their opponent.

Aldon reappeared near one of gate posts. He yanked the length of metal from the ground and sent it whipping toward the barn. Most of the men and women in the way managed to lower themselves to the ground but a couple of them were nailed with the beam. They went down and didn't get back up.

Sadie emerged behind Aldon. Dropping the sword, she went at the vampire with her fists. She hit him in the side and followed it up with a devastating knock to the back of his head. He pivoted, snarling at her. Trey's heart sank to his stomach, terror and fear swirling together. He couldn't lose her now. Not after he'd finally faced his darkest fears. Not when they finally had a chance for some kind of future together.

"Damn you," Aldon spat, throwing up his hand. "You'll learn."

An invisible force lifted Sadie into the air. She flew back several feet and hit the wooden fencing. The wood broke under her weight, cracking in two as she crashed to the ground. Trey scented her blood, knew that she had been hurt. The beast roared in his skull, his hackles rising. He would rip the motherfucker apart.

"I'll kill you!" Trey snarled, leaping at the male.

He let the wolf rise, welcoming its presence. His claws extended, fangs dropping in his mouth. He tackled the vampire, forcing Aldon to the grassy earth. The pent-up aggression Trey'd carried for so long finally had an outlet. He sent his fist into Aldon's side over and over again. An ear-splitting crack informed Trey he'd broken several of the vampire's ribs. A spattering of fur erupted from his skin, the wolf trying to force him to shift. He managed to keep his human form, using the animal's strength.

His breath caught when something changed, a force like no other slamming into him. There was no feeling like it—raw power and strength. He wanted to bray in relief, finally given the one thing he needed. The pack had finally pulled together, offering him their solidarity. Their combined energy suffused him, making him stronger and faster. Each time Trey's knuckles slammed into Aldon's side he felt the bones give. Just a little bit more and he'd puncture the fucker's lung.

A blast of fire seemed to come from the vampire beneath him.

Trey tried to hold on but something dislodged him. He skittered to the side, not far away but unable to strike the man. Aldon didn't rise, phasing from the ground. Trey's head moved, his eyes taking in the area. At any given second the asshole would materialize and go for someone else.

"She's not here," Ava yelled, her high-pitched wail tinted by fear. "She left hours ago. The woman you want is gone."

"Who's gone?" a pack member growled, his gaze darting wildly into open space.

"Are you sure about that?" Aldon asked, the inquiry full of menace.

Trey froze, the wind knocked out of him.

Aldon stood behind Ava, his hand wrapped around her neck.

"Choose your answer carefully," Aldon seethed.

"Fucker!" Sadie thundered, jumping on Aldon's back.

Trey's stomach bottomed out. He hadn't seen his mate appear.

Ava ducked—getting free as Sadie went at Aldon's eyes with her fingers—and made a mad dash for Diskant. Trey ran to his mate, his feet pounding against the soft ground. Each of his breaths was short and stinted. He'd never tried to direct the pack's power to someone else but found himself sending all his energy to his Sadie. He willed everything he was to her, sending the pack's influence to his female. She wrapped her legs around Aldon's waist, holding on even as the male tried to shake her off.

"I spared your life and this is how you repay me?" he snarled, fangs shining and lips drawn back. His blond hair mixed with Sadie's, one shade slightly lighter than the other. "No more. It's time you were introduced to humility."

They vanished, evaporating before the pack.

Trey forced his weight back, coming to a stop. He used his nose, trying to find Sadie's scent. Alarm sent the wolf into a mad frenzy. He tried to keep it back, flexing his muscles. The animal didn't want to listen, ripping at his insides.

He heard Diskant snarl and glanced up.

Aldon stood across the field with Sadie in his grasp.

Trey's chest tightened, a phantom hand squeezing his heart. He watched — horrified — as Aldon threw his mate from him and Sadie soared through the air. She was headed toward the barn, her body moving too fast to catch. The momentum would kill a person. He wasn't sure that she'd survive the impact. Only a few feet from the barn, she disappeared.

"Sadie!" he screamed, fisting his hands. His claws pierced his skin, causing blood to flow. He'd never run faster, going for the barn. Praying he'd find her. "Sadie!"

Then she was there, standing directly in front of him.

He almost sagged, thankful she was still alive.

Until he saw the deep, jagged wounds running from her neck to her stomach.

Blood covered her shirt, seeping down her torso. It looked like four claws had been pierced her skin and torn the flesh all the way to her bones. She tried to lift her arms, her eyes dulled by pain. Her legs buckled and she fell, sinking to her knees. She tried to talk, lips moving though she made no sound. Bringing a hand to her chest, she tried to stem the bleeding.

Oh God. No.

He made it to her, catching her before she landed on her face.

"Is he gone?" a pack member questioned, followed by someone else asking, "What was that?" Another voice chimed in, "Why would a vampire attack one of its own?"

Confusion turned into concern.

"What's wrong with her?" someone yelled. "Is she all right?"

Irony. How he hated it.

They'd wanted to toss her aside, leave her on her ass and forget all about her. Yet she'd tried to protect them anyway, putting herself between them and danger.

His inhale was ragged, his fingers trembling.

If she hadn't have gotten Aldon away from Ava the pack would have lost Diskant. The Omega wouldn't continue living without the tiny woman. He'd rather die. Where would that leave them?

Alone and searching for a place to call home.

"Back off," Zach ordered coolly. "Give them space."

The Beta's influence spread over the pack, reaching out to their beasts. He wasn't as powerful as Nathan but he had definite potential. Even Trey felt the power of Zach's wolf, the way it stretched itself to soothe the turmoil of the pack. It gave them a center of gravity, replacing chaos with order.

What had started as loathing had somehow turned to worry.

The pack's anxiety slammed into Trey and he experienced their regret. Although they weren't sure about Sadie they'd seen what she'd done. They created a circle around the fallen woman and their Alpha, forming a protective barrier around them. Trey wanted to be angry, to tell them all to go to hell. But he didn't. He had to take care of Sadie. She needed blood and she needed it now.

"What did he do?" Ava shouldered her way through the wolves, Diskant on her heels. She was ruffled—her blonde hair messy and her face splotched with dirt—but unhurt. "How bad is it?"

"It's not good." His voice shook but he didn't give a shit about that. Trey tried to be careful when he hoisted Sadie into his arms. "I need to get her inside."

"All of you," Diskant said, his tone dark, "stay out here and keep watch. If you want to leave now's your chance. But if you chose to split don't bother coming back. I'll escort you out of my city if you ever show your face here again."

Trey marched to the house, trying not to jostle the woman in his embrace. She'd lost so much blood. He felt it coating his arms, staining his skin. He didn't want to look down and see the damage but he had to look at her face. She was so pale, her skin an eerie white. Her eyes were open but he could tell she was close to losing consciousness.

"Don't give up on me."

"*I won't.*" Even her voice—whispering through his thoughts—was weak. Then, with a pain that sliced through him, she thought, "*I'm sorry.*"

Son of a bitch. He wanted to kill something. To destroy the first thing he saw.

After everything she'd done, she thought she'd failed.

"I've got you, darlin'," he whispered, eyes burning as his vision blurred. "I'm never letting you go. Fuck them all."

"I do love you." Her fingers drifted to his forearm, weak and uncoordinated. "I have for a long time."

Forcing back panic, he increased the pace.

She wouldn't have made that confession if she wasn't afraid. With her injuries he didn't blame her. She was surrounded by people who'd turned their backs on her. She had no way of knowing if they'd keep her safe or toss her out.

Her head lolled back and she went limp.

At the very least she wasn't feeling any pain. Once he got her inside he'd pry her mouth open and force his blood down her throat if he had to. His number one priority was getting her well. Then all bets were off. Once he'd healed her properly he was finished.

He'd thought the pack was more important than her.

He'd believed he couldn't live in a world without them.

He'd been wrong.

Chapter Sixteen

ಹ

"Stay and find out what's going on. Use my private number for updates. Keep me informed."

"Yes sir."

Kinsley MacGregor returned the phone to the cradle and rested back in his chair. His spies had seen Aldon attack and wanted to put him on alert. Kinsley wasn't surprised. In fact he'd suspected it would happen. Often he had premonitions about what was to come. A nifty gift when one dealt with creatures and insane humans who wanted to kill him.

He rocked back and forth, trying to compartmentalize his thoughts.

The timing was bad but the pack didn't have to have him in New York.

He knew Sadie was good for the wolves.

His gut told him the pack shifters wouldn't welcome a vampire with open arms but something would transpire that would make them see the light. Apparently Sadie had placed herself in harm's way to save Ava. Very smart. None of the wolves could turn their backs on anyone who'd protected the Omega's mate, especially with the female being pregnant.

She'll carve her niche. That's one problem solved.

As for the other woman—the vampire named Leigh.

He had a strange feeling about that one but he couldn't put his finger on what nagged him. Something was going to happen and it wasn't entirely good. Yet he couldn't pinpoint why he had the feeling something was going to go wrong, nor could he get any kind of mental impulse that forewarned of what might transpire.

Was it Aldon?

He let the question sink in, mulling it over.

No. It wasn't Aldon. There was a threat but it came from somewhere else.

Aldon was a danger to be sure but what was going to take place didn't involve him. Not yet. The scenario was one Kinsley couldn't see. Knowledge existed but remained out of reach.

Perhaps it had to do with some form of magic.

He'd always had issues sensing future events when that element was involved. Since they were taking Leigh to an enclave Kinsley wasn't surprised he didn't have a solid grip on what he was experiencing. Maybe it was even more than that. Perhaps it was Ava's brother and the amulet everyone seemed so keen to get their hands on.

Better wrap things up. You're out of time.

He felt the presence of his butler before the man had a chance to enter the room. Going still, he anticipated his guest. This was the one thing he'd waited for. Something he desired beyond measure. But it wasn't going to come easy.

When it came to matters that involved him, Kinsley's gift never helped.

He'd never been able to gauge his own future.

He'd never seen what was in store for him.

"Master MacGregor?"

Lifting his head, Kinsley looked at George.

The human had served him faithfully for decades, never asking any questions. It was a relief, really. Everyone always wanted him for something. Over the centuries he'd grown accustomed to it. Whenever things got crazy they asked for his help. He was old, having seen a lot of things. He shared his knowledge and gained favors from shifters all over the world. It had been easy, offering his aid. And why not? He'd gained a fortune and notoriety. Wonderful things considering what he was about to face.

It was his time to take a blind leap of faith, to venture into unknown territory.

"Is everything ready?" he asked, even though he knew it would be.

"Yes sir. They've loaded the car. The plane is ready and waiting at the airport."

His eyes flicked up to George's and he gave him a curt nod. "Have the car brought around back. I'll be down shortly."

Tension knotted the back of Kinsley's neck as he watched George leave. He rolled his head, trying to loosen the aching muscles. Visiting Diskant had actually been a welcome distraction. He'd needed time away from his home to put a bit of space between him and his...guest.

She's more than that and you know it.

And there rested the shame of it all.

The first time he'd laid eyes on Persephone Maples he'd known what she was. Like all shifters, he'd felt the animal within shouting its content, telling him he'd finally found the woman meant for him. But she wasn't what he'd expected when he'd pictured his mate.

It wasn't that she lacked beauty.

In her mid-twenties, Persephone still retained the youthfulness that radiated from women. Her hair—a long, lush mahogany—was wavy and thick. And her mismatched eyes—one brown and one blue—were utterly captivating. Unfortunately she'd lived a hard life, experiencing more than she should have in her short years. She'd done a good job of hiding it but he'd eventually seen right through her.

He went back in time, recalling their first encounter.

He'd used his charm to seduce women in the past but it hadn't worked on her. He'd tried thickening his brogue, giving her the look so many women adored. When that didn't help he'd dressed to impress, wearing clothing he thought she'd appreciate. He ditched the business suits, going for jeans and casual shirts. She'd actually laughed at his attempts, giving him the cold shoulder. She'd even poked fun at his muscular form, asking if he'd heard the story about steroids and the male anatomy. He bore her insults, letting them slide off his back. Frustrated that he didn't take a hint and kept returning to her place of employment, she'd made fun of his hair, asking if he was giving Fabio a run for his romance cover model glory.

She taunted him.

She refused him.

But he didn't let her *stop* him.

He bided his time, returning to the antique store she worked at several days a week. She'd asked the owners to make him stop coming to the store but he was a good customer so they refused. She had been polite but aloof after they'd informed her to get over it, answering his questions but remaining unmoved by his charm. He tried everything he could think of to get her to open up to him, if only a little. When he couldn't get answers from the source he'd decided to search for them elsewhere.

With his connections it hadn't taken him long to find out everything about her.

Married at eighteen, she'd had a child—a son—when she turned twenty. She'd moved with her husband from a small town in Alabama. New York had been foreign but exciting. She'd gotten a job at an antique shop, using her years of combing through flea markets to her advantage. Things were going well until destiny had thrown her a cruel curveball. As fate often did, it had taken all of her hopes and dreams away.

Everything she loved. Gone in an instant.

He suffocated his rage, locking it away.

The thought of her with another male infuriated him, as did the fact she'd had a child with someone else. But that anger had died when he learned what had become of her family.

Her husband—a wild and reckless youth with a penchant for heavy drinking—had taken their infant out for a spin to the local supermarket. The moment the moronic human had lost control and veered into the oncoming traffic, slamming headfirst into an eighteen wheeler, he'd snuffed out the one thing Persephone lived for.

The guilt that crept over Kinsley wasn't new. He'd been dealing with it for a little over a week. He hadn't liked having to intervene and interfere with his mate's life but she'd given him no choice. If he'd had his way he'd have given her more time. But she'd forced his hand, her will to live slipping away.

His eyes drifted shut, rage no longer content to remain hidden.

She'd hated it when he prevented her from jumping from the Brooklyn Bridge. She'd lashed out at him, screaming through a river of tears. He'd expected her to be embarrassed. What he hadn't prepared himself for was her misery at being denied the death she longed for. He knew then that he couldn't watch her walk away. If she was given another chance to end her life, she'd take it.

He'd waited too long for her. He wasn't about to let her go.

Over the course of the week he'd tried to talk to her without success. She threw things at him, called him a kidnapper and threatened to turn him over to the police. What she hadn't realized was each day she'd developed the fire she'd lacked. In hating him she'd found something to look forward to. Her consuming loss had turned into a raging fury. Even if it was in destroying the things he'd acquired over the years—she'd already demolished two of his guest bedrooms—she'd found the spark she'd long forgotten.

He laughed quietly, imagining what she'd do when they reached Caledonia. The private island in the Bahamas was secluded and private. She could run all she wanted but she could never escape. There he could finally set her free. She'd be able to roam and explore the beautiful location. Of course he'd watch over her, keeping her safe. Eventually—he hoped—she'd come to him for some kind of companionship. He'd already instructed the staff to stay away from her unless she engaged them in conversation.

The trip would give her what she needed to heal.

Maybe one day she'd find it in her to forgive him.

Or maybe you're being a hopeless romantic with happily mated fantasies.

True, he'd thought about what his mate would be like. What male didn't? He'd assumed she'd be a feline, with lean muscles and curves. A woman who'd meet his passion with a healthy dose of her own lust. He'd never expected that she'd be a human female who was so thin she looked like she'd break with a strong wind. That was the first thing he'd worked on. He'd made sure his cooking staff prepared the finest meals, so he could put weight on her tiny frame. She'd refused to eat for a day or two and then hunger had gotten the better of her.

Thank heavens for that at least.

Knowing he couldn't delay any longer, he rose from his seat. He dreaded taking the trip to her room, braced for what she'd do next. She hadn't accepted any of his visits, telling him to get the hell out or let her go. For that reason he'd kept their upcoming trip under wraps. She'd spook if she knew what he was up to. He couldn't take the risk she'd harm herself.

He retrieved the syringe he'd gotten from the doctor in Diskant's pack and rolled it between his fingers. Doc had been curious about Kinsley's request, asking what he needed a sedative for, but he'd given the medication to him without receiving answers to his queries. Thankfully the male knew Kinsley shouldn't be questioned. The pack needed him too much. In a pinch, he'd always come through.

This is it. No more waiting.

He loathed the shame he felt. Hated what he had to do.

All you're going to do is let her rest. She needs it. When she wakes up she'll be in paradise. You can start anew and let her see the beauty of the world. Give her a reason to greet each day. Take your time and let her rise from the ashes. She'll be beautiful when it happens. And you'll get to witness her rebirth.

Sliding the capped needle into his pocket, he silently prowled from the room. Any woman from the pride would have given anything to share a night in his bed. He could only imagine how receptive they would be if he accepted any of them as a mate. They threw themselves at him, fawning over him. Sometimes he welcomed their advances, finding them amusing. After all he was a male with an enormous sex drive.

But that wasn't going to happen ever again.

He'd found the one meant for him. She'd have to adapt.

Especially when she figured out he wasn't human.

He knew she had an idea about his nature. Most mortals were nervous around shifters, their natural instincts warning them something was off. Persephone was no different. She watched him warily, as though she knew he could pounce at any moment. Despite his attempts to put her at ease, she remained cautious and unrelenting. Once she discovered he could change into an animal he was certain she'd really give him a run for his money.

She'll probably bolt from you screaming and try to swim the length of the ocean to get away.

Leaving his office, he crossed the foyer and started climbing the stairs. He was grateful he moved without sound. Persephone freaked out whenever she knew he was coming. Even if he'd not taken her body, he could easily sense her emotions. She'd been rattled for so long fear and hatred practically oozed from her. In a way her animosity was a relief. He'd rather see her angry with him than heartbroken by what she missed with all her heart.

He reached the top of the stairs and walked to the door at the end of the hall. The guards he'd placed there acknowledged him and moved aside. He stood at the entrance to her door, knowing she was on the other side. The hair on his nape rose, the panther slithering under his skin. Being around one's mate did all kinds of things to a male.

Taking a deep breath, he opened the door.

She sat on the windowsill, gazing outside. Her eyes saw nothing, her brows smooth as she looked into the night. His heart broke at the sight, the wrenching agony like a fist to the chest. Slowly she turned her head, her thick hair falling over her shoulder. The emptiness in her features changed as he expected it to, shifting from vacant to livid.

"You!" she spat, rising to her feet.

She looked around, trying to find something to throw at him. Since she'd done this plenty of times in the past he'd had most of the things she could toss with ease taken from the room.

"Aye," he said softly, observing her. "It's me."

"You can't keep me here." It was an argument they'd had more than once. Her soft, Southern lilt—even when she was furious—was like a symphony to his ears. He could listen to her talk for hours. "Eventually I'll find a way out. When I do you're screwed. You're going to jail. You're going to rot behind bars. This is illegal. You're crazy for thinking you can get away with it. Your face will be splashed all over the news!"

"We're about to leave." He continued speaking quietly, not wanting to upset her further. "I've come to take you downstairs."

"Leave?" Contempt turned to suspicion. "Leave for where?"

"A special place." It was the truth. He'd always loved the island. "Somewhere safe."

"It's not your right," she hissed, her beautiful brown and blue eyes furious. "This is my life." Pounding a fist to her chest, she snarled, "My. Life." She lowered her arm, glaring at him. "You don't have any say in it."

Not your life. Your death. If allowed such a thing.

Never.

"That's where you're wrong, little one." Sliding a hand into his pocket, he carefully removed the plastic shield from the needle and crossed the distance to her. "When it comes to you I have more of a say than you think."

She tried to get away but there was nowhere to go. When he cornered her, she gazed up at him with terror in her mismatched eyes. "I'll scream. I swear I will. I'll bring the house down."

"I won't hurt you, *Mo chride*," he promised, edging nearer to her. "Easy, lass."

"You take it easy!" If she could have vanished into the wall he was certain she would have. "Stay back. Don't come any closer."

He admired her attempt to fight, although she didn't stand any real chance. As a human she'd never match his speed or strength. He pinned her to the wall, preventing her from seeing the syringe. Before she could break into a full-fledged fight he slid the needle into her arm and pushed the plunger.

As she'd warned him earlier, she screamed. "No! You said you wouldn't hurt me!"

"And I will no'. I'll never harm you."

He hated the way her anguish and obvious feelings of betrayal corroded his insides, eating away at him like battery acid. The sedative was strong and he only had to hold her for a couple of minutes before she rocked unsteadily on her feet. For the first time since he'd brought her to his home he was able to sweep her into his arms.

Christ, she felt so right.

Nothing was more perfect.

"Put...me...down." Her words were slurred, almost impossible to make out.

"But I like having you like this. So close and warm," he murmured against the shell of her ear. "You're a sweet little armful. If I could I'd keep you this close all the time."

The panther within loved the nearness, urging him to swipe his tongue along his female's throat. It ached for the taste of her, wanting to lap at her skin. His cock went instantly hard, his fangs dropping of their own accord. She wasn't aroused but he knew the first time he smelled a hint of her cream the beast would want to lick at her slit, discover exactly how sweet she tasted. Thankfully the panther also felt her pain and wanted to take it away. It knew she needed more than it could give her so it took a backseat. As long as he was able, he'd make sure the man and not the animal stayed in charge.

"Sleep for me, wee little creature." With care he swept heavy strands of hair from her face. Like this, with her peaceful and resting in his arms, he never wanted to let her go. A surge of protectiveness and longing spiked through him. He'd attend to her. Give her good memories. Love her beyond measure. "When you wake up you'll find a whole new world waiting for you."

He strode from the room, carrying her with ease. She settled against him, her deep breaths telling him she'd fallen asleep. The guards stood aside but followed him as he carried his female down the stairs. He turned in the foyer and made the trek to the back of the house. The car would be waiting. Soon they'd travel to the airport and be on their way to paradise. It was beautiful at the island. The water was so clear you could see the sand. She could frolic and play or spend her days gazing up at heaven.

Whatever she wanted would be hers.

If it took everything he had, he'd make her happy. No matter how long it took. No matter if she hated him and would never give him her heart and soul. He'd gotten everything in order for the packs and the prides in the area. Diskant was going to have to hold his own for a while. This was his moment and he wasn't letting anything else get in the way.

He'd finally found his female, the most important thing in his world.

God knows he'd done enough for everyone else.

Chapter Seventeen

Finally. Her injuries were healing.

Thank God.

Trey brushed the back of his hand across Sadie's cheek.

At first the horrible gashes in her chest had kept filling and spilling over, covering the sheets in stains of vibrant red. He'd opened his mate's pale lips, slashed his arm and dripped his blood into her mouth. She'd swallowed despite being out for the count. Certain she'd had enough, he'd taken a seat beside her.

Then he'd waited.

Each second had felt like minutes, the minutes in turn like hours. When the bleeding had stopped he'd put her in a button-down shirt Ava had provided, so he could inspect Sadie's chest without shifting her body. She hadn't healed as fast as she should have and it terrified him.

He never wanted to see her like this again.

If he had his way he wouldn't.

"They're asking about her," Diskant said quietly. "We should tell them something."

"How about fuck off," Trey growled, not turning to look at the man. "Do you think that'll do?"

"Trey, please," Ava said, imploring him to listen. "You've gotten their attention. Do this right and we can work things out. They want to understand. Go to them and explain. You wanted to plead your case. Now's your chance."

"They can kiss my ass." Whipping his head around, he narrowed his eyes and growled at Diskant. "And don't even think about using your mind juju shit on me. You can wear me down but you can't change my decision. We're not staying. Fuck it. As soon as she's well we're leaving."

Over the years Trey had been careful with his money. He wasn't the richest man in the world but he had enough saved to find a place Sadie would love—a place they'd call home. Perhaps they'd venture to a distant location where no one would find them. There he'd keep her safe. He didn't need anything else.

At least that's what he told himself.

Grief kept rearing its ugly head. He didn't understand it. The pack had hurt the woman meant for him. The only female he'd ever be given. But knowing he'd soon leave everything behind—no longer be able to turn to other wolves that understood and embraced him, a part of something much larger than himself—created an enormous divide in his soul.

Are you fucking serious? Think about what they've done.

Remember how they treated her.

The wolf tried to make him think logically. No one in the pack had behaved in a manner he wouldn't have. If someone had brought a vampire to him and asked for his blessing on the mating he probably would've turned him or her away.

Right?

He shook his head. He didn't know what he'd have done. Circumstances had changed. His opinion had drastically shifted when it came to mating and vampires. And it all made sense, didn't it? After all he was mated to a vampire. That was enough to make the most arrogant and disagreeable bastard see the light.

Shifting emotions confused him, making him see things both ways.

His growl deepened as he stared Diskant in the eye. "Don't mess with my head."

"I'm not," Diskant snapped in return, eyes going from green to gold. "If you want to go it's not my place to stop you. I can't say I blame you for being pissed. I'd want to rattle a few heads if I were in your shoes. But I won't let you look back on this and blame me for making you leave. If you go it's on your conscience."

"I wouldn't." No way. Diskant had done everything he could to help. "I can't blame you."

"Then you have to understand something." With a step to the side, Diskant placed an arm around Ava's shoulders. She leaned into him, wrapping both arms around his hips. "What I told the pack applies to you as well. Leave this city and you'd better not ever try to come back. If you do I'm not reaching out to help you. The mess you leave won't be easy to clean. You're on your own."

"S'okay."

The heavy weight of dread lifted and Trey tuned Diskant out, placing all of his concentration on Sadie. She'd finally woken up. He wasn't sure how hurt she was since she'd communicated with him telepathically. Perhaps the wounds were deeper than he'd thought. A few had scored through her flesh down to the bone but he hadn't noticed more than that.

He gazed down at her face, begging her silently to open her eyes and look at him.

Her lashes fluttered, thick wisps beautiful against her fair skin. She blinked a couple of times, like she was fighting sleep, then he was peering into her beautiful blue eyes, the color so magnificent it challenged the bright colors of the ocean.

Someone nudged him and he almost lashed out.

His gaze drifted to Ava who had one had on her stomach and another covering her mouth. The teensy female had tears in her eyes—eyes that were shifting colors. The trait of a human mated to an Omega. She'd never change forms but slivers of Diskant's beasts resided in the fragile female. Usually Ava didn't give off emotion. She'd always been strong when it came to such things, keeping herself apart in a small way from the pack. Now he could feel how grateful she was to Sadie, how much she wanted to repay the favor.

"Thank you." Ava choked out the words, pulling in a soft breath as she tried not to cry.

Sadie's eyes flittered to Ava.

She studied the woman for several seconds and then she gave her a small smile and nod. The motion caused her to wince and Trey inserted himself in front of Ava, crowding Sadie's body. She needed time to rest. Werewolves healed during sleep. More than likely his female would do the same.

"*Talk to me,*" he pleaded, reaching out to her.

"*What do you want me to say?*"

Hell yes. There was humor in the question. That meant she was going to be fine. "*Tell me what to do.*"

He couldn't rationalize clearly, worried only for her. The man in him wanted to get the fuck out of town. The wolf wanted to stay. He was fighting an inner battle he wasn't sure he could win. He felt torn right down the center. As much as he wanted to get into a car, drive away and never look back the idea haunted him.

"*Don't run.*" She closed her eyes but kept the line of communication open. "*I never wanted or expected that from you.*"

"*I don't want to see you hurt.*" Her well-being was more important. His pride be damned. "*Not ever again.*"

"*Then be the man I fell in love with. Don't turn your back on what you love. Don't cut and run when things get tough. You found me, didn't you? Even when you thought it was impossible you didn't give up. You kept going. And you saved me. Without you I wouldn't be here now.*" Her thoughts became broken, a messy, convoluted tumble. "*I need to rest. If I were at the caverns I'd have been ordered to sleep by now.*"

He wanted to ask what the caverns were. Then he knew she'd picked up on his curiosity. She was too tired to respond so he thought back to her, suffusing the words with all the feeling inside him. "*Then sleep. I'll watch over you. I'll be here when you open those beautiful blue eyes.*"

"*Don't you dare run.*" The order was weak. "*Be fierce.*"

Her chest rose as she drew a deep breath and closed her eyes. She returned to sleep as quickly as she'd ripped herself away from it. His skin prickled, frustration eager to find an outlet. She'd told him to stay. He wasn't sure if he could. The pack wanted to ask questions but he didn't know what answers to give them.

"If you go there's a chance she won't find Leigh again," Ava said. She hadn't moved, standing slightly behind him. "Diskant can keep her informed. She doesn't have to stay in the dark."

Damn it. He'd forgotten about Leigh and Nathan.

Sadie would want to know about her friend. She wouldn't allow them to push her out of Leigh's life.

"We're not going to be able to keep any secrets." It was hard to find words. He wasn't sure how to phrase things. "If you're going to give them answers they deserve to know everything. But packs have a tendency to gossip. We have to make sure they stay quiet."

"We can weed out the deserters," Diskant offered, shrugging his large shoulders. "Sort out who's going and who's staying." His deep, threatening growl filled the room. The grim upturning of his lips and the glimpse of his fangs screamed vengeance. "Ava and I can take care of Brandi and Andrea. If their friends decide they want to leave we'll make sure they don't remember much about what went down."

Trey had never known how the couple manipulated people's thoughts. Honestly, as long as it didn't involve him, he'd normally never cared. There was more on the line now. The slightest slip and they'd all be fucked.

He pondered the future, working out the angles.

Sadie had told him not to run.

If that's what she wanted he'd stand down hell itself.

"Do it." A part of him remained with Sadie as he moved from her side. The connection kept growing, bringing them closer together. "Take care of the bitches first. Then I'll talk to the pack. But I need to speak to Zach first. We have to be up to speed."

"I figured you would. He's in the living room."

The smugness in Diskant's voice was almost too much to take. The male had known Trey wouldn't go. He'd been banking on the Alpha standing his ground. Trey faced his friend, trying not to lunge at him and unleash the fucking fury he'd held inside for too fucking long.

Son of a bitch. "You knew I'd stay."

"Call it a gut feeling."

Gut feeling my ass. "How did you know?"

"Ava is my life," Diskant answered with a heavy dose of gravity. "I'd die without her. But your life and living are two different things. You have to choose what's most important to you and work everything else out around it. You'll find your way. For now everything is new."

"And you want me to lead?" He couldn't understand how Diskant could fathom such a thing. "You think I'm capable?"

Diskant didn't respond. Not right away. After a pause, he closed the distance between them. The Omega stopped inches away, looking at Trey, his eyes brimming with respect and admiration. Trey remembered when the Omega had been born. The moment he'd arrived everyone in the pack had felt the newborn's power. They'd known what he'd eventually become. Trey had taken Diskant Black under his wing, guiding the young man to maturity, much like an older brother would a sibling.

"I wouldn't trust anyone else," Diskant said. "You're who they need."

"Tell me that after I speak to them." Turning his head slightly, he gazed at Sadie. "Someone needs to stay with her in case she wakes up. I don't want her alone."

"I'll stay." Ava walked to a chair on the other side of the bed. "I won't leave until you come back."

At least he had that small consolation. Ava wouldn't let anyone near Sadie. He actually felt sorry for anyone who tried to get into the bedroom. Ava—even in her condition—would likely throw them out by their ears. Then they'd have to deal with Diskant.

Anyone with half a brain would know better.

"I'm going to speak with Zach." Swiveling around, Trey faced Diskant. "It won't take long. You'll need to take care of the females. I want them gone before I address the pack."

"Consider it done. Ava mine," his voice softened as he spoke to his female, "be ready."

"I don't want them near Sadie." *Hell no.*

"Trust me," Diskant said, a menacing glint in his eye, "they won't be."

It took all of his will to walk out of the room. He detested the distance, hated each step he took away from his mate. Sadie's request, "Be fierce," kept him going. This was what she'd wanted, for him to be the man she admired. He could do no less. Not after what she'd sacrificed. He'd be the Alpha the pack needed, commanding their respect. Trust would be slower to achieve but eventually it would come as well.

Zach was where Diskant had said he'd be, seated on the couch. The male had changed drastically since Katie had died. Physically he was thinner, his frame no longer as wide or muscular. His hair was long and unkempt, dark blue eyes constantly brooding. Once Zach had been a consummate joker, easy to laugh and exchange witty barbs. Those days were gone, leaving behind a shell of Zach's former self.

How in the hell he'd survived the loss, Trey had no idea.

Perhaps it was his need for revenge.

Maybe Zach couldn't rest until he'd made the Shepherds pay for what they'd done.

"I need to be clear," Trey said, striding into the room. "If you want the position, you have to be ready for what comes with being a Beta. It can't be done half-assed."

"I don't do half-assed," Zach grumbled, rising from the couch.

"Are you sure you're up to this?" To keep the pack balanced Zach would have to cage his grief. It was all about stability and management. "Can you honestly tell me you won't buckle under pressure?"

The male's intense gaze didn't falter. "I need this," he rasped through clenched teeth. "I have to have a reason to wake up each day. I..." He exhaled through his nose, a tic visible in his jaw. "Katie wouldn't want me to follow her to the grave. My existence—her memory—keeps her alive. I won't let her be forgotten."

"Is that how you do it?" Trey didn't want to be cruel by asking but he was curious. Most males would have withered and died after the loss of their mate. "Is that what's kept you going?"

"I'm not sure." A bit of the tension left Zach's face. "I ask myself the same question. I can't explain it."

There has to be another mate for him.

Such a thing was rare but it had been known to happen with shifters and humans if the third stage of the bloodbond hadn't been established. Zach had to know it. The male wasn't a young cub.

He'd been around, seen a lot of things.

And he'd endured the worst loss imaginable.

Zachery Taylor didn't appreciate the way Trey looked at him. Hell, he didn't appreciate the way the pack did. He loathed their sympathetic glances, hated the way they whispered behind his back. He knew what they were thinking and it pissed him off.

Katie couldn't have been his mate. He'd have died if she had been.

So far from the fucking truth.

A familiar pain lanced his chest. He thought about Katie every minute, longing for her touch, wishing for a trace of her sweet scent. He'd gone through the second bloodbonding stage with her, had been ready to put a permanent stamp on their union. If he'd been smart he'd have pushed for the third as well. She wouldn't have survived the explosion but at least he could have joined her in the afterlife.

He hated memories, especially when they took him back to the night she'd been killed. Yet they rose unbidden, plaguing him with torment. The moment her life had been taken he'd felt it. The sensation had been like an amputation of his heart, an invisible enemy punching through his torso and ripping away the most vital part of his soul. He'd fallen to his knees, stricken by the blow.

But somehow—someway—he'd managed to make it to his feet.

At first his pain had kept him strong.

He'd wrapped the feeling around him like a blanket, using it as a weapon. He wasn't sure when things had changed, failed to notice the shift in his beast. The animal was the reason shifters dwindled away and died following the death of a mate. At first his wolf wanted to do just that. It told him to find a place to rest and never get up again. The man, however, had wanted to kill the people who'd taken Katie from him. Over time the wolf's gloom had eased.

Why? He didn't understand it.

Even worse? Each day became a little easier.

He wasn't sure he liked that.

"I stayed after you left," Zach said. Instead of lingering on Katie's memory, he got to work. Trey wanted to see what he was made of as a Beta. This was his opportunity to show the Alpha what he could do. "The pack has calmed substantially. They're mystified by what they saw, which is why they're willing to listen. Most of them have never seen anything like Aldon before."

"Did Diskant tell you everything?" Trey questioned.

"Yes." Zach hadn't wanted to believe it but he'd seen Aldon with his own eyes. With a creature that powerful Diskant didn't have to sugarcoat the issues the pack faced. "I know what's coming."

"And you still want to be my Beta?"

"I do."

As the second wolf in charge he'd be privy to information. He wanted to be the first in line to kill Shepherds when they returned. And they would return, coming back to New York with reinforcements. To him Aldon was merely an afterthought. He didn't care about Trey's mating or any of the rest. He wanted to feast on the blood of his enemies, watch the life drain from their eyes.

"Nathan will eventually return." Trey rubbed the back of his neck. "When that happens you'll have to step down. Are you willing to do that?"

Oh yeah, he was willing. But not for the reasons Trey expected. "Yes."

"Then I guess..." Trey lowered his arm, crossing to him. "It's official."

Zach took the hand Trey offered, shaking firmly.

He'd do what he had to, be the Beta the pack needed. In the meantime he'd continue collecting all the information he could, storing it away. The wolf snapped its teeth, squirming under his skin. With effort he made the beast subside. That was his ability, his gift. Like a mask that never slipped out of place. He could control emotion, use it to his advantage. Trey didn't know what Zach had in mind. The Alpha wouldn't, either, until Zach let him in on his secret.

A vision of Katie's face floated before him—beautiful, sweet. Perfect.

He wanted to growl but didn't. He'd gotten what he needed.

With addresses and names he'd finally be able to leave New York and start hunting.

When the time came, he was going to kill them all.

One by fucking one.

Chapter Eighteen

೮౨

Sadie woke but didn't open her eyes. She studied her surroundings using her other senses, her nose homing in on Trey's scent. The rhythmic ticking of a clock sounded like a drum, voices drifting to her ears from the other end of the house.

She and Trey were alone in the bedroom.

It was safe to reveal that she'd finally healed.

Warmth spread through her, a love like no other speeding the beat of her heart. Trey rested in the chair, his chin nestled against his chest. He was too large for the furniture, his long legs sprawled out. Shadow spread over his chin and jaw, the dark circles under his eyes proof of his fatigue.

Flexing her muscles, she assessed her injuries.

No pain. Zero stretching in her torso. The wounds had closed and mended.

Sleep was just the thing she needed.

How long was I out? A day? Two possibly?

She didn't want to move and disturb the peace but she knew Trey would want to know she'd finally come around. Her limbs were shaky but as always they adjusted quickly, allowing her to peel back the comforter. Trey's eyes shot open, his face brimming with alarm. Then he saw her and his brows relaxed, relief smoothing his features.

"Hey stranger," she murmured, rising to a seated position.

"Don't move." Trey jumped from the chair, hurrying to the bed. He ran trembling fingers down her cheek, his eyes drinking her in. "Take it easy, darlin'. Do you need more blood? Do I need to get anything for you?"

His sincere concern melted her.

"Trey." She captured his hand with hers, pressing her face to his palm. "I'm fine."

"Your chest closed yesterday." He tried to hide how nervous he'd been but she could see past the image he tried to project. "I thought you'd wake up but you didn't."

Yesterday? "How long have I been asleep?"

"Two days."

Shit. That was two days too long.

"What happened with the pack?" She hated shoving him to the side but she needed to get out of bed. There was a lot to do. If things had gone badly they needed to discuss where they were going to go. "What did they decide?"

"Should you be getting out of bed so soon?" He balked at the idea of her getting on her feet, trying to still her by grasping her arms. "Don't you need to take it easy for a while?"

"I'm not human," she reminded him, swinging her legs over the edge of the mattress. "And I'm not a shifter."

Her rate of recovery was better than others'. That's why vampires used healing caverns. There they could sleep off their wounds. All they needed was an ample meal and a good rest. She'd been shot, stabbed and nearly had her head sliced off. None of those things had put her in the ground. It'd take more than Aldon's claws to keep her on the sidelines.

Spying her bag on the dresser, she rose. "Tell me about the pack."

"Sadie..." Trey growled.

She stopped, lifting her head, really looking at Trey. The poor man had been through hell. Getting dressed would have to wait. He needed to be comforted and reassured. Winding her arms around his neck, she pressed her chest to his. The heat from his body radiated against her, the hands he placed on her hips were almost painful as he snatched her closer.

"I told you," she skimmed her lips over the deep hollow of his throat, "I'm fine."

"You have no idea how petrified I've been." It almost sounded like an accusation. As though she'd made him suffer on purpose. "I could see you breathing but you didn't move. Not even when Diskant came to talk to me. You just kept sleeping. You've been in the same position. You didn't even shift your arms and legs. Every hour that you didn't wake up I thought…" His fingers dug into her skin, his body shaking hard. "I thought that maybe…"

"I might not wake up at all?" How could she not love him when he was like this? There were no barriers, no lies. He was like an open book, revealing everything. "I'm sorry. I should've told you what to expect. A healing sleep is just that. We don't wake up. That's why we have to do it in a safe place."

"Is that what the caverns are?" He'd stopped shaking, gaining a hold of himself. "The place you heal?"

The fragrant aroma of his blood tempted her. She tried to stifle her hunger, pulling her head from the enticing curve of his throat. "Yes." But she couldn't return to the caverns. Not until she knew what Geneva was up to. She put away that concern, fixated on the here and now. "Tell me about the pack."

"They had a lot of questions." Nuzzling the top of her head, he said, "Some of them I could answer. Some of them I couldn't. When I told them about Aldon they responded better than I expected."

"You told them everything?"

"I did." His fingers drifted from her hips to her lower back, his touch leaving behind a fiery imprint. "Diskant thought it was best."

"What about Leigh? Did you tell them about her?"

"I didn't think I should but I told them about her. They aren't pleased but they adore Nathan. With everything going to shit they want him to come back. They're willing to give Leigh a chance if she and Nathan agree to the same terms we did."

"The same terms?" she echoed despite knowing precisely what he meant. "They'll kill her if she pisses them off?"

She could live with a target on her back. Unfortunately Leigh wasn't as capable of protecting herself, not until she learned how to control her magic. Maybe it would be best for Leigh to stay where she was, out of reach of the pack and Aldon.

"Yes," he answered softly, pacifying her.

There wasn't much else he could do, really. She'd never like placing Leigh in harm's way. Trey was smart enough to know he couldn't change her stance on the subject.

"What do we do now?"

"We call another meeting." His shifted his feet, rocking her side-to-side. "They want to meet you. You'll have to answer the questions I couldn't."

More questions. More answers.

What she wouldn't give for a mental health day.

"I'll do my best."

She had a lot of knowledge but she wasn't a vampire dictionary. As much as she knew about white mage vampires she knew just as little about black mage ones. Her kind avoided their counterparts. The Fallen were dangerous and unstable. Aside from killing a few she'd done her best to avoid them altogether.

Think about all that later. Enjoy the moment while you can.

Silencing her worries, she just let him hold her, taking him in. His hard body felt substantial against her, strong and proficient at delivering damage. But when he held her like this—gently, reverently—she knew he was far more than he seemed. He could destroy walls with his fists yet those same hands were tender with her. His fingers were capable of working her body like the strings of a guitar.

How could I ever have thought I could hate him? If he keeps this up, I'll happily wrap myself around his little finger. I'll be his to command. A hot lick of heat slithered from her stomach to her pussy. *Or maybe I'll wrap my entire body around his. See how many positions we can figure out.*

"Damn," he growled, rolling his hips. "You are feeling better." He took a deep breath, drawing in the air. "I love the way you smell when you're turned-on."

"I should probably take a shower." She'd have to face the members of the house soon, as well as the pack if her hunch was right. There was no way she was doing so in nothing more than a shirt and panties. "I need to change into my clothes."

"Later," he expelled in a rush, pushing her back so he could dip his head.

Their lips met in a kiss wild and wicked. The hunger she'd tried to smother returned, creating an itch at the back of her throat. She rotated her tongue around his, flicking the tips together. Her gums tingled and her fangs descended. His pulse beckoned, thrumming in her ears. The spicy and alluring scent of his blood called to her, she could almost feel the warm liquid splashing over her tongue.

He tried to take her to the bed, bending her back.

Not so fast.

She wasn't as strong as she should have been but he was being so cautious with her that she easily wriggled free. With a quick glance to make sure the door was closed she sank to her knees. He wasn't denying her this again. She'd fantasized about it for too long. Next time he could do whatever he pleased. Right now she was taking what she wanted for a change.

Trey tensed, his eyes forming into thin slits. "Careful," he warned, words rumbly. "You might bite off more than you can chew."

"I hope so." She popped the front of his denims open and lowered the zipper. He had gone commando, had nothing but bare skin to greet her.

Excellent.

"Sit down and lay back," she ordered, tugging at his pants. He'd forgone shoes so undressing him wasn't going to be difficult. "You'll like this."

And so will I.

It wasn't in Trey's nature to submit but when Sadie looked at him like that—with lust and hunger in her gaze—how could he possibly say no? He plopped down and scooted back, allowing her to remove his jeans. With a snarl, he ripped his shirt over his head. He'd waited so long for her to wake up, fearing she never might. When she finally did so he'd meant to be courteous, seeing to her every want and need.

He'd never expected her to get aroused.

The succulent scent of her pussy was a sexual stimulant, making his cock go rock-hard. The wolf was also eager for her, longing for her touch. He didn't care what she did to him so long as she kept her hands on his skin, her body in contact with his.

I've wanted to do this for so long.

Sadie's thoughts were easier to hear, sometimes coming out of nowhere.

In her sleep, when she dreamed, he picked up fragments from her mind. Strange images and impressions. When the dreams were good she felt elated, flying on a constant high. On the other hand when her dreams were bad she felt desolate and empty, her sadness a nightmarish tomb.

Her palms brushed his inner thighs, obliterating rational thought.

He sank back in the pillows, making sure he stayed upright so he could watch. She ditched her shirt, ripping it open, sending buttons flying through the air. Her bare breasts bounced, ripe pink nipples pebbled and hard. Before he could enjoy the visual, she'd lowered her head. Her lips breezed up one of his legs, her breath cool on his skin. Her hair cascaded over his thigh, the blonde strands a stark contrast with his darker complexion.

He fisted the comforter to stop himself from reaching out for her. "Sadie."

She tisked at him, gazing up and meeting his eyes, flicking her tongue over his flesh. Her fingers carefully squeezed and massaged his sac, using just enough pressure. Her irises lightened, turning sky-blue. His gaze went to her mouth. Her full lips were parted, her tiny fangs visible. His wolf snarled and his claws lengthened. He itched to feel her hot little mouth wrapped around his cock, drawing him deep, sucking him down.

"Tease me now," he warned, fighting to breathe, "and I'll tease you later."

Amusement lit her face. "Is that so?" She slid the tip of her tongue from the base of his cock, gliding it all the way to the crown.

"It's a fucking promise, mate." He'd show her how it felt. She wouldn't like it much. He'd see to that. "I'll keep you on the edge for hours. You'll be begging me to make you come."

"In that case…"

She took him into her mouth, lips parting and making way, her tongue cradling the underside of his dick. Then there was suction, the most intense pressure imaginable. His eyes rolled back in his head, the comforter ripping to shreds as his claws tore through the material. He pumped his hips, feeling the softness at the back of her throat. She compensated for what she couldn't do orally, working the base of his shaft with her hand.

His sac tightened and his cock pulsed. She moaned, the vibrations almost enough to send him hurtling over the precipice. Since the comforter was ruined he had to make do with destroying the bed. He sank his fingers into the soft mattress, determined to let her finish.

"*So good.*" Her voice flowed through his mind. "*I knew you would be.*"

He groaned, grinding his teeth. Why did she have to go and say that?

Son of a fucking bitch.

The pressure in his balls built, his entire body quaking. He wasn't going to be able to hold off. He'd waited too long to see her like this, worshipping his cock with her mouth, enjoying the act as much as he did. His wildest fantasies weren't shit. The real deal was so much better, so much fucking sweeter. With a plunge of her head, she took him all the way to the back of her throat and swallowed.

That was all it took. "I can't hold back," he grated, losing the battle.

"*Then don't. I want to see how you taste.*"

His came with a roar, the sound so loud it echoed through the bedroom. It dawned on him that the others could hear but he didn't give two shits what they thought. His female not only met his expectations, she kept exceeding them. Her clever fingers continued stroking his cock, her mouth going up and down the length. She swallowed blast after blast of his semen, drinking him down. It seemed to go on forever but forever would never be long enough.

Not when it came to Sadie.

"Mmm," she hummed, sliding her lips from the head, slowly backing away.

She fed him the image of what she wanted to do next.

The vein on his thigh beckoned, the blood pulsing under his skin. She wanted to feed from him there, watch him come a second time. But if that happened there was a chance he wouldn't be able to go another round. His mate might be content to give him release without achieving her own but he wasn't keen on letting it happen.

Another time, baby.

"No you don't." He moved before she knew what hit her, yanking her up his body, flipping them over and changing positions. His fingers drifted over her slit, finding her folds soaking wet. "It's your turn to scream."

There was no precursor or warning. He fed his cock into her tight little sheath, working the head into her pussy. As soon as he was lodged inside her he thrust. She took all of him, arching her back, her fingernails piercing his skin. He didn't stop, pulling out only to return with more force. Bringing his mouth to her breast, he sucked her nipple into his mouth, rubbing his tongue over the nub.

"Yes." She moaned, grinding her cunt against his cock. "Oh yes."

Reaching down, he cupped her ass. Again and again he rammed into her, upping the pace. She gripped him like a glove, her cunt wrapping around him. He released her hard nipple and turned his head, giving the other breast equal attention. Her pussy clamped down on him and her breaths changed from even to ragged.

"Come, Sadie," he growled, nipping at her skin. "Show me how good I make you feel."

With a muffled cry, she did.

He abandoned her breasts, getting in place. Sliding his hand behind her head, he lifted her and offered her his neck. He didn't stop moving, plunging in and out. Sweat slicked his skin and beaded down his back. The air felt charged with electricity, thick and alive around them. Her tongue darted over his flesh, bathing the area covering his vein. Anticipation prickled up his spine, muscles tense as he waited for her bite.

She scored his skin cleanly, her fangs sinking deep.

He came again, groaning in pleasure, snapping his hips. The wolf snarled in his head, voicing its satisfaction. Their bodies crashed together, skin slapping against skin. She moaned as she drank, sucking, her lips soft and gentle. The sound broke something inside him. He slowed his motions, changing his thrusts from violent to tender.

"Love you," he panted, clutching her to him. "So much."

Before Sadie he'd existed only to kill. His sole purpose had been to make those who'd wronged him suffer before they died. The wound was still fresh but it no longer festered, eating away at his compassion, destroying what remained of his humanity. His mate had not only managed to ease his suffering, she'd found a way to piece the man he used to be back together again. Making him whole. Complete. He didn't deserve a second chance but he was fucking grateful he'd been given one. His life would have gone on but he wouldn't have known what it meant to exist.

She gave him that.

His cock softened, his body spent. He thrust his length into her one last time and remained there, buried deep inside her. Keeping his head turned, he closed his eyes, dazed as she drank her fill. Her fangs eased from his skin, her tongue darting out to skim over his neck. He shuddered, enjoying the way she caressed his throat, her long fingers drifting through the hair at his nape.

"Trey?"

She tugged at the strands trapped in her fist, bringing her other hand around to cup his face. He lifted onto his elbows, gazing down. Sadie's irises were a dark shade of blue, her cheeks rosy pink. Her hair had tangled around her shoulders and neck. She looked like a woman who'd been ridden good and hard. He was a smug asshole because he loved knowing he was the one who made her look like that.

Her hesitation revealed her nervousness. "Say it again."

His heart broke all over again. If she needed to hear the words, he'd say them over and over again. Until she knew just how profoundly she affected him and understood that he never had — and never would — feel this way for anyone else.

"I love you." Bending down, he brushed his lips over hers. "I love you."

"One more time," she sighed, relaxing beneath him. "Tell me."

He brought his mouth around, raining kisses over her cheek.

Winding down to her ear, he whispered, "I love you, Sadie Dumus."

Chapter Nineteen

"They're ready for you," Zach said, motioning to the door.

Sadie squeezed Trey's hand, trying to steady her nerves. It was time to run with the big dogs. She stole a look at the male beside her. He was equally alert, ready to throw down and kick ass if anyone gave her shit. A thrilling bolt of happiness cascaded over her like a warm wash of morning sunshine.

He loved her.

She'd felt the gravity of the declaration when he'd said it aloud. He meant it all the way down to his very soul. He'd do anything she asked of him, regardless of the cost. That level of dedication deserved equal respect and commitment. She'd prove she was worth the trouble. With time the pack would know she'd do anything for them. She'd offered them her fealty so long as they accepted her place at Trey's side.

"Why the long face?" She teased him, wanting to lighten the mood. They weren't facing their deaths. The pack wanted to see her. She needed to answer their questions. "Relax."

His head turned, his amber gaze loving. "I'll relax after this is done."

"Come on, then," she said, leading him to the door. "It's time."

Instead of gathering at the barn, the pack had taken up the area surrounding the swimming pool. They stopped chatting with each other, going quiet as she stepped outside. The sun hadn't set but it wasn't of any consequence. It had started to descend, making room for the night. The rays no longer beamed from above, draining her strength and scorching her skin. The fact that she appeared in the dwindling daylight seemed to surprise them. A few whispered to each other, their voices soft in an effort to keep her from hearing.

"She can't be all bad," she caught a man saying. "She's in the daylight for fuck's sake."

"Thank you for coming," she said, wanting to engage them. "I know you have a lot of questions. I'll do my best to answer them."

A large male stepped forward. The way the pack moved behind him indicated he spoke for the entire group. "Did you mean what you said that first night?"

"I said a lot of things," she answered slowly, unclear of his meaning.

"Do you truly mean to accept the responsibilities of the mate to our Alpha?" the man asked. "Are you willing to lay down your life to protect us? No matter the threat? Even if it means giving up what you love most?"

Trey's hand nearly crushed hers, his body trembling. He still worried for her, afraid of the idea she could be hurt or killed. She held back a wince, accepting the pain. He wasn't even aware he was squeezing her so hard, locked in his own thoughts, imagining her dead and gone. She wanted to comfort him but couldn't. If she did he'd seem weak. They had to project a strong image, united in front of the people before them.

"I do and I am," she replied, staring at the faces studying her.

"And if other vampires attack, you'll kill them?"

She didn't hesitate. "In a heartbeat."

"What about our other enemies?"

"The same applies."

The male paused, gazing at her. "How can we know you mean it?"

"You can't." That was the bitch of it. She'd never be able to reassure them with words. She'd have to use action. "But if you'll give me a chance, I'll prove it to you."

He didn't stop staring, considering her words. The shifters behind him remained still, watching him closely. She expected more questions but none came. They had to want to know more than this. Why weren't they bombarding her with their uncertainties? Why hadn't they started an outcry to find a chink in her armor?

After a moment he said, "Bring them."

Bring them? What the hell does that mean?

She thought to Trey. *"What's he talking about?"*

"Not what," he thought back, fingers loosening. *"Who."*

A male standing at the side gate opened it wide, waving at people she couldn't see on the other side. Women and children appeared, squeezing into the area one by one. Some of the females carried infants while a few others held the hands of toddlers. The older children gawked at her, eyes bright with curiosity.

She thought back to the first pack meeting.

Women had been there but no children. Come to think of it, she'd rarely ever seen the youngest members of the pack. And why should she? Children were the future. They had to be protected.

This was what she'd be fighting for.

Life with Trey took on new meaning. And it was a glorious thing. She'd protected a coven of scheming bitches, doing whatever she was told. But there had been no real pleasure in it. Here she'd have an actual family, just as she had in her childhood. It was inconceivable. Vampires usually joined covens and roamed the world. They didn't settle down. For once, she'd plant roots. This would be home.

The idea more than appealed to her.

It suited her to a T.

Once everyone was inside and the gate closed, the male addressed her again. "Give us your word. Swear that you'll put them before anything else."

She'd never take a more important vow. "I swear."

Her lips parted as they kneeled, heads angling to the side. The older children mirrored the actions of their elders while the babes cried out softly and clung to their mothers. All heads were bowed, so she couldn't see their faces. Concerned, she reached out to their minds, finding that all of them were resolved and accepting.

Accepting of what?

"You," Trey rasped. The male would never cry but she heard the emotion in his voice. "They're taking you into the pack."

It couldn't be that easy. No way. She hadn't done anything to deserve it yet.

"*You saved the life of one of their children,*" Trey thought to her. "*There is no greater gift in the pack. When you protected Ava you showed them that you value the same thing. Apparently they're willing to take you at your word.*"

A child—no more than five or six years old—broke position and stood.

Sadie grinned when he scowled, shaking off his mother's hand when she tried to make him kneel. He was an adorable little thing, still chubby in his youth, maintaining the roundness in his cheeks, his brown hair streaked by the sun. He cocked his head to the side, looking straight at her, resting his cheek on his shoulder.

"Do you really drink blood?" he yelled, like he couldn't believe anyone would want to do something so repugnant. When she didn't answer immediately he asked, "What about flying? Can you do that? I heard you could fly if you wanted to."

His mother shot up, trying to shush him.

"Oh Mom," he complained, squirming out of her hold. "You said questions are important." His poor mother looked mortified, eyes darting to Sadie. "That's why we're here, isn't it?" He kept going, embarrassing the hell out of the poor woman. "Why can't I have a turn? Why does it always have to be grown-ups? It's not fair."

She released Trey and phased, appearing in front of the youth. His mother startled, taking a step back. Whispers surrounded Sadie, the accepting pack wondering if they'd made the wrong decision. The child reacted differently, apparently pleased. An enormous smile lit his face, his chocolate-brown eyes excited.

"Wow," he exhaled. "You can fly. You moved so fast I didn't see you!"

"I can do all kinds of things."

"Tell me!" he exclaimed, rushing at her. "This is better than a bedtime story."

Normally she didn't touch other people's children unless she was given permission. Such a thing was considered rude. But since the little boy was coming at her like a steaming locomotive she didn't have a choice. She couldn't let him fall. That would probably tick the pack off more than her holding him.

Catching him midway, she hoisted him up. Everyone around her was anxious. Their worry ate at her, robbing her of breath. She needed to give them a reprieve, allowing them to become comfortable in her presence. Trey gave her a disapproving look when she turned around and faced him. He didn't like her doing things unexpectedly.

Barbarian.

"I'm sure you have a lot of questions." She eased down, taking a seat at Trey's feet. She faced the pack but talked to the boy, speaking loud enough for everyone to hear. "I'll do my best to answer them."

"I'm Arkin," he told her proudly. "Momma named me after my grandpa."

"I'm Sadie," she murmured. She didn't tell him her parents took the name from Hebrew, or that it meant princess. "It's nice to meet you, Arkin."

"So how do you fly?"

How did she answer that? Would it freak everyone out?

She'd promised to be honest but could she really share all of her secrets?

The coven has already shunned you. You can't sink any deeper.

Trey kneeled at her back, resting his hand on her shoulder. Electricity zipped down her back, winding down her spine. His touch exorcized her demons, forcing her fears to retreat. She'd made this decision. This is what she wanted. In order to be a part of the pack she didn't have to merely earn their trust, she had to give them hers as well.

She gazed at the men and women in front of her.

They were listening, just as keen as the child to know an answer.

"I don't fly. Not really. It's called phasing."

"How do you do that?"

Settling in, she answered his question. He'd chosen a good one. "Well you see," she said, looking at Arkin, "it starts with a bit of magic."

His face bunched together, lips pursed. "Magic is for sissies."

She brought her hand to Trey's, resting her fingers on top of his. She felt their connection, growing stronger by the minute. "Why do you say that?"

"It's mostly fake," he informed her briskly, bored now. "I've seen it on TV."

Her eyes settled on a scrape on his leg. It was nearly healed but not quite.

"It's fake, huh?" She peered up, meeting the stares of the pack.

They didn't trust her but they wanted to. She remembered what her father had used to say, chiding her when she'd complained about her studies in her youth, saying that Rome wasn't built in a day. He loved to quote Roman Emperor Hadrian.

Brick by brick, my citizens, he'd say, *brick by brick.*

This was the start, the first block in her foundation.

Releasing the child's waist, she called on her magic, gazing at his knee. Energy buzzed through her, warming her blood, heating her from the inside. Trey knew what she was up to, gave her shoulder a squeeze. She intended to start things off on the right foot. There was no better way than revealing her gift for healing.

A simple touch and the wound disappeared.

The child was amazed. The pack, stunned.

She turned to Trey, giving him a smile. He lowered his head, skimming lips over hers.

Brick by brick, she'd become the woman they needed.

This was only the beginning.

Epilogue

What a quandary.

Aldon Frost studied the fireplace, watching the wispy red flames dance and sway. He didn't like to brood. It wasn't his style. Normally he didn't have to. Smart people avoided him. They certainly never fucked with him.

Not if they wanted to keep their heads attached to their shoulders.

Sadie Dumus, how you've thrown a wrench into things.

He'd put her down more than once but she kept coming back, determined as ever. He'd actually found her stalking rather amusing at times. She'd truly believed he hadn't been aware of her. A shame, since a true member of The Fallen would have killed her. For all her slyness she wasn't intelligent. Likely she'd never even encountered a member of The Fallen in her life. The silly vampire had no idea what she was dealing with.

The fire spurted, wood splintering. The sound matched his dour mood.

Thrumming his fingers on the edge of his chair, he contemplated his next move.

Although he wanted the vampire who could locate objects using touch, he didn't have to have her. So far he'd gained much information about the whereabouts of the zephyr. The ignorant human dog that had the mystical creation managed to maintain a low profile but he left a paper trail. After Aldon had gotten a name it was as easy as phoning in a few favors. Thomas Brisbane was tightening the noose. Soon he'd jump the gun and strangle himself.

Irritation was a waste of time but he let the sensation flow through him.

Foolish mortal.

His brothers wouldn't like it if Aldon didn't obtain the relic. As the self-proclaimed hunters of The Fallen, they wanted the tainted thing wiped from existence. Certainly they could use it to their benefit but his family would never allow that. They operated under a strict code of ethics. True, they did use black mage magic to accomplish their tasks but only when absolutely necessary. Otherwise they'd be lost to the allure of the dark. Besides, if they didn't use their gifts they couldn't blend in, spying on those they picked off one by one.

Fooling everyone around them.

Much like he'd duped Sadie Dumus.

His fingers stilled, thoughts turning in another direction.

So now the female was claimed. Mated to a werewolf.

Good. She wouldn't be a distraction.

The head of her coven was an outright bitch but he could handle Geneva. The arrogant female was much like Sadie, thinking she was smarter than she actually was. She wanted to take control of New York? Good luck with that. When Sadie found out she'd wipe the floor with the woman's ass. He often wondered if overconfidence was a feminine trait, but that wasn't fair. Not all women were created equal. Especially in his eyes.

Olivia.

Her name suited her perfectly.

Regal. Beautiful.

Forever out of his reach.

He knew he shouldn't go to her but in a blink he'd phased from his hideaway to the small diner where she waited tables. As per the norm he took the booth in the back, so he could watch her without notice. To be safe he put a veil in place so no one would see him. Mortals were drawn to him but also terrified of him. Best to let them think they were safe and sound within the secure little bubble they placed around themselves.

A flash of blonde drew his attention. There she was, coming from the back.

All of his troubles evaporated.

He hadn't seen her in weeks.

He inhaled deeply, wanting to draw her scent into his lungs. He had to sort out the other unwanted aromas—cheap beer, greasy food, stale sweat—until he locked onto what he was searching for. His shoulders relaxed, eyes drifting closed, his mind awash in bliss. The female bathed in lily of the valley. He loved that about her. Hell, he loved even more than that if he was being honest with himself. And to think she'd once been a willing vampire slave, allowing them to feast on her blood and body.

Such a pity.

He drew another breath, taking it in, letting it pervade his senses.

The first time he'd seen her—resting on rounded cushions placed upon the floor with a glistening gold collar on her throat—he'd accepted his first defeat. Blonde curls had fallen to her shoulders, her piercing purple eyes like newly bloomed violets. Dressed in white, she'd looked like an angel who'd been trapped in a den of depravity.

He'd wanted her like hell on fire.

In most cases he'd have requested her services and claimed his due. While he didn't use slaves often, he'd been tempted once or twice. He needed to sate his needs once in a while. Who better to get him off than a human female who used vampire blood to remain forever young? As an added bonus, his involvement and participation tricked The Fallen into thinking he was just like them. Twisted and sadistic, manipulating humans to be whatever they wanted.

So he'd approached Conrad Masterson and asked about the girl seated at his feet.

To his dismay her master refused to share, stating the angelic creature that belonged to him was off-limits. It had made no sense. The Fallen didn't care about mortals. They were toys, mere playthings used at their leisure. Conrad had instructed the angel—Olivia—to collect their things and take them to her quarters. Aldon had no choice but to watch her stand and walk away, her curvaceous backside taunting him as she strolled from the room.

The memory was scorched into his head.

He couldn't forget her, even when he tried.

Over time the image of her had become an obsession. He couldn't bed other women without seeing her face. Even when he drank he pictured her, allowing himself to wonder what it would be like. The softness of her blonde curls would caress his face, her silken skin soft as she begged for his bite. She'd shatter into a million pieces when he sank his fangs into her flesh, crying out as she came.

The truth was he'd found something he wanted but couldn't have.

It lit a fire in his ass.

So he'd returned to Aurora Palace—an exclusive mansion on the outskirts of Georgia where members of The Fallen dwelled—determined to change Conrad's mind. He didn't know the male very well but all black vampires were pretty much the same. Everything had a price. Once he found out what Conrad wanted, Aldon could take the woman to his bed, drink until he was full and be done with it.

He hadn't been prepared to learn that Conrad had been killed.

With her master gone Olivia had been set free. It had taken him a couple of weeks to find her—here, at this place. Her departure had made little sense. Most would have stayed, grateful to be treated like a pampered pet, content to be a belonging and not a person. But not her. The perplexing mystery of a woman baffled him. She'd taken her things and left, vowing never to speak of her former life.

It was a sealed deal too, inked in black magic. If she ever revealed what she knew to other mortals, the curse placed upon her would kill her in an instant. She was free to speak with other slaves—or other vampires for that matter—but never to those who knew nothing about the supernatural world.

Where is she?

Lost in his thoughts, her scent had drifted from him.

He inhaled, searching for her, wanting to feel her presence all around him.

One day he'd ask her why she'd left. Perhaps when he'd figured her out he'd lose interest. Over the years many women had attempted to snare him but he'd never stuck around. He bored of them easily, casually pushing them aside. He was what humans referred to as a player, moving from one partner to the next.

There. His lips curved into a smile. *There she is.*

Another scent mingled with her blood, burning in his nose. He frowned, trying to block it out. He attuned everything to Olivia, wanting to be crystal clear. If he hated one thing about her working—as he didn't think she should be working at all—it was the place she'd chosen to earn her living. At the diner she catered to others like she did as a slave, cleaning up their messes, doing precisely as she was told.

He stopped breathing, eyes flying open.

That scent. It can't be.

Something was very, very wrong.

Panicked, he searched for her, eyes wild as they darted across the room. Her glorious curly hair was gone, cut into a short pixie. And she was rail fucking thin. So slight he'd break her with a stiff fucking. There were circles under her eyes, her frame barely strong enough to support the tray she carried.

Even in her current state she smiled at the family seated at her table, carefully placing their meals before each one of them.

He took another breath, staring straight at her. There it was, bright as day.

No, damn it. No.

He knew what the smell meant, even when he tried to tell himself it couldn't be. He'd encountered it on numerous occasions from the various mortals all around him. There wasn't another smell like it, almost like a citrusy acid. The stronger the scent, the worse the condition.

She's dying.

Everything inside him rebelled, screaming it would never happen.

He dropped his guise, doing something he never did, acting on instinct.

Everything for him was carefully planned. In order to stay alive and one step ahead of his enemies, it was a necessary precaution. His brothers would kill him when they found out he'd dropped his guard, asking him what the hell he'd been thinking. He'd tell them the truth.

He'd never seen it coming. He'd never seen *her* coming. There had to be a reason he couldn't stop thinking about her, drawn to her in a manner that would never dissipate.

She had to be the one for him.

He'd just never touched her. If he had, he would have known for sure.

That ends now.

"Livvie," the hostess called out, giving Aldon a strange look. Her mind was easy to read. She wondered where he'd come from, thinking there was no way she'd have missed someone like him. "You've got a table."

"Are you set?" he heard Olivia ask the people at her table. "I'll be back to check on you. Enjoy your dinner."

He grinded his teeth, keeping his fangs from dropping.

How he loathed her waiting on others.

Ever since he'd tracked her down he'd wished she'd find another line of work. He'd refrained from giving her the idea, wanting to figure her out without invading her head and depositing his own thoughts. That was the danger with mortals. If you weren't careful you could change who they were, influence their decisions.

When Olivia came to him, he wanted her. Not what he'd created.

She walked over, pulling a pad from the apron at her waist. As she retrieved her pen she lifted her head. Her purple irises were no longer as bright, her skin a sickly shade of yellow. Mortals wouldn't notice it but he wasn't a mortal. The last time he'd seen her she'd been the picture of health. Vibrant and youthful, the vampire blood in her system slowed the aging process considerably.

But no more.

The last blood she'd taken had obviously left her, returning her to a completely mortal state. She'd grow old now, her body susceptible to illness and disease. He guessed her to be in her mid-twenties, but since she'd been drinking from vampires she could be much older. His eyes took her in, his cock hardening despite the changes in her body and face.

Once she drinks from me she'll heal. She'll never look like this again.

At first she struggled to place him, her lovely brushstroke brows furrowing. Then her eyes widened, the scent of her fear punching into his nose. She stopped a couple of feet away, terror etched on her face, hands visibly trembling.

Her reaction made no sense whatsoever.

She knew about his kind. She'd lived with them for God knows how long.

Why would she be afraid? What has her so spooked?

"Come here, *luvena*," he instructed quietly, staring into her eyes.

The order broke her from her trance. She scanned the diner, looking to see who might have seen her reaction. He understood that much at least. If she gave anything away she'd die on the spot. Doctors would think she'd suffered a heart attack or stroke. But it would be magic that killed her, the curse she'd accepted sending her to her death. He noticed her relief when she discovered no one had noticed her slip.

Lifting her shoulders, she walked to the table and asked, "What can I get you?"

Holy Mother of God.

She'd never spoken to him directly. Now he wished she had.

The sound stroked his nerve endings, his already stiff cock jerking in his trews. Her dismissal — pretending she didn't remember him — agitated him a way he didn't appreciate. Likely he'd tan that luscious little ass of hers so she wouldn't do so again.

Touch her now. Be certain.

"I gave you an order," he rasped, fingers twitching. "Come here."

She'd broken away from the palace but she'd know not to disobey. It wasn't an enormous request. If she didn't do as he said she'd draw attention to herself. He waited, blood rushing through his veins, gums burning with the effort to keep his fangs retracted. As if it pained her she complied, inching nearer to the table. Her fear doubled and he could hear the frantic drumming of her heart.

Like a bird flapping its wings against the bars of a cage. She's afraid.

The instant she was within reach his hand shot out.

He encased her tiny wrist in his fingers, holding back a groan when their skin touched for the first time. Like magic, a white-hot burst of blistering fire seared him, winding up his arm, traveling to his chest. Quickly as it came the sensation vanished. The deed was done.

He'd found her and imprinted on her, claiming her even if she didn't know it yet.

His gaze ventured from the wrist he held to her face. She had felt the same thing but he was sure she didn't comprehend its meaning. Not yet. The color had drained from her face, her pupils had completely dilated. A tremor shot through her, her skin going cold. He needed to get her away from this place, the sooner the better.

Before he could phase she yanked her arm away, standing upright. "Y-you n-need to l-leave," she stammered, horror and revulsion evident by her tone.

"I'm not going anywhere." *Not without you.*

He searched the minds in the area. There couldn't be a scene. If he wanted he could use black magic, creating an illusion. Fortunately that wouldn't be necessary. There was more than one way to skin a cat. Olivia needed to exit the establishment without causing a fuss. He followed mental pathways until he located the person he needed to influence.

Her boss. The cook.

In a second it was done.

Placing a thought into the man's head was as easy as lifting a newborn.

"Livvie!" the mortal yelled from the kitchen. "I need you!"

Her terror returned, uncertainty wafting from her. "I'll be right there," she called in response but didn't move.

Beautiful and clever female.

"Go. Do as he instructs then return to me."

After tonight she'd never work again. The transition needed to be smooth. He'd let everyone around them think he was a normal customer coming to eat a meal. They wouldn't notice a thing. He'd wait, get her alone and phase them out. Questions might be asked but without any clear answer Olivia would be safe.

With a final, petrified look at him she rushed away. He watched her go, resting in the booth. Once he'd taken her from this wretched place she'd be his to command. He couldn't wait to uncover her body, exploring every soft curve.

No more wishful thinking. Tonight he'd have the reality.

Finally he'd see her on her knees.

Waiting for instruction at his feet.

Holy shit. Why is he here?

She willed her heart to stop pounding. If anyone noticed how shaken she was, they'd ask questions. She couldn't risk that. Cancer might be taking her life but she had a little bit of time left. She didn't want her heart to stop beating in an instant because she couldn't keep a secret.

Entering the kitchen, she asked calmly, "What do you need?"

Harry—the owner and cook—shot her a look. He seemed almost dazed. "You need to clock out and go home."

"What?" She was the only waitress on the floor. There was no way she could leave.

"You need to clock out," he repeated like he was in a trance. "Go home."

Then she knew. Her blood ran cold, terror returning with full force.

The vampire was responsible. He'd gotten inside Harry's head. But why? Why would he show up here? He'd only seen her once and that had been months ago.

Have The Fallen come for me? Are they going to force me to go back?

If so she'd tell the entire world about them. She'd rather die immediately than return to that hell. The things they did to men and women sickened her. The only reason she'd agreed to exist there with Conrad was due to the bargain they'd struck. She wasn't like the rest, used as a receptacle of lust. The things she'd seen had made her nauseous. She shivered as she pictured some of the acts, hating to recall that she'd sat there and watched.

Sex, blood, torture.

She considered asking Harry who'd work the floor but thought better of it. Under a compulsion he wouldn't have an answer. Until she left he'd be oblivious to what he'd done. He'd certainly question why he'd sent her away, but eventually he'd figure out a reason that made some kind of sense to him. Human minds tried to repair themselves in strange ways after they'd been manipulated.

Her gaze swept to the back door. She could run but she didn't think she'd make it far. The vampire could track her scent. If he wanted her badly enough to come here—for reasons she wasn't sure she wanted to know—he wasn't going to let her slide from his grasp easily. The strange sensation she'd experienced when he'd grabbed her wrist warned her things were not as they seemed.

She felt a migraine coming on, likely the tumor in her head preparing to burst.

Wouldn't that be fitting?

Defeated, she untied her apron and strode from the kitchen.

The blond vampire had wanted her the night he'd appeared at the palace. She'd seen the glimmer of lust in his eyes, noticed with disgust that his light-blue irises had started to change in the centers, becoming red. To her mortification she'd felt a trickle of awareness stir to life. For the first time in years her body reacted to a male.

To a vampire.

Her breasts had tingled, her nipples growing hard. A gush of wetness coated her panties and her clit had started to pulse. She couldn't tear her eyes away from him. He wasn't dressed like the others, fully clothed in rich materials without a hint of leather in sight. His long coat had fit his broad shoulders perfectly, his thick blond hair falling past his shoulders.

Stop it!

It didn't matter if she was attracted to the man or not. There wasn't enough sexual gratification in the world to be what he'd expect. She didn't like pain. The others had accepted it but the thought of being bound to objects and lashed with whips terrified her. She also didn't want to be shared, given to anyone with a passing interest. At the very least she'd been spared that. She'd never taken part in the bloody orgies or been forced to endure the shame of being fucked by strangers.

Conrad. She thought of him fondly, even now. *Why did you have to die?*

Theirs had been an unlikely union but it had worked.

Now she was left to face the future without him.

Maybe the blond vampire only wanted to take her to his bed. That wouldn't be so bad. One night and she could pretend she was a normal girl. A sliver of hope surfaced. If he allowed her to drink from him she'd also be given more time. Depending on his age her cancer would either go into remission or would recede all together. Conrad hadn't been old enough to stop and reverse her malady but maybe this vampire could.

She walked back into the dining room and the iron will she'd tried to create crumbled around her. He was still there, studying her with those all-seeing blue eyes. He didn't merely look, his gaze almost seemed to devour her. She felt like a deer caught in headlights, unable to turn away as she walked to him. There wasn't enough distance between them, not nearly enough time to consider what she was doing.

"Are you ready?" he asked, rising from the booth.

So he had done what she'd thought, making Harry send her home. "Ready for what?" she whispered, hoping he wasn't cruel. Many of the vampires she'd seen enjoyed tormenting their slaves, feasting on misery. "What do you want from me?"

Something crackled in the air, encasing their bodies. Her gaze darted around the small space. Had they been seen? Everyone continued with business as usual, as though she and the vampire weren't even there.

Magic.

Dear God, help me.

He was much older than Conrad. Only the oldest of vampires could cast spells.

"Shh, *luvena*," he murmured, reaching out, placing his hands on her waist. He drew her to his body, standing so tall she had to crane her neck to see his face. "Close your eyes."

She did as he said, screwing them shut.

The air sizzled, burning her skin. Then the ground felt as though it disappeared, her body tumbling into nothing. Emptiness swirled all around her, the world vanishing into thin air. But she wasn't alone, captured in his arms.

Everything returned with a jolt.

She opened her eyes, finding her equilibrium off balance.

They weren't in the diner anymore. He'd taken her to another place.

A fire roared a few feet away, the furnishings were expensive and old.

She started to pull free of his embrace when he lifted her from the ground, her feet dangling inches from the floor. His lips found hers, the touch not painful but tender. She tensed, waiting for his violence to appear. Vampires loved to deceive. It was like a game to them. The instant she relaxed, he'd strike. But she also knew not to fight. That's what vampires loved—to destroy things and see them fall to pieces.

To her shock he pulled away, his ice-blue eyes full of wonder.

She didn't understand it. Nothing made sense. He wasn't acting like any vampire she'd ever met. Was it an act? A way to gain her trust so he could turn around and break it? He seemed so sincere. It couldn't possibly be all for show.

"Welcome home, Olivia."

Welcome home? She gasped, thinking he'd lost his mind. *What does that mean?*

He dipped his head, kissing her again, drawing her close. Her traitorous body responded, heating from the inside. She tried to hold back, telling herself it wasn't safe to give in. Then his tongue slid past her lips, delving into her mouth. She lifted her hands and clutched his shoulders, holding on tight.

It had been years since she'd felt like this.

Swept into a maelstrom of desire and need.

Stupid as it was, she gave herself over, meeting the soft strokes of his tongue. He groaned, thrusting his hips against her, his thick erection hard and long against her belly. She'd never made love to a vampire before but she had a feeling that was about to change. Just when she thought she was going to die—right as her body had started to fall apart and stop working—she remembered why she desperately wanted to live.

Surrendering to a vampire—an immortal.

Something she'd sworn she'd never do.

Damn it to hell.

She writhed against him, wanting to ease the ache between her legs.

She'd just gotten herself into a lot of trouble.

The End

Also by Aline Hunter

eBooks:
Alpha and Omega 1: Omega Mine
Alpha and Omega 2: Enemy Mine
Alpha and Omega 3: Vampire Mine
Alpha and Omega 4: Alpha Mine
Changed
Make Me Shiver
Kiss Before Dying
Marked
No Strings

Print Books:
Alpha and Omega 1: Omega Mine
Alpha and Omega 2: Enemy Mine
Make Me Shiver
Marked

About Aline Hunter

ଛ

Aline Hunter is the alias of multi-published author J.A. Saare, who has written stories featured in horror magazines, zombie romance anthologies and flash fiction contests. Her work has a notable dark undertone, which she credits to her love of old eighties horror films, tastes in music and choices in reading, and has been described as "full of sensual promise," "gritty and sexy" and "a breath of fresh air."

Currently she is penning multiple projects within the urban fantasy, erotic and contemporary, and paranormal romance categories.

ଛ

The author welcomes comments from readers. You can find her website and email address on her author bio page at www.ellorascave.com.

Tell Us What You Think

We appreciate hearing reader opinions about our books. You can email us at Service@ellorascave.com (when contacting Customer Service, be sure to state the book title and author).

Why an electronic book?

We live in the Information Age—an exciting time in the history of human civilization, in which technology rules supreme and continues to progress in leaps and bounds every minute of every day. For a multitude of reasons, more and more avid literary fans are opting to purchase e-books instead of paper books. The question from those not yet initiated into the world of electronic reading is simply: *Why?*

1. *Price.* An electronic title at Ellora's Cave Publishing runs anywhere from 40% to 75% less than the cover price of the exact same title in paperback format. Why? Basic mathematics and cost. It is less expensive to publish an e-book (no paper and printing, no warehousing and shipping) than it is to publish a paperback, so the savings are passed along to the consumer.
2. *Space.* Running out of room in your house for your books? That is one worry you will never have with electronic books. For a low one-time cost, you can purchase a handheld device specifically designed for e-reading. Many e-readers have large, convenient screens for viewing. Better yet, hundreds of titles can be stored within your new library—on a single microchip. There are a variety of e-readers from different manufacturers. You can also read e-books on your PC or laptop computer. (Please note that Ellora's Cave does not endorse any specific brands.

You can check our website at www.ellorascave.com for information we make available to new consumers.)
3. *Mobility.* Because your new e-library consists of only a microchip within a small, easily transportable e-reader, your entire cache of books can be taken with you wherever you go.
4. *Personal Viewing Preferences.* Are the words you are currently reading too small? Too large? Too... ANNOYING? Paperback books cannot be modified according to personal preferences, but e-books can.
5. *Instant Gratification.* Is it the middle of the night and all the bookstores near you are closed? Are you tired of waiting days, sometimes weeks, for bookstores to ship the novels you bought? Ellora's Cave Publishing sells instantaneous downloads twenty-four hours a day, seven days a week, every day of the year. Our webstore is never closed. Our e-book delivery system is 100% automated, meaning your order is filled as soon as you pay for it.

Those are a few of the top reasons why electronic books are replacing paperbacks for many avid readers.

As always, Ellora's Cave welcomes your questions and comments. We invite you to email us at Service@ellorascave.com or write to us directly at Ellora's Cave Publishing Inc., 1056 Home Avenue, Akron, OH 44310-3502.

Discover for yourself why readers can't get enough of the multiple award-winning publisher Ellora's Cave. Be sure to visit EC on the web at www.ellorascave.com to find erotic reading experiences that will leave you breathless. You can also find our books at all the major e-tailers (Barnes & Noble, Amazon Kindle, Sony, Kobo, Google, Apple iBookstore, All Romance eBooks, and others).

www.ellorascave.com

CPSIA information can be obtained
at www.ICGtesting.com
Printed in the USA
FSOW01n2005120815
9895FS